Amelia Splint

AND THE DOORWAY TO HOPE

Amelia Splint

AND THE DOORWAY TO HOPE

Written by

Henry Elmo Bawden

Illustrated by

Marcelo Vignali

Bawden Studio Press

Writing, art direction, book layout, many of the chapter head illustrations, and decorative elements were done by Henry Elmo Bawden.

Visual style treatment, character designs, cover illustration, first and last interior illustrations, young and teenage Amelia illustrations, and many chapter head illustrations were done by Marcelo Vignali.

The following fonts are used in this book:
Garamond, created by Claude Garamond
Abadi MT, created by Ong Chong Wah
Cavolini, created by Carl Crossgrove
Comic Sans MS, created by Vincent Connare
Times New Roman, created by S. Morison & V. Lardent

Published By Bawden Studio Press
Columbus, Ohio

Library of Congress Control Number: 2023917841

ISBN: 979-8-9891908-1-2

Printed in the U.S.A.

Dedication

To my wife and children.

Thank you for your endless love and support.

CONTENTS

CHAPTER ONE

The Doorway

 It was a room full of chickens, or so you would have thought. Not pretty chickens with bright white, orange, red, and yellow, but a room full of chickens pretending to be crows. Dark and scary crows. The crowd was clucking away like mad, but the color was black.

Even little Amelia Splint was sitting in her silly black dress. She wanted to be out of it. She wanted to be out of all of it. The roomful of clucking drab people with the nauseating combination of casseroles, deviled eggs, perfume, sweat, and old people smell was overpowering. It created a toxic mist among which the mourners sat.

Amelia looked at one hand as she covered her nose with the other. She held up four fingers. She knew how old she was. She tugged at her brown hair. Her mother had called it "flowing brown hair," which made Amelia feel elegant along with her mother's description of Amelia's hazel eyes and thick eyelashes. If she knew so much about herself, why couldn't Amelia wrap her head around all of this?

Amelia quickly looked down as a hook-nosed, tall, hunchback, thin-handed, and thick-knuckled woman made eye contact. Yes, the whole crowd could be chickens, but this lady was a vulture. Seeing her prey, the vulture woman worked her way toward Amelia.

Amelia shrunk down and tried to hide behind the large woman next to her. Sandy patted Amelia on the head and sat up, soaking in the attention she was receiving. The vulture woman, looking for some juicy gossip to feast on, was met by attention-craving Sandy. One was a vulture, and the other was a rotund hyena. Both hoped to share in the feast of the same child.

"So, everyone was killed except for the youngest?"

Amelia tried to make herself smaller as the vulture spoke. Amelia hoped that Sandy wouldn't answer but knew that she would. Sandy stood up and spoke in a larger voice

than she normally used.

"Yes. Just like I told the reporter, and I'm sure that you read in the newspaper, our neighbors were all killed except for this one, whom we have graciously decided to take in until a permanent home can be found. Who knows why people do the things that evil man did. To think that a murder-suicide would happen in our neighborhood."

The noise level rose as Sandy, smelling like she had been dumped into a bathtub of cheap lavender perfume, and the vulture lady continued performing for their audience.

Amelia didn't like them. Everyone knew who had been killed. They had just come from the funeral after all. "Closed casket," the vulture woman pointed out with raised eyebrows, subtly clawing for more explanation, while still raising the clucking level of others in the room.

The ongoing scene was becoming more uncomfortable. The questions were changing from what was reported and into what only Amelia knew. Amelia shrank into her chair further and tried to be as inconspicuous as possible. She knew what was coming next and dreaded it. It had been the same since she was found.

First it was the police officer, then the doctor, then the inspector, the distant relatives, and now the neighbors. Amelia had become tired of the routine. They would ask a

question, which she would answer as best she could. They would always act shocked and scandalized but would continue asking questions anyway.

"Do they know if there's anything wrong with the little one?" asked the vulture woman, practically drooling as she looked at Amelia.

"The psychologist said not to talk to her about it, and she would likely forget most everything," said Sandy. "She is too young to understand what happened. In a year or two she won't remember anything at all."

"Oh. I guess it won't do much good to ask her about it then," said the vulture woman, looking instantly deflated.

The vulture lingered, making idle chat, until she found a good moment to exit the confrontation, eventually wandering off for an easier bit of gossip to pick at. Sandy had unknowingly saved Amelia.

Amelia relaxed but was angry at the same time. She knew much more than the adults gave her credit for. She knew that there was no way that she could ever forget what happened.

"Mommy, Daddy, Sister..." began Amelia, under her breath.

Feelings of pain and emptiness welled up inside of her like a temperamental snake that was getting ready to

strike. If she stayed in the living room, she would cry again, inviting more unwanted attention.

Amelia quietly got up and weaved her way through the whispering adults. Occasionally hearing snippets of conversation, the pain continued to grow. Each remark was a new dagger hurled right into her soul.

"Really?" asked a tall man.

"What led up to it?" asked the wrinkled man who lived two houses away.

"What did the inspector say?" asked another person.

"How did it happen?" asked Mrs. Cumberly, a lady Amelia had met at church.

"When did they find the youngest daughter?" asked two more people in totally different conversations.

The endless faces and clucking conversation in the stench miasma of the dark-clothed ones created a disturbing, otherworldly feeling. Nothing was distinct, but this crowd and their questions were pressing in relentlessly. If Amelia didn't leave soon, she was going to explode.

She pushed her way through the crowd and tried her best not to be stopped. Whenever someone did make a comment about where she was going, Amelia would mumble the word "potty" and they would let her go. She had learned that trick from her sister when they wanted to get out of

boring, grownup, meetings and go play. As she thought of her sister, the tears began welling up and she nearly lost control of herself.

The crowd thinned as Amelia left the living room, went past the kitchen, and down the hall to the stairs leading to the basement. Proceeding downstairs, she could hear the voices trailing away and she started to feel better.

Amelia opened one of the doors at the bottom of the stairs and went into a room in the unfinished basement. She closed the door and sat down on the cold concrete floor. As she felt the cool basement air soak into her, she relaxed for the first time all day. She could hear a humming chatter and the footsteps of the people above her, but they were now quiet enough that she could block them from her mind.

The pain inside of her chest had calmed down, and it was now replaced with an intense feeling of solitude. Her mind became a silent and airtight coffin with no one to hear her screams as she slowly lost her ability to breath.

Amelia's thoughts flashed through who she could possibly confide in. There wasn't anyone left. The one face that came to her mind was Grandma Splint. But grandma had passed away a year ago, and the thought of her funeral just brought Amelia back to her current situation.

"What did I do?" Amelia asked herself aloud.

She could picture everything that had happened. She knew all the events leading up to that horrible night. Amelia had done her best to help fix things. Hadn't she and her sister told her mom and dad about the gardener? Hadn't she done everything she knew how to?

In the end, it didn't matter. Her family was gone, and Amelia couldn't help but feel like it was her fault.

"Mommy, Daddy, Sister... I'm sorry!" Amelia sobbed.

"I'm sorry! I'm sorry! I'm sorry!" Amelia began to chant as she sat curled up on the cold concrete floor. She rocked back and forth with her arms folded on her knees and her head tucked down, staring at her dress, which was becoming wet with tears.

"I'm sorry! I'm sorry! I'll be a better girl. I'll be better next time. I didn't mean to make bad things happen and to have you go away. I'm sorry!" She continued to sob, as if by apologizing enough the last few months would disappear, and her family would return. "I'm sorry! I'm sorry! I'm sorry!"

Amelia cried until she had run out of tears. She had gotten used to this over the last two weeks. Now she would get extremely tired and probably fall asleep.

She sniffed and let out a few more whimpers before lifting her head and wiping her nose and eyes. Amelia wanted the pain to end and for things to go back to the way they

were. She wasn't allowed back into her home and was instead stuck in a basement.

This was the home of Sandy and Bill. Amelia was regularly reminded that it was a temporary arrangement until a "suitable habitation" could be found. There were a few toys in the room to play with. The frame walls had posters and blankets tacked up to offer privacy. There was even a little bed she had been sleeping in.

Amelia thought that she was familiar with everything that was in the room, but as she was wiping her eyes she noticed something very different about it. In the far corner, at the edge of the basement, there was a door she'd never seen before. It looked like it had been built into the solid concrete wall but looked older than the rest of the house. It sat slightly open, and there was a warm, golden, light shining through.

Amelia wiped her eyes again and gave one final big sniff before getting up. She walked to the door and carefully inspected it. It was beautifully carved. It looked very old and had a delicately decorated brass handle. Amelia was amazed. Something about this door felt natural. It felt like it was supposed to be there, and in a way, like it always had been. She slowly opened the door, and the small light that had been shining through grew brighter until the room looked like it was filled with sunshine. For the first time in a few months,

and particularly since that horrible night two weeks ago, Amelia felt the guilt, pain, and sorrow leave her body. As she stepped through the doorway, little Amelia did something she hadn't done since the problems had started.

She smiled.

CHAPTER TWO

Bartholomew

A slight breeze was shifting the foliage of the lush green jungle. The flowers on the vines that covered the broad leaf trees gave off a sweet and slightly tart fragrance. It was a lovely afternoon, and the weather was just right for a calm picnic. At least it would have been if not for the loud popping noises and the chaos that ensued.

"Hey, Binky, you better keep up," Amelia yelled playfully as she sprinted through the dense jungle.

It had been eleven years since the funeral. Her hair had grown thicker, but her eyes were the same hazel. Slightly

behind her huffed a dwarfish figure with a long, highly manicured, beard.

"I've told you a hundred times..." the small figure panted and bellowed in his gruff voice. "...now that you're older I want you to use my full name. Sir Bartholomew Anthony Frederickson!" Bartholomew said with the emphasis on "Sir."

"Whatever you say, Binky," called Amelia, mischievously.

"Dinosaurs," yelled Bartholomew. "Whose brilliant idea was it to see dinosaurs?"

"Mine obviously," hollered back Amelia. "I have to start school next week and wanted to do something fun first."

"Yeah!" screamed Bartholomew. "But who wakes up in the morning and says 'Gee, maybe I should go out and get eaten by a prehistoric monster today'?"

"Oh yeah? Whose idea was it to play the practical joke on Betty Sue?" yelled Amelia. "And just happened to bring along firecrackers and duct tape?"

Amelia could hear the panting Bartholomew chuckling to himself. She was torn between the hilarious look of surprise on Betty Sue's face, and her concern over Bartholomew not thinking through the consequences of his actions. Amelia looked back at Bartholomew as he nearly

tripped over a root that was sticking out of the ground. He recovered quickly and strained to catch up to her.

"You have to admit," said Bartholomew with a sheepish grin on his sweaty face, "it was pretty funny though. Likely the most interesting way she's ever been woken up before."

They looked at each other with straight faces for a second while running, and quickly broke out laughing. They kept running and laughing, until they burst through the last of the undergrowth into an open field.

"I'm just glad her hide is tough enough that she wasn't hurt, otherwise it would not be funny. Don't you ever do that to anyone again. That is seriously dangerous," scolded Amelia.

"The doorway's ahead!" yelled Bartholomew, changing the subject quickly. "Think we'll make it in time?"

"We always have before," called back Amelia, still scowling with her "we'll talk more about this later" face.

Across the open field was a bare cliff sticking out of the tall grass and rising straight into the sky. At the base of the cliff, was an ancient-looking, intricately carved door with a fancy brass handle. The door looked like it had been built into the wall. It began to open as they approached it.

There was an enormous crash in the tree line behind

them. Betty Sue, an eight-ton tyrannosaurus, ran out onto the tall grass behind them with one leg covered in melted tape and scorch marks.

With a powerful roar, the great beast lowered her head and continued to charge after the two of them. Amelia and Bartholomew were nearly at the door. Bartholomew rushed through, followed closely by Amelia. As Amelia went through, she looked back to see that Betty Sue was only yards away. Amelia quickly shut the door, knowing that it would disappear from the other side and once again turn into a solid stone cliff face.

Safely back inside Amelia's bedroom, she and Bartholomew felt a small tremor as the last trace of the door disappeared. They looked at each other for a moment and broke into a fit of chuckles and guffaws.

"Must not have been able to stop in time," said Bartholomew through tears of laughter.

"That was awesome!" yelled Amelia, as she settled onto her bed, giggling. "I hope she didn't get hurt though."

"Of course not," said Bartholomew. "She's a tough old gal. I'd be more worried about the side of that cliff. You remember the times she's hit things to try and get us. Betty Sue's got a battering ram of a head."

"But itty, bitty, little arms," they both said in unison,

imitating the frantically waving miniature arms.

They started laughing again. It took a bit, but Amelia finally caught her breath.

"Narrow escape though. When was the last time we cut it that close with something?"

"Giant slugs," said Bartholomew, looking sick. "Only we didn't cut it close. I got slimed along with everything else. Thankfully it wasn't fatal. But after being stuck in that stuff, I almost wish it had been."

"Awwww, poor Binky," said Amelia, using a baby voice. "Are you sad because you got a little messy?"

"Messy nothing!" hollered Bartholomew. "Do you have any idea how long it took to get that slime off? Not to mention the nightmares I still have when I think about being covered in it after getting run over by the equivalent of a giant tongue. I'm scared to death of slugs now. They creep me out. The only reason you aren't sympathetic is because you got out of the way in time."

"Well, you started the stampede by yelling and beating that drum."

"I had no idea that they could move so fast though. Slugs are supposed to be slow."

"Now you know better."

"Yeah, I'll know better," muttered Bartholomew. "I'm

gonna really get 'em next time. They'll wish they had never run over me by the time I'm done with them."

"Yup," said Amelia. "I'm sure you'll show them. Then again, if slugs could taste what they were sliming over, they would have already received their punishment."

"Why you… you…"

As Amelia laughed, Bartholomew started laughing too. It continued until Amelia felt thoroughly laughed out. It was a good feeling. Amelia had missed this because of everything that had been happening recently.

Peaceful feelings started to turn into anxiety, and an awkward silence filled the room.

"So…, what's going to happen now?" Bartholomew quietly ventured. "You have been thinking about it, haven't you?"

"Of course I have," said Amelia. "After Russell and Sally, I know that something has to change."

"That fire wasn't your fault," said Bartholomew.

"How do I know if it was or wasn't," Amelia retorted, her temper exploding suddenly. "I was on an adventure with you when it happened. They couldn't find me. I don't know if I was outside wandering around lost in my imagination, or if I did start the fire and just don't remember it. I still don't know what happens to me when I go with you. I'm almost

sixteen. I'm too old for imaginary friends."

"But, Amelia, I…"

"No! I don't want to hear it," said Amelia, cutting Bartholomew off. "I know what you're going to say, but it isn't true. We've gone over this. I'm not okay. I'm messed up. I am, but I'm tired of it. I'm tired of being treated like a freak and an outcast! Maybe all the doctors are right. Maybe you are just an imaginary friend. Maybe you all are…"

"Amelia," said Bartholomew, calmingly. "Your anger…"

He left the reminder hanging. Amelia knew she was being unreasonable. She didn't mean to lose her temper, but she didn't know how to control it either.

"I wanted to talk to Russell and Sally. I wanted to tell them about you and about my adventures. But that would have just meant more doctor visits to figure out what is wrong with me. Instead, I didn't say anything. I get why they didn't feel like they could trust me, especially around the new baby. They didn't have to kick me out though."

Bartholomew patiently listened. Amelia knew it wasn't his strong suit, but he could be sweet at moments like these.

"Fifteen homes now," said Amelia. "Fifteen different homes, three orphanages, and two rest centers. Something has to change."

"Are you mad at me?" asked Bartholomew. "Did I do something wrong? I'll try to make it better."

"No, of course not," said Amelia. "It isn't you. I'm mad at myself. I screwed up again. Now I start all over. New home, new school, but same me. The 'same me' is the broken part of every equation. I need a new me."

"You mean you don't want to keep having adventures like we did today?" asked Bartholomew.

"It's not that," said Amelia. "I just can't anymore. I can't."

Amelia started to cry. Bartholomew stood up and walked over to sit by her on the bed. He gave Amelia a hug. She stiffened at first because she wanted to be strong and not give in to her emotions. She looked at his short arms, trying to stretch around her, and couldn't help but soften enough to hug him back.

"I don't want to lose you," Amelia said, fighting back tears. "I don't know what to do. I'm tired of being broken! I'm tired of being the weird one in school! I'm still worried that I'm crazy because I can see you, and I don't know what to do."

She held Bartholomew as she cried again. His beard was filling with her tears, but he put up with it.

"Pirates," muttered Bartholomew. "That's when

everything went topsy turvy."

"What?" whispered Amelia.

"You remember when we first met?" asked Bartholomew.

"Of course," she responded. "The day I walked through my door for the first time."

"Right," he continued. "You, pretty las, show up on my ship in a black dress that's fit for a pirate queen. I tell you that we'll become the most fearsome pirates ever to sail. I give you the finest offer you could ever receive. What response do you give back?"

"I said that we shouldn't be mean to people," said Amelia, using her lazy "we've done this a thousand times before" voice. "We should be seafaring explorers instead."

"Right," said Bartholomew. "That's where it all went wrong. We should have just stayed pirates."

After Bartholomew left, Amelia watched as the last traces of her door disappeared. She flopped on her bed and stretched.

"Pirates," she whispered, looking at the ceiling. "I would have made a cute pirate."

CHAPTER THREE

A New Home

 Bacon! Glorious bacon!

Hair was covering her face, and there was still too much sunlight. Amelia could only get one eye open because the other one was refusing until someone closed a shade. She sat up just enough to survey the landscape.

"Okay," she said to herself, looking around with one eye. "Bacon in the morning, fancy old room in the tower, Victorian home, and it's another Sarah this time. Sarah Buttonley. Right, I'm in Pickleton."

Amelia flopped down into the comfy quilts on the

soft bed and burrowed underneath like a mole. She loved sleep. Staying bundled up all day would be heavenly. Unfortunately, this mole loved bacon even more than sleep, and the smell left her tummy rumbling.

Amelia sat up in her bed. She rubbed the last of the sleep out of her eyes and put on some slippers. As she stepped out of her room, she went to the railing that overlooked the staircase and let the wonderful smell of breakfast waft up to her. She then grasped the banister and went downstairs to the kitchen.

"Good morning," Amelia heard as she entered. Sarah hadn't even looked up, but instead seemed to know by instinct that someone was there. She was humming and kept her attention on the eggs to make sure they wouldn't get overcooked.

"Morning," replied Amelia mechanically.

She had planned on snacking and running back to bed, but like previous mornings Sarah had set out a full feast. It was as if it would be the last one in the world. Bacon, eggs, sausage, biscuits and gravy, fruit, pancakes, homemade butter syrup, muffins with butter and jam, orange juice, and fresh milk.

"Sit down anywhere," said Sarah.

They said a prayer and started to eat.

"So, what do you want to do today?" asked Sarah. "I already watered the garden this morning and aside from paying the utilities sometime today, my schedule is open."

"I dunno," mumbled Amelia with a mouthful of pancake.

"Well, what if we went over to see your new school?"

Amelia wasn't sure how she felt about this. "How many kids go to the school?" asked Amelia. "I mean, well, it's a really small town so there can't be that many kids my age, can there?"

"I believe that you will have about twenty-seven that are your age," said Sarah. "There are only about ninety students total in the high school. They are split up between grades nine, ten, eleven, and twelve."

Amelia's jaw dropped, and she had to catch the orange juice that spilled out. "Twenty-seven!" she said with shock. "My last school had thirty-five in each classroom, but there were hundreds of kids in my grade."

"Well, part of Pickleton's charm is that it's in the country," said Sarah. "I know you haven't been in a small town like this before, but I think it will grow on you."

After breakfast, Amelia got ready for the day and they headed out. People were up and about. They smiled and waved as they passed each other on the street. Many were

watering their gardens as Amelia and Sarah passed. More often than not, Sarah would stop and chat for a few minutes about the weather with them.

When they got to the main street of town, Amelia noticed all the little old-fashioned shops that were attached to each other. A combination ice cream parlor and pharmacy, a cafe, a clothing store, and a few other fun little stores made up one seemingly continuous building. There was even a little single screen movie theater pinched in between the bookstore and the vacuum and sewing machine repair shop. At the end of the street sat an old, granite courthouse that was also used as the city building. To the side of it was an old library that looked like it had been built at the same time as the courthouse. Wrapping around the courthouse and library, on the sides and the back, was a small park. Through the center of the park ran a little stream that meandered through the rest of town.

Two blocks away from the courthouse were the red brick schools. There was an elementary, middle, and high school that all sat next to each other and shared the same baseball field, track, football field, and a large grassy play area. Like everything else in this community, the schools were very old, quaint, and small.

Amelia had never seen anything like Pickleton before.

She had seen the whole town on a short walk. No malls, no noise, and no smog covering the town. There was also a pleasant but unfamiliar smell that Amelia later discovered was a mix of wildflowers and alfalfa. There were so many flowers in the country, and so much plant life, that the scent was carried on the wind like some sweet perfume.

Sarah left Amelia to explore the school while she went back to the courthouse to pay the utilities bill. Amelia walked around the corner of the school and saw a group of kids that were sitting on a swing set.

"Who are you?"

Amelia was so distracted with the new experience of the town and the school that she had trouble responding. The kids looked about her age. The group consisted of two girls and four boys. The skinniest of the group had noticed her and spoken up. He was a boy in blue jeans, sneakers, a bright red shirt, a baseball cap, and was covered in freckles.

"I said, who are you?"

"My name's Amelia," she said, feeling a little silly about not answering faster. "I'm new."

"Obviously," said the same freckle-faced boy, dripping with sarcasm. "I've been here my whole life and have never seen you, so thanks for stating the obvious."

"I bet she's the one that moved in with freaky old

Sarah," commented a girl who had black hair and was starting to get zits all over her face.

"Nah..." said the other girl. "No one would move in with her. She's disturbed."

"That's the truth," said a boy with hair that almost covered his eyes. "She's a witch. She once flew over my uncle's farm and scared the chickens into not laying eggs."

"I heard she ate her parents," said the zit-faced girl.

"My cousin said that she was put in an insane asylum for twenty years and was only let out because she tricked one of the guards," said a short, round boy in overalls.

They continued until they realized that Amelia was still standing nearby, looking very dumbfounded.

"So, do you live with crazy Sarah or not?" asked the zit-covered girl.

They all looked at Amelia expectantly. Amelia hesitated for a moment, but the anger she felt welling up inside took over.

"Yes, I do. I've been there for a few days, and she is wonderful. I don't think it's right for you to be spreading rumors that can hurt people… especially when you don't even know them," said Amelia, recognizing her own hypocrisy. She didn't really know Sarah yet either.

"Yeah..., normal if you're a freak," commented the

short, round boy. Everyone in the group started laughing at that, and they began to call Amelia a freak.

Amelia didn't want to start a fight on the first day she met kids from her school. She bit her tongue, turned around, and walked away. As she rounded the corner of the school and started toward the courthouse, she could hear that their name-calling had turned into a chant.

"Freak, freak, she's a freak. Freak, freak, she's a freak."

Amelia felt her heart sink and the tears well up. School hadn't even started and she was already an outcast. It wasn't fair. Why couldn't things ever just work out? Why couldn't she ever have people who would like her for who she was and accept her from the start? Why did it always have to be like this? Why?

Amelia was so wrapped up in her thoughts and anger at her situation that she almost ran into Sarah, who was coming out of the courthouse.

"Sorry. Didn't see you," said Sarah. "Already done looking around your new school?"

"Yeah," said Amelia, wiping her eyes quickly and trying to hide her emotions. "I've seen as much as I want to."

They walked in silence on the way home except for when Sarah would occasionally say hi to people as they passed. When they arrived home, Sarah began making lunch.

Amelia tried to help, but just got in the way. Instead, she went outside to walk around in the orchard.

She thought about what the kids had said about Sarah. They couldn't be talking about the same person. Also, if people were spreading those kinds of stories about Sarah, why was everyone so nice to her when they were out walking?

When Amelia was called in for lunch, she ate quietly and brooded to herself.

After lunch, Amelia went to her room. She sat on her bed, looking around for something to do. She was angry and bored. She pulled a small box out from under her bed, opened it, and spread the contents out on her bed to help calm herself. As she placed her treasures around, she spent time examining and trying to figure them out. These were all items that she had picked up when she had gone on adventures. Most were rocks or shells that were pretty or unique. Those were easy enough to explain as to how she could have found them while she was in pretend mode, but there were a few that were more difficult to explain, and so they had become puzzles for Amelia as she would try to figure out where they had really come from. Despite doing research, some of the gems were still unidentified. Some of the small dried fruits didn't look like anything Amelia had ever seen in the real world.

She had a section of clockwork parts that she had gotten from a robot that once tried to kidnap Bartholomew. After the kidnapping, and spending some time listening to Bartholomew, the robot quickly returned him with an apology, a gift, and many condolences to Amelia. Bartholomew took the insult personally. As Amelia smiled to herself about the memory, she could only think that the pieces must have come out of something broken around the house that she had picked up while wandering around in her imaginary state of mind.

She held a bat-like wing, a ring made of hair, pinky-sized shoes, a marble that would glow the evening before foggy mornings, and a pendant of a beetle that was silver with a turquoise-like inlay. As she picked up each in turn, she would try to figure them out for a moment before returning the objects into the box.

After storing the box back under the bed, Amelia looked up at the one picture she still had of her family. She let the mixed emotions linger until another emotion took over.

"I'm so bored," shouted Amelia.

She couldn't take it anymore and went downstairs to find Sarah, who was sitting on the front porch swing and reading a book. Amelia plopped down next to Sarah.

"Isn't there anything to do?" asked Amelia.

"There's lots to do," responded Sarah, looking up. "It's really about what you want to do. You can garden, you can read a book, you can go for a walk, the options are limitless."

"But those are all boring right now," said Amelia, flopping back on the swing.

"What's wrong?' asked Sarah.

"I'm bored," said Amelia.

"No. What's really wrong?" pressed Sarah. "You were fine this morning. You went silent during our walk, and now you are getting surly."

Amelia had the morning events repeating in her mind and was running through scenarios of what she should have said or done. It didn't help and only made things worse. Even her efforts to distract herself didn't work.

"Was it something I did?" asked Sarah.

"No, nothing like that," said Amelia, sitting up.

"Spit it out," said Sarah, smiling. "It's better to be straight forward than to let it fester."

"Fine," said Amelia. "At the school I ran into a bunch of kids. They apparently knew you and started saying all sorts of mean things about you being a crazy witch that cannibalized your parents."

"Wow," said Sarah. "And now you're scared? Look, if you had put anywhere in your paperwork that you would have an issue with this kind of lifestyle, then we could have called this whole arrangement off. Which child told? We'll start by devouring them. Would that make you feel better?"

It was hard for Amelia not to laugh at the absurdity of the conversation.

"Maybe," chuckled Amelia.

"Rumors are nothing new," said Sarah. "Especially in a small town and about a woman who lives by herself. Some things are true. I was with my parents when they passed away. My father died of cancer, and my mother died a few years later of Alzheimer's disease. A lot of what you will hear though is not true. I didn't eat my parents. Stories can get twisted and changed in retelling."

"Don't they bother you?" asked Amelia.

"Why should they bother me? It doesn't matter what other people think about me. My opinion of myself is the only thing that matters," said Sarah.

"But then, why was everyone so nice to you while we were walking around if they all think those crazy things about you?"

"It doesn't really matter now, does it?" said Sarah. "The main thing is that I feel good about myself. Regardless

of what they say, I will continue to be nice to the people around me and be genuine in my friendship. What they do in response is up to them, but I can't waste time letting their decisions affect me."

Amelia felt like Sarah was trying to teach her something important, but she also felt like Sarah was lecturing her. Instead of pursuing it, and getting lectured further, Amelia opted for silence.

"Truthfully," confessed Sarah. "It bothers me a little, but I have learned to let it go and I make the choice to not have it damage my life anymore. It isn't worth the frustration over something I can't control."

"I still wish the morning could have gone differently," said Amelia.

"I know," said Sarah. "Anything I can do to make things better?"

"Nothing. Unless," said Amelia, smiling wickedly. "Out of curiosity, if you were a witch…"

"Yes?"

"What kind of seasonings would you use to prepare a bunch of high schoolers to be palatable?"

"Most any kind of seasonings will work," said Sarah, with an equally devilish grin. "Like chicken, they have potential to work in a lot of dishes. The problem is the

aftertaste that you can never be quite free from."

CHAPTER FOUR

Island Hop

 "Quiet or I'll de-feather every last one of you pompous, noisy, lunch-stealing, accomplices," howled Bartholomew.

The noises of the tropical birds increased and drowned him out. Amelia and Bartholomew walked into the clearing with the familiar small grass hut at the center of the island, and Amelia knocked on the door.

When there wasn't an immediate response, Bartholomew grew visibly agitated.

"You in there, Ohma?" hollered Bartholomew.

"Yes," called back a voice from inside. "Have you

arrived to partake in the luminous glow of my wisdom?"

"No, we're here to take you with us," responded Bartholomew.

Amelia and Bartholomew looked at each other and had to stifle their giggles when they started hearing the crashing. Pots and pans were clanging, things were being upturned and thrown all around, and they even heard Ohma catch himself mid-curse a few times after extra-loud crashes. There was a short silence, more clanging, and then the door opened and Ohma was outside with a backpack on that was as green as his suit. It was overflowing with pots, hats, a picnic basket, an umbrella, and other things tied on and hanging down the outside. He put on his glasses and smoothed back the hair on his head before putting on a tight green bowler cap.

"So, are we departing to discover that illustrious maiden to bask in her presence also?" he asked, beaming with a huge grin on his thin and slightly wrinkled face.

"Yeah," said Amelia, elbowing Bartholomew to stop giggling. "We'll be going to pick up Amy next."

"Glorious! I had been contemplating when we would embark together once more. It's been absolutely ages since our last excursion. How long has it been since I've laid eyes on that wonderful beauty of a maiden?"

"Two weeks, you dirty old loon," muttered Bartholomew.

"He only looks old," Amelia whispered to Bartholomew with a giggle. "This is my imaginary world, so he can't be older than me."

"He's still a loon though," said Bartholomew.

"Even a moment away from the one that you love can be an eternity," continued the love-struck Ohma, oblivious to Bartholomew's comments.

They walked through the jungle, and when it gave way to the white sand beaches of Diplump island, they boarded the rowboat to return to Bartholomew's ship. The double-masted ship stretched about a hundred feet. It had a cabin sticking out of the deck in the rear. The cabin had a door leading into a sitting room and stairs on the sides leading to the helm on top. The whole thing looked like a proper pirate ship.

It wasn't painted, but instead had polished wood that was a beautiful mixture of light and dark colors. The masts were made of wood, but also had large iron bands that held them together and iron settings that attached them to the deck of the ship, where they ran down through the deck and into the base of the ship. The two masts had stunning white sails and plenty of ropes and webbed rope for climbing. On one side of the ship, the name "Mistress" was carved, which Amelia ran her hand across to help slow the rowboat as they pulled alongside.

Amelia immediately went to the helm while Ohma helped Bartholomew secure the rowboat.

"Pull up the anchor," called Amelia.

Ohma and Bartholomew worked the wheel to pull the anchor out of the water.

"Drop the sails," called Amelia again.

"Are you going to do any of the work today or are you just gonna bark out orders?" yelled Bartholomew, panting with the exertion of climbing up the rigging to reach the sails.

"Woof," said Amelia. "Captain Woof."

"I'm the captain," muttered Bartholomew, almost to himself. "It's my ship."

With the sails down, they began heading toward the island of the fleora when a storm came upon their ship.

The rain pelting Amelia was cold and harsh. Yet, in a strange way it was revitalizing as well. The wild storm was finally helping take away her painful numbness and allowing Amelia's senses to return. She gripped the helm of the ship and worked to keep it under control.

"Can't you clear up this stormy weather?" said a grumpy Bartholomew, joining Amelia.

"Maybe," responded Amelia, "but I'm not going to." She flashed him a mischievous smile and looked back in the direction the ship was headed.

"What good is having total control with your imagination if you don't use it?" ranted Bartholomew.

"You know that isn't true," whispered Amelia, feeling her playfulness leave.

She wished it were though. Amelia thought that if she had that kind of power, she would be able to imagine her problems away. Her extremely limited control over her imaginary world was only another sign of how unstable she was.

"It looks like it's going to clear up soon anyway," said Amelia. "Stop your complaining."

Bartholomew playfully stuck his tongue out at Amelia and went back to grumbling under his breath, through his dripping beard.

As the storm lifted, the sun shone brightly and began to dry them and their vessel. The wind blew more of the clouds away, and they could see the island of the fleora on the horizon.

The first time Amelia saw the fleora, they reminded her of illustrations of fairies that she had seen. They were extremely tall and graceful. To Amelia's delight, some even

had wings. They did have one major flaw though. In Bartholomew's words: "They are beautiful and wonderful creatures without a thought in their heads."

The fleora, although graced with many things, could not count intellect among them. Most were so flighty that they couldn't even remember what happened the day before. For them, every morning was a clean slate, and every experience was a fresh new one. There were exceptions like their friend Amy, but even she was quite forgetful and innocent.

Amelia giggled to herself.

"What's so funny?" asked Bartholomew.

"Nothing," said Amelia, straightening her back and hiding her smile. "We're almost there. Get ready to secure the sails and drop the anchor."

"Yes, Captain Woof," said Bartholomew, saluting.

"Grrrrrrrrr," said Amelia, doing her best dog impression.

"Praytell, who's Captain Woof?" asked Ohma.

"Help secure the sails," yelled Bartholomew.

The island was covered with giant flowers. Some were so large that they drooped over the ocean and created a ramp that the group could simply climb up directly from Bartholomew's ship. They were greeted by a large gathering

of the fleora that were fascinated with the newcomers because they hadn't seen anything like them all day. Amelia, Bartholomew, and Ohma slowly worked their way past the crowd and started walking through the flower forest until they reached the home of Amy.

Amy lived in one of the flowers of a giant hyacinth. With someone different living in each of the flowers, it looked like a strange apartment building.

Amy's flower was filled with furniture that appeared to be made entirely of plants. Her dresser had two doors that looked like giant leaves. Her desk looked like it had grown out of a rose bush. Even her tea set and other china looked like they were large flowers that had grown into those shapes.

"My most felicitous salutations! How does this fine and glorious day find you?" asked Ohma with a deep bow.

Thankfully, they had forced him to leave his backpack on the ship. Otherwise, it would have been an extremely strange sight: a thin, green-suited, turtlish man wearing a backpack that looked like an overgrown shell, bowing inside of a flower and making eyes at a tall, elegant girl who had clear, gold-veined, wings and wore a long flowing dress of what looked like large flower petals and leaves.

"I'm okay," said Amy staring off at a cloud, watching it change shapes, "except for..." Amy looked down for a

moment and seemed to be trying hard to remember something. "Well, there's been this bee that has been trying to pollinate my home. It wouldn't be so bad except that when it comes in to find nectar and only finds me, it's been getting angry. I don't know where its pollen and nectar went. I moved in after someone else moved out. Besides..." she said, as she straightened up and looked very indignant. "I don't think that I'm such a bad thing to find. In fact, I think that I'm pretty special and it should be happy to meet me."

Amelia could sense that Ohma was about to say something about Amy being special and that Bartholomew was about to make a sarcastic comment about the bee. To save time, she piped in, "We still have to go get Raskiel. I've already been here an hour, and if we want to have an adventure tonight, then we better get going now. I have to leave in a couple of hours to get some sleep."

"Alright, let's get moving," said Bartholomew.

He grabbed Ohma's arm and had to forcibly drag him through the door. Amelia followed them out of the flower so that Amy could change into clothes that would be more functional. By the time they got back to the ship, Amy had caught up to them. She was now wearing a set of jeans, a shirt with holes cut in for her wings, and a pair of sneakers.

"You really do wear those better than I could," said

Amelia, feeling frumpy suddenly.

Amy didn't say anything but simply smiled. Amelia knew that Amy adored attention. Amy was careful to preen herself and straighten her clothes as she went, just so that the other fleora would pay attention to her as well. Amy wasn't mean spirited at all, and Amelia knew that. It was just frustrating to never be the pretty girl in the group.

As they left the island of the fleora, Bartholomew pulled out his compass and looked up at Amelia.

"So what are we going to do today?"

"I don't know," she responded. "I needed to get away."

"I thought that you didn't want to do that anymore," said Bartholomew in a serious but gentle tone. He obviously wanted to say more but was being careful to choose his words.

"I thought so too. I still don't know what to do. Things are already going bad. I thought that this time it would be different. I thought this time I would be able to fit in. It's just, everything stinks so badly again that I don't care anymore."

"You'll probably feel different in the morning after you get a good night of sleep. You'll go back to wanting a normal life, and to forget about us. However," he said looking

up at her, "I'll always be here if you need me."

Amelia smiled and sighed deeply. "Have I really become that predictable?"

"Yes, and so have those two idiots," said Bartholomew, motioning to the source of noise on the ship.

"Please, oh wonderous beauty, please alight so that I may converse with you. I shall repair to the pantry and prepare us some victuals if you will only allow yourself to grace my presence. Please, won't you come down?"

Ohma was on the deck, looking up at the mast where Amy was roosting and acting as lookout.

"But if I come down, won't it be hard for me to keep my post and spot land?" Amy asked, thoughtfully.

Ohma thought about this for a little and seemed to be devising a good argument. Finally, with a look of resolve, he returned to begging.

Amelia exchanged glances with Bartholomew and smiled. "They really are oblivious about each other, aren't they?"

"Yup," said Bartholomew, grinning at the two.

They watched Ohma and Amy until Amelia bent down by Bartholomew and whispered, "Thank you for always being here."

"You're welcome," said Bartholomew.

"Help, help, it's got me. It's got me," screamed Ohma.

Ohma had been trying to climb up the netting on the mast to be with the diligent Amy at her post, but he had been wearing his full pack and had gotten stuck. Ohma so closely resembled a flailing green fly that had gotten caught in a spider web that Amelia and Bartholomew started laughing all over again. Through the laughing, Ohma kept screaming for help.

"That looks like so much fun," said Amy. "If I didn't have to watch for land, I would have loved to join you."

Amy's comment only helped fuel the laughter.

After Amelia and Bartholomew helped to free Ohma and take him into the cabin to rest, they heard Amy call, "Land ho!"

CHAPTER FIVE

The Warning

 A landscape of heat and gray. The lush island was filled with trees, plants, birds, and animals that were all unsaturated, ashen hues. The giant volcano on the side of the island, with its streams of red lava, was the only color punctuating the otherwise monotone environment.

"Hey Raskiel, you old puffball pain in the neck! Get out here!" called Bartholomew.

"You aren't still mad at him, are you, Binky?" teased Amelia.

"Of course I am," said Bartholomew. "He set my

beard on fire."

"Well..." mused Amelia. "You did shave your name and a smiley face into his fur."

"His grew back in!" yelled Bartholomew.

"So did yours!" hollered back Amelia, doing her best Bartholomew impression.

"But it's one thing to wake up and have some hair missing. It's another entirely to wake up with your face on fire." he said, exasperated.

"That must be Binky out there!" came a voice from the cave.

"That's great! How did you know?" asked Amy as a giant ash-colored creature, which looked like a cross between a wolf and a bear, appeared in the mouth of the cave.

"Only as obnoxious an idiot as Binky..." said the creature, with an emphasis on Bartholomew's nickname, "could have whined loud enough to knock the books off my library shelves."

"Library," scoffed Bartholomew. "You live in a cave. I don't believe any of what you say is in there. That's why you never let us in."

"I never let anyone in because I don't want you to destroy my art, instruments, or my collection of porcelain dolls," growled Raskiel.

"You coming with us tonight?" interjected Amelia, attempting to stop another argument.

"Sure, just give me a second to lock up first," said Raskiel, suddenly polite and with his fur turning a light brown.

Raskiel went back into the cave, and the group could hear what sounded like dozens of dead bolts being shut. He came out after a short while and said, "I'm ready."

"Do you really have to lock up every time?" asked Bartholomew. "It's just a bunch of stupid dolls... supposedly."

"They are not a bunch of stupid dolls." responded Raskiel, his fur going back to gray with highlights of red. "For your information, they are one-of-a-kind, hand-painted, porcelain dolls."

Amelia couldn't help smiling to herself. She was grateful for the stability and comfort that her friends brought to her life, even if they did fight a lot.

"Like a hairy, overgrown, stuffed animal needs to collect dolls. I'll bet you're really hoarding a giant dog food collection, you mangy mutt."

As they loaded up into the now-cramped rowboat, Amelia watched Raskiel's fur change colors to the brown of the boat. His chameleon-like tendencies always amazed her.

His personality was the same as his fur. He shifted between being a great intellectual to being a fearsome beast when danger arose.

By the time they reached the ship, they were glad to be out of the confining space. They got on, secured the rowboat, and took up their positions. Amy went to her perch atop the mast, Raskiel went on top of the cabin by the helm to help navigate, Amelia and Bartholomew went to the helm to control the ship, and Ohma wandered around aimlessly on the deck trying to get Amy to notice him until he was sent to deal with the anchor and sails.

"Where are we going?" asked Raskiel.

Bartholomew simply looked up to Amelia. She realized that they were all waiting on her. She didn't have any ideas. She just wanted to spend time with people who cared.

"What about the glowing lagoon?" Bartholomew whispered so quietly that only Amelia could hear.

"That sounds perfect," she responded. She then spoke loud enough to be heard by Raskiel. "We're going to the glowing lagoon."

"It's been one of those days, huh?" asked Raskiel.

Amelia nodded with a sour face.

"Works for me," said Raskiel. "I'm easy."

"Plus, I don't think the other two will mind one way

or the other," said Bartholomew, staring at the deck.

The sun had set, and it was starting to get dark. Bartholomew and Raskiel were both good navigators, though, so Amelia wasn't worried. They set sail and continued in the moonlit night. It wasn't far, but it was hidden. They reached an island that was sheer cliff that reached up as far as the eye could see. If someone had sailed all the way around the island they wouldn't find a single place to even get a foothold to be able to start climbing up, let alone getting to the top to see what was there.

Amelia walked to the front of the ship and held her arms outstretched in front, and her hands together. She concentrated and tried to visualize what she wanted to happen. She then opened her arms so that they stuck out to her sides, and yelled, "Open!" The solid cliff face responded by cracking. Two major chunks of the cliff then rumbled to the sides and created an opening just wide enough to allow the ship to pass through.

Because a small breeze always came out of the passage and the current always went into it, they secured the sails and had to rely on their momentum and the current to get them through the long passage to the opening in the center of the island. Once the ship reached the opening, the passage sealed behind them, and they dropped anchor.

In the center of the island was a lagoon that was fed through underground tunnels connected to the ocean. The cliff walls were so high that there was never any daylight. The sun never went directly overhead, and so it was even possible to see the stars during the middle of the day. The lagoon itself produced enough light to see below the water and a short way up the cliff. Because of the lack of sunlight, life in the lagoon learned to compensate. The coral, fish, and even the plants all glowed red, blue, green, and everything in between.

For Amelia, the most interesting thing about the lagoon were the drawings along the cliff walls. They depicted the various adventures that Amelia had been on. She loved to lie on the deck, looking up at the stars and the glowing lights that shone up from the water below as they danced on the cliff faces. Even though this world was a safe place to escape to, the glowing lagoon was her absolute safe haven. This was the one place that she could truly feel secure and untouchable.

"Cannonball!" bellowed Bartholomew, after quickly stripping off all his clothes except for a pair of trunks and an undershirt.

He jumped into the water and splashed Ohma and Amy, who were watching from the edge of the ship. Raskiel

then jumped in and tried to outdo Bartholomew. As a result, a second sheet of water came flying onto the deck of the ship, and Ohma ended up totally drenched. Ohma went into the cabin and changed into an old fashioned, full-body swimsuit and rubber cap that were the same awful color of green as his regular clothes. Amelia felt like it made him look even more like a turtle without a shell than his regular green suit. Ohma quickly joined the others in the water by slipping on the wet deck, hitting the edge, and flipping in with a splash.

"Hurry up, slowpoke!" hollered Bartholomew. "What's the holdup?"

"Nothing," yelled back Amelia, who realized that she was the only one left on the ship after Amy had also changed and gone into the water. "I'll be right in."

She quickly kicked off her shoes and socks and dived in. They took turns diving down and tried to catch the glowing fish with their bare hands. Bartholomew was the only one who succeeded. He came up with two glowing crabs.

"Those don't count," said Raskiel. "They aren't fish."

"Yes," replied Bartholomew. "But they were in the water, and so they are fair game."

"If that's the case, then I can just break off pieces of coral."

"Even at that, I doubt you could beat me. You soggy rag mop."

Amelia was starting to feel a little worn out and headed back onto the deck of the ship. Ohma and Amy decided to have a breath holding contest and Raskiel joined them. As the contest started, Bartholomew followed Amelia onto the ship.

"Amelia," Bartholomew began tentatively, "would it be all right if I asked you something?"

"Sure," said Amelia.

"I know that you have been having a hard time, so I haven't wanted to bother you. I just... um..."

Amelia could see that he was struggling to get out what he wanted to say. She smiled and tried to be encouraging.

"Well, I've just been wondering... umm... what will happen when you don't want me around anymore?"

Amelia was caught off guard by the question. She hadn't thought about it before. He was only an imaginary friend, wasn't he? Why would he worry about what happens? Maybe it was her own concerns manifesting.

Amelia sat stupidly for a moment before finding any words. "The truth is..." began Amelia, "I have no idea. I guess I didn't think about it from your point of view. I'm happy you

are here. You're my best friend. I just don't know."

"Don't worry about it," whispered Bartholomew, giving a reassuring smile.

Amelia sat awkwardly for a moment, and then finally flopped onto her back and stared up at the night sky.

That's odd, thought Amelia. The shadows at the top of the cliff seem to be moving. It must be my eyes playing a trick on me.

Amelia tried squinting to see more clearly. Right as she did so, she heard a blood-curdling shriek from Amy.

Amelia and Bartholomew jumped to their feet and ran over to the railing of the ship. Something was very wrong. Amy never shrieked. She didn't have enough intelligence to know when to be scared of something.

"What happened?" hollered Bartholomew.

It was a wasted question. They stood there with their mouths open, staring at the writing. Sections of coral and fish had gone dark in a pattern to spell out the message that had frightened Amy.

Leave this place, return to your room, and beware the Rha' Shalim. Leave now! You are being watched.

Raskiel and Ohma helped Amy swim back to the ship.

Raskiel's wolfish paws became more bearlike so he could haul Amy up the webbed rope and onto the deck, while Amelia and Bartholomew helped to pull a struggling Ohma the rest of the way up the side of the ship.

"What does it mean?" asked Raskiel, talking to Amy.

"We must leave this place at once!" screamed Amy. She was lying on the deck, eyes wide with fear, pupils fully dilated. "I saw them. The Rha' Shalim. The shadow spawns. I saw what they've done. It's... It's..."

At this, her mouth was wide with a silent scream. Her eyes widened more, and her pupils contracted. She turned and looked at Amelia. "You must leave right now. You are in great danger." The next thing she said froze Amelia's spine. "They're here."

They could feel a cold audible silence. They looked up. The stars had gone out. There was something darker than shadow moving down the walls.

"Let's go!" shouted Bartholomew. "Raskiel, pull up the anchor!"

Bartholomew took command and continued barking out orders. Amelia opened the cliff face so that they could leave, but it was slow work and they could see the darkness descending even faster.

"We need more wind!" shouted Bartholomew, looking

at Amelia. "The current draft won't get us through fast enough."

"You know I can't do that!" said Amelia. "It only worked the one time."

"Well, now would be an ideal time to try again!" shouted Raskiel, his hair turning red and orange as he grew slightly and his claws got longer.

Amelia immediately began to concentrate, and a short gust of wind came blowing down into the lagoon, filling the sails, and pushing the ship through the opening. It wasn't much and didn't last very long, but thankfully it pushed them much faster than normal. They had to rely on the regular draft to push them the rest of the way.

"That helped," said Bartholomew. "But it may not be enough. Look!"

Bartholomew pointed back into the lagoon, and Amelia could see that the shadows had reached the bottom and were starting toward them.

"What's that?" asked Raskiel.

A single figure had appeared out of the darkness. It was wearing a long flowing cloak that was darker than anything Amelia had ever seen. The creature drew out a dark sword that looked like it had smoke pouring off it.

"Quick, we're almost through! Close the lagoon now!"

barked Bartholomew. "If you wait any longer, that'll make it through as well!"

Amelia concentrated, clapped her hands together, and yelled at the wall to close. It began to shut. As it did so, the water swelled underneath them and the air rushed faster to push the ship out right before the cliff sealed itself together.

The shadowy figure was nowhere to be seen. Amelia waited only a moment to make sure there was no immediate danger, and then ran down to the main deck to check on Amy. Amy had passed out during their escape, and Ohma had stayed by her side the entire time.

"Are you okay?" asked Amelia, as Amy started to stir.

"Why? Is something wrong?" asked a puzzled Amy. "Oh, I must have fallen asleep. I was having a lot of fun swimming. I don't know why I fell asleep. I'm sorry. I must have missed the party."

"Do you not remember anything else?" asked Amelia, now being joined by Raskiel and Bartholomew. "What happened at the end of the breath holding contest?"

"I'm not sure?" responded Amy, straining to remember. "Did I win?"

"We need to get you home," Bartholomew said to Amelia. "Use the door right now and get out of here. I'll make sure that everyone else gets home safely."

Amelia was too frightened and confused to argue. She quickly said goodbye and walked through the wide-open door that had appeared in the wall of the ship between the stairs to the helm and the door that led into the cabin. She had one thought going over and over in her mind. What are the Rha' Shalim?

CHAPTER SIX

School

The look of nausea on the faces of the people around her were delightful. The mention of the act wasn't enough. The description of the scalpel cutting through the flesh and the smells described got such wonderful reactions that Amelia smiled with some sadistic pleasure as she watched.

The first day of school was already going poorly, much as Amelia had been expecting. What she didn't expect was the excitement from the small, freckle-faced girl with braided light brown hair and Coke bottle glasses that had been assigned to sit next to her.

"Frogs! We get to dissect real frogs! It's gonna be so cool to learn how stuff works," the girl said. "By the way, my name's Cindy."

Amelia already caught her name as they were being assigned seats. Cindy Pattersly. She seemed nice enough. Amelia couldn't have asked for a better science partner. With the reaction the teacher just got, it looked like they were the only two girls who were interested in the class.

"My name is Amelia. I moved here a few weeks ago."

"I know," said Cindy. "It's nice to have someone new in the class."

"Look, the freaks are starting to group," came a taunting voice from behind them.

Amelia turned to see that it was a short, round boy named Clyde Jones. He was one of the boys who she had met on her first walk around town. Amelia now had names to put with the faces of all the kids from that miserable encounter.

The zit-faced girl, and seeming leader of the group, was Becky Bicks. The other girl who had been in the group that day was a pretty, scarlet-haired girl named Jessica Grant. The freckle-faced boy's name was Bobby Hunsick. The boy with long hair and bangs nearly covering his eyes was Billy Jessop. The final boy, a tall, quiet, boy with short blond hair, was named Spencer Maxis. He seemed to be the only one not

snickering at Clyde's remark.

"I thought Cindy was pathetic and had to be alone. But I never knew she was weird enough to hang out with this new girl," said Becky.

"Just ignore them," whispered Cindy and Amelia to each other at the same time.

They had a moment of insight and realized that they had both dealt with this a lot. It was so funny that they couldn't help but laugh. It was then their turn to hide a fit of giggles. Becky was visibly confused at this strange reaction and became angry.

"What's so funny? Huh? You freaks!"

"Miss Bicks," came the teacher's voice. "Is something wrong?"

"No sir," lied Becky.

She kept trying to retain some of her poise and dignity as the teacher went back to lecturing, but she stared daggers at them throughout the rest of the class.

Amelia was able to mostly avoid a lot of the hazing for the next two classes, but it all changed when they arrived in their English class. She noticed that it was solely sophomores again. Amelia and Cindy ended up sitting far apart when they found where their names had been placed on their assigned seats.

Feeling isolated, Amelia was already on edge when the chanting began. It started from one of the boys near her. It was slow and quiet at first but spread quickly throughout the class.

"Freak, freak, she's a freak. Freak, freak, she's a freak."

Amelia could feel her temper rise along with the volume of the chanting. She gripped her desk and could feel the throbbing of the veins in her head. The class immediately went quiet as the door to the room opened. In walked a wrinkly, leather-skinned lady who looked something akin to a sun-dried prune. She was followed by a younger woman.

"We are going to be trying something different this year," said the older woman. "We will do a new kind of English course. I'll let her explain it to you though."

"My name is Tristen Copnet," said the younger lady, stepping forward. "I recently graduated from college, and this is my first year as a full-fledged teacher. The principal has agreed to allow me to start up a new program that has worked wonderfully in other schools. It is called 'Honors English.' It is going to be a much more difficult class, but it will also be much more rewarding in the long run. Rather than only focusing on grammar and the rules of the English language, it will focus on literature. It will use all the things that you would be learning in this English class, but will

expound upon it through prose, style, and the ability to convey a message. Anyone that feels like they would be able to handle it, and is interested, please raise your hand."

Amelia raised her hand immediately. It seemed like the only chance she would have to get away from these people. She was happy to see that Cindy's hand was in the air as well. There were six other kids who slowly raised their hands, and the little group left to follow this new teacher to another classroom.

"Pull those desks in a circle," said Ms. Copnet. "There's not many of you, so let's keep this informal and get started."

Amelia was happy to sit next to Cindy. She glared at Spencer Maxis though. While he was quiet, he was still part of the playground group.

Ms. Copnet handed out the syllabi, and they reviewed it together. They spent the rest of class talking about various things they had read in the past. Amelia had fun finding out that Cindy had a lot of the same tastes in books that she had.

The bell rang and ended their discussion. Amelia hadn't even been aware of how quickly the time was passing.

"I have a sack lunch," said Cindy, picking up her bag. "If you give me a bit to grab it from my locker, I can meet you in the lunchroom."

"I brought something from home too," said Amelia. "Do we have to eat inside, or can we take our food and go somewhere else?"

"We can go out onto the grass," said Cindy.

They began walking to their lockers, and passed the other students coming out of class. Amelia fell into the wall as something caught her foot.

"Watch your step," said Becky.

Amelia could feel the blood rising, burning hot. She got tunnel vision that was tinged with red as she jumped up and got right in Becky's face, startling Becky for a moment.

"What is your problem?" Amelia hissed, rage building inside of her.

"You," said Becky, now recovered. "Learn to take a joke and back off."

Amelia felt a light tug on her elbow.

"Let's just go," Cindy said in a quiet voice.

Amelia turned to see Cindy panicking, and it helped to cool her anger down.

"Fine," said Amelia. "We can go."

As Amelia turned to walk away, she was shoved in the back and had to force herself to keep walking straight ahead despite the mocking laughter that arose behind her.

Amelia couldn't stand the contradiction she was

experiencing. She felt like she was being noble by not fighting and going with Cindy, while at the same time feeling like a coward because she was leaving and not defending herself.

There was a familiar and unpleasant sensation in Amelia's chest and gut. She hated this feeling.

"I'm sorry," said Cindy. "I didn't know what to do."

Amelia pulled her lunch out of her locker and then waited for Cindy to finish getting hers.

"It isn't your fault," said Amelia. "Let's just find someplace to eat."

They eventually found a quiet spot to scarf down their food. They didn't say much to each other while they ate. The fun of lunch had been stolen. Even the nice weather did nothing to break through the pain and anger that seemed to be a shell around Amelia.

"I'll see you after school," said Cindy, almost imploringly, when the bell rang to signal that lunch was over. "We can walk home together."

"Alright," replied Amelia, still caught in a whirl of thought about what she should have done during the confrontation.

She was hoping that things would get better the rest of the day. It didn't. Not only was she in a different class than Cindy, which left her alone again, but she was in the same

geometry class as Becky, Bobby, Jessica, and Clyde. The class was led by an older looking man who wore brown suit pants, thick-rimmed black glasses, a pocket protector in his white shirt, a black bow tie, and a permanent slight hunch in his back. After taking role, he introduced himself as Doctor Bernaird. He insisted that they call him Doctor because he had worked so hard to earn his doctorate degree in math. It didn't take long to find out that he became extremely touchy about it when anyone forgot his title.

The class was nothing but tension, glares, whispering, and discomfort. Amelia was glad to be done with the class when the bell rang. She almost ran to her final class of the day, just wanting it to be over. Cindy was in the band, and Amelia had choir for the last hour. Amelia went into the new classroom and sat in a corner, trying her best to disappear while the rest of the students filed in.

A short lady with gray curly hair and a long floral dress came in and stood at the front of the classroom.

"Hello, everyone," said the teacher. "For you freshmen that were not part of the middle school choir, my name is Mrs. Witherpot. Please come up by the piano so that we can figure out what section to put you in. Everyone else, please get your folders and form up in your groups to start running through your sections together. This is the same

number we ended on last year. We will use it as our starter piece for the season."

Amelia felt empty and lost as people started moving. Without knowing what else to do, she followed the few students who were heading to the front of the class. While the different groups were quietly running through their parts, the freshmen were going through their scales as Mrs. Witherpot guided them with the piano. At the end of their scales, when she had determined what their vocal range was, she gave them a folder of sheet music.

"Write your names at the top and join your section," Mrs. Witherpot repeated for each student. "Bass is there, tenor is there, soprano is there, and alto is over in that corner."

Amelia ran through the scales, first going up, and then going down.

"You have a wonderful range," said Mrs. Witherpot. "You could fit in either section. Would you prefer alto or soprano?"

"Soprano," replied Amelia, taking the folder that Mrs. Witherpot handed her.

"Right over there," said Mrs. Witherpot, pointing toward the corner nearest the shelves.

Mrs. Witherpot called the bass section over to the

piano and started running through their part with them. As Amelia reached her group, she heard a voice that made her skin crawl and her stomach sink. The pain in her chest became more acute, and her stomach felt sick.

"Was that supposed to impress us? You no-talent hack," said Becky.

Becky and Jessica were also sopranos.

"Leave me alone," said Amelia.

"Why? You gonna run away again?" said Jessica. "You shouldn't have come here. Freak."

"Go practice by yourself, you loser," said Becky.

They closed their circle, and Amelia was forced to stand to the side, running through her part as best she could while listening in to the rest of the sopranos that made up the circle.

"Why aren't you practicing with your group?" came Mrs. Witherpot's voice.

"She said that she's better by herself," said Becky, before Amelia could get out a response.

"That won't do at all," said Mrs. Witherpot. "Part of being a choir is that we all have to work together to create something more beautiful than any of us can do apart. It is a group effort. You must work as a team. Now, join your group and start participating."

Amelia went numb. The best she could do was to angle herself to look like she was part of the circle, while still being blocked off from actually getting into the circle. Her singing was half-hearted, and time slowed to a crawl through the rest of the class.

Amelia scrambled out of the class as fast as she could at the sound of the bell. She raced to her locker, grabbed her stuff, and went to the front of the school. Amelia waited, and waited, as bodies swarmed out of the school building. The longer Amelia waited, the more her panic rose. Every time someone came out of the doors, Amelia could feel her heart rise up to her throat, and the panic rose with it. She waited as long as she could until the panic was too much, and she couldn't wait any longer.

Amelia ran straight home, avoiding getting too close to any of the students who had been in her classes that day. She walked in the front door and ran straight up to her room. She locked the door, lay on her bed, and began to cry. Sarah knocked on the door to see if she was all right, but Amelia didn't feel like talking. Eventually Sarah stopped and left Amelia alone.

Amelia didn't feel like doing anything. She didn't want to do homework. She didn't want to talk. She didn't want to see anyone. Three hours later, she also didn't want to eat. She

was angry and hated everything. Why did things always have to go so bad for her? Why couldn't anyone appreciate her? It wasn't fair. Things were supposed to be different this year, but everything was still the same. Things always went wrong at school. Amelia's thoughts turned to Cindy.

So much for getting a friend, thought Amelia. It was too much to hope for that something would go right.

Amelia broke out into a fit of tears. She lay in her bed and didn't feel like moving. When she saw the light start to dim in her room, and knew it was getting late, she heard Sarah's footsteps outside the door. She prepared to tell Sarah to leave her alone again when she saw a note slip under the door. Amelia waited until the footsteps left and then quietly got up and went to see what it had to say.

Dear Amelia,

You seem to have had a very bad day. I don't know exactly what is going on. I don't need to know and don't want to pressure you into talking. I do know that you are hurting and I'm sorry. I was hoping your first day would be wonderful for you. I was hoping that you would come home excited today and be ready to go back tomorrow. As it sits, I am sure you don't feel like doing much of anything.

I just wanted to remind you of something though.

However terrible your day might have been, I am here, and I love you. If you don't feel like talking, that is fine. I am here. If you do want someone to talk to so that you can let it out, that is also fine. I am here for that as well. No matter what happened, I am here for you. Even if you fight and get suspended like you have told me happens so often to you, I am not angry. I am here for you. I want you to understand that.

You are special. You are a good person. I hope that you will be able to have a better day tomorrow. I won't force you to go back to school, but I hope that you won't let one bad day ruin the rest of the year for you. Things will get better. Even if they don't, I am here for you to come home to after a bad day. I love you. I hope that you will be able to start feeling better. Take care.

Love,
Sarah

P.S. There is a plate of food in the fridge for when you get hungry.

Amelia felt like the letter was filled with hollow sentiments. She had heard similar things from her foster families before. Even so, it brought a small hope, and it was enough to allow her appetite to return.

Amelia waited until she heard Sarah's bedroom door

close. She then quietly snuck downstairs to get food. The pain in Amelia's chest didn't go away, but having a full belly helped.

CHAPTER SEVEN

Amelia's Song

"I don't know what happened, officer," said Amelia, trying her best to fake sincerity. "It was an accident. I hadn't ever driven a combine before. I can't help it that all of them got in the way. So sorry. Chomp, chomp, chomp."

"Don't you think that's a little too morbid for the dinner table," said Sarah, setting down a platter of fried chicken.

"No one would be the wiser. I'm just a kid after all," said Amelia, grinning innocently.

"Are they really as bad as you are making them out to

be or is it like the Cindy incident after the first day of school."

"Alright, so I got that wrong. Cindy didn't hate me. She just took a little too long to put her tuba away."

"You mean you were impatient," interjected Sarah, smiling.

Amelia rolled her eyes. "I was impatient. But this is different. It's every day now. They are looking for ways to make my life miserable."

"Have you talked to your teachers about this?" asked Sarah. "Maybe they could help."

"Maybe," said Amelia. So that everyone can add snitch and tattle tale to their list of names for me, thought Amelia to herself.

"Wasn't Cindy going to finally come over?" asked Sarah.

"She was going to, but she has to take care of her baby brother for her parents' date night."

"That's too bad," said Sarah. "I keep hoping to finally meet her."

Amelia brooded during the rest of dinner. She couldn't tell Sarah what was really happening at school. Sarah wouldn't believe her anyway. The daily shoving and tripping, the name calling, things being thrown at her during class. All

part of being the new kid, thought Amelia.

She reached down to rub her calf and winced in pain. A little reminder of Becky and Jessica from choir today. The bruise would probably get ugly over the next few days.

As Amelia ate her green beans, she felt helpless. She was staying out of fights, but she kept getting picked on. She was doing the right thing by following Cindy and being calm, but she really wanted to hit someone in retaliation. She felt powerless, hopeless, and pathetic. Yes, that was the word.

I am a pathetic eater of green beans, Amelia mused to herself.

"Grumpypants," said Sarah. "We have got to do something to cheer you up tonight. Did you want to go for a walk? Did you want to watch a movie? Did you want to sit on the front porch swing? What would you like to do? I'm happy to do anything that will help you feel better. It's Friday, so we could go to the dollar theatre."

Yuck. The thought of her first meeting with Cindy's parents being one where she sees them making out on the front row of the movie theatre wasn't exactly appealing to Amelia. She didn't want to deal with any of the kids from school tonight either.

She didn't want to be stuck. She didn't want to feel like a coward. She didn't want to feel useless. But what did

she want? She wanted to be empowered. She wanted to be free. She wanted to be happy. Amelia realized how to get what she wanted.

Feeling suddenly inspired, Amelia said, "I need some alone time tonight."

"Are you sure," said Sarah. "I don't want you getting lost in your headspace and withdrawing again. I would be happy to spend time with you."

"No," said Amelia, smiling. "You have that book you've been wanting to finish. We can spend time together tomorrow."

Amelia was feeling energized, and a bit defiant, when she got to her bedroom after helping do the dishes. Not from the dishwashing, of course, but because of her plan, which had become much clearer as she worked. She needed to go back to the glowing lagoon, and she needed to get rid of the pain that had been sucking the joy out of her life.

Once her bedroom door was shut, her special door had appeared. Amelia opened it and stepped out onto the deck of Bartholomew's ship.

He didn't seem to be around, but Amelia knew that wherever he was, he couldn't be far. She looked around and saw that the ship was anchored right next to Raskiel's volcanic island. She pulled off her shoes and socks, dove off the edge

of the ship, and swam to shore where she could see the rowboat had been pulled onto the sandy beach. She headed up to the base of the volcano where the entrance to Raskiel's home was. In front of the cave entrance Bartholomew fidgeted impatiently next to Amy and Ohma.

"So," said Amelia, "about to head off somewhere?"

They all turned with surprise and ran to greet her.

"Are you okay?" asked Bartholomew. "I thought you weren't coming back."

"The consensus was that you would be expeditiously absent for a prolonged hiatus," said Ohma.

"You're back," said Amy, running to give Amelia a hug.

"It's only been a few weeks," said Amelia. "What's the big deal?"

"The big deal was the creature with the giant smoking sword," said Bartholomew. "Come to think of it, you shouldn't be here now. It's not safe. We should get you back."

"No," said Amelia flatly. "I'm here to face whatever it is. We're going back to the glowing lagoon tonight."

Amelia needed this. A chance to prove that she was brave. A chance to show that she was special. A chance to be with her friends.

"Well, if that's what you want," came a familiar voice.

They turned to see that Raskiel had finally come out.

"You finally got all your locks taken care of?" grumbled Bartholomew.

"Yes. So, let's be off," said Raskiel.

They headed back to the shore and then out to the ship. Taking up their normal positions, they sailed toward the glowing lagoon.

"What were you all doing before I got there?" asked Amelia.

"Well..." began Bartholomew, looking a little embarrassed. "Just jawing about how much we miss you."

Seeing Bartholomew acting so sheepish, Amelia bent down and gave him a hug. It didn't last as he quickly turned to yell at Ohma for "not being able to tie a blasted knot correctly."

They soon arrived at the cliff face of the lagoon's island. Amelia opened the way and they headed in. They were expecting the worst, but everything was back to normal. It looked like nothing had ever happened.

"We need to cleanse this place and make it happy again," announced Amelia. "We shall now have a cannonball competition."

There wasn't much said, and everyone was mostly going through the motions. But by the end, after Ohma's

decidedly painful belly flop, the somber mood had begun to lift. It would still take time before this felt safe again.

"Where to now, Amelia?" asked Bartholomew as they left the glowing lagoon.

"Let's go to see the singing crystal glade tonight," said Amelia.

"You're the boss, Captain Woof," chuckled Bartholomew. "Last time, I promise."

Amelia sighed and smiled.

As they neared their destination, Amelia felt a panic in her chest. She was reminded of the weeks before her eighth birthday when she was trying to make the decision about whether or not life was worth it. It wasn't until after she made the decision to keep trying that something changed, and this island appeared.

"Land ho!" called Amy from her perch.

The group got to their tasks and then loaded up the rowboat and headed to shore.

The exterior of the island was similar to many of the surrounding islands with its white sandy beaches and tropical plants. The interior was another story. The foliage quickly changed to that of an overgrown oak forest with old, gnarled trees as the group walked toward their destination. Moss and vines seemed to be covering everything. The ground was

littered with mushrooms and fungus poking up through the debris. Chunks of marble sat intermingled with the roots of the great trees. Where the leaves had been dug away, Amelia could see and smell the rich black soil that seemed to be teeming with life.

The trees eventually pulled back and opened into a clearing that was near a large stream on the island. In the center of the clearing sat sixteen large, gray stones laid out in a circular pattern. While the stones didn't look like anything special, Amelia knew their worth.

Amelia walked into the middle of the clearing. With her hands, she brushed away the leaves and debris to reveal a circular stone platform that was set in the very center of the sixteen upright stones. Bartholomew, Raskiel, Amy, and Ohma found places to sit at the treeline so they could get a full view of the clearing, the stones, and Amelia.

Amelia stood on the platform, closed her eyes, and prepared herself for what was coming. She waited and let herself calm down. Her breathing became slow and regular. She could feel her racing thoughts slow as well. As she accepted the calm, she began to sing.

The song was a serene melody that sounded and felt ancient. Anyone listening would have felt like they were hearing a sister performance to Ave Maria.

Gradually, the sixteen stones began to glow and transform from stone into vibrating crystal. When the transformation was complete, they joined in the song, singing their respective parts. The song became more powerful, beautiful, and peaceful at the same time. It reverberated through everything around it.

Amelia let her voice flow freely with as much passion and skill as she possessed. She knew the song by heart. It was the first one she ever truly learned. It was the song her soul would sing in desperation when things were at their worst. It went through the creation of life and the meaning of existence. It brought hope and peace.

The air in the glade began to change and lighten. The glade's colors became stronger and deeper, until it felt like another, beautiful, world. As the song wound down, the crystals glowed even brighter. The light was so intense that Amelia had trouble keeping her eyes open while she continued to sing.

After the stones finished, Amelia sang her final two lines and let the closing silence fill the glade. Now it was time for the reason she came. Once the song ended, the light left the crystals and drifted toward Amelia like dandelion seeds in the wind. She opened her arms and let them come to her. They flowed into her body and made her skin and hair glow.

She could feel love. It was all the feelings of love that she had been longing for her whole life. It was as if her parents were with her again and were holding her close. She could feel her sister near. She could feel so much love that she began to cry. The light whispered that she was special and important. That she was worthwhile.

That was why she came to this glade. She came to sing and to be reminded of all the love that people had ever given to her. She came to let go of her self-loathing and to feel like she was worth something. This place reminded her that life was worth living.

She had, of course, felt this outside of the glade before. On late, desperate nights when all hope seemed gone. She would go for a walk in the cool night air and be reminded that she was alive, and she would feel hope again.

Here it was the same hope, but in a concentrated form. As the crystals turned back into stone, she knew that the healing was almost over, but she also knew that the memory of being loved and cared for would stick with her.

She moved to step off the circular platform she was on but stopped abruptly. Something was wrong. The stones had gone dark. In fact, the whole glade had gone dark. This hadn't happened before. She couldn't see anything.

Amelia started to panic but didn't want to move. She

didn't want to risk hurting herself. She could hear faint voices but didn't know where they were coming from. When they finally became clear enough to understand, she recognized them as her classmates from school.

"Stupid, crazy Amelia," one of the voices said. "She's losing her mind."

"Yeah," said another, "she can't even tell what's real or not."

Amelia saw shadowy figures emerge from the rest of the darkness. They were strangely darker than the black, like condensed darkness. They looked like silhouettes of her classmates.

"You are going insane," confirmed one of the closer figures. "Normal people don't have these illusions. You need to be locked up in an asylum."

"Been seeing fairies and stuff too, I'll bet," said another, laughing.

Amelia thought about Amy. She did see things that looked like fairies.

"Fairies aren't real," said another shadowy figure. "None of your imagination is real. You are going to end up just as crazy as Sarah."

More voices and shadowy figures joined in on the conversation, attacking Amelia and telling her she would

never fit in. It turned into a chant.

"Freak, freak, she's a freak. Freak, freak, she's a freak."

"No, stop it!" hollered Amelia. "I'm not crazy! I'm not a freak!" The chanting continued unheeding.

"Freak, freak, she's a freak. Freak, freak, she's a freak."

It was too much. Amelia ran as hard as she could, despite the darkness. She tripped and stumbled until she was cut and bruised all over. The chanting followed her. She was in pain, but she kept running. It was the only way she could escape the overpowering shadows. The darkness without wasn't nearly as bad as the darkness she felt within. All the pain and self-doubt she had been trying to avoid by pretending things were fine while using the glade as a crutch to fill the emptiness. Those questions were now given a voice, and it was impossible to ignore anymore.

Amelia's grasp on reality was slipping, but she had to keep going. She heard a loud crack, saw a flash of white, and then searing pain filled her head. She felt her body hit the ground, and everything stopped.

"Amelia! Amelia! Amelia! Are you okay? Amelia!"

She opened her eyes. She recognized the voice but couldn't place a name to it. She tried to move but couldn't.

"Amelia! Are you all right?"

She blinked some more and finally things came into focus. The person talking was Bartholomew. He was surrounded by Ohma, Amy, and Raskiel.

"Let us requisition a stick and poke the young lass to ascertain her state of mortal vicissitude," said Ohma, rubbing his chin.

"You really are a twit," said Raskiel.

"Thank you," responded a pleased looking Ohma, mistaking the insult for a compliment.

"Both of you be quiet!" shouted Bartholomew. "Amelia! Talk to us! Are you okay? Tell us you're okay!"

She was having a hard time saying anything. Her head was pounding, and there was a tingling in her mouth like her tongue had fallen asleep. It took some effort, but she finally squeezed out a few words.

"What... happened? Where am I?"

"I don't know," said Bartholomew. "Everything went black and when it disappeared you were gone. We only just found you."

"You've got a nasty bruise on your head," said Raskiel.

"But it went dark," said Amelia. "That's not supposed to happen."

"No," said Raskiel, "it's not. Are you alright?"

"Yeah, are you all right?" asked Amy, who had been quietly staring at Amelia up until now. "It felt strange at the end of the song."

"What happened to you?" asked Bartholomew. He turned to Ohma and growled, "And don't say anything stupid while she talks, you yammering gallunda."

"Be nice," said Amelia, still feeling dazed. "Stop picking on him."

Amelia thought for a minute. She could remember voices, and something about a shadowy form. No, it was multiple shadows that looked like people from school. They were telling her something. What were they saying?

Suddenly, the whole experience came flooding back.

"I'm losing my mind!" cried Amelia. "I'm going crazy!"

"No, you're not," said Bartholomew. "You're fine. We're here to help if you need anything."

Amelia looked up horrified. "Yes, I am losing my mind. I'm sitting in a fantasy land with imaginary friends after running away from imaginary shadows and getting an imaginary concussion."

Her head throbbed. She didn't know if her injury was imaginary or not. Where was she really? Was she in the garden during this delusion? Was she at the school? Amelia

didn't know where she was, or what she was doing. She was trapped in a fantasy and didn't know what was going on in the real world. She just knew that she was getting hurt. Or, was she?

It was too much. Amelia began to cry. Bartholomew tried to comfort her, but she pushed him away.

"I can't keep doing this. You aren't real," said Amelia, between sobs. "I can't keep losing my mind like this. I don't want to be crazy."

"You aren't cra..." began Bartholomew, but Amelia cut him off.

"Yes, I am!" Amelia screamed. "I've been crazy and delusional my whole life! You aren't real! I don't want to be crazy anymore!"

She got up and started running again. She kept crying but yelled back as she ran. "I'm never coming back! I don't want to see any of you ever again! You aren't real! I don't want to be crazy! Go away and don't ever come near me again! Leave me alone! I hate you!"

That last line hurt her. She didn't hate them. She loved them, but they weren't real.

Amelia ran through the open doorway that had appeared in one of the overgrown oaks and burst into her bedroom. She lay on her bed and cried. She hurt all over. Her

head was throbbing, her heart was aching, and she wanted everything to go away.

When her crying slowed down, Amelia looked at the wall to see that there was no door. It would never be back again. She couldn't allow it.

CHAPTER EIGHT

The Secret

 Amelia carefully inspected her flattened peanut butter and jelly sandwich. The insides were dripping out of the end of the folding plastic bag it was contained in. She watched as a large gob of it plopped to the concrete with an oddly satisfying splort.

"I really don't think she meant to," said Cindy. "I think it was an accident."

"Accident or not, she stepped on it, and then went on to yell at me instead of apologizing," said Amelia. She held up the flattened lunch bag as proof.

"At least the teasing has died down a little. People

aren't bothering us as much anymore."

"Except for Becky and the gang," retorted Amelia. "Even when the boys aren't around, the devilish duo is bad enough."

"Would you like to share?" asked Cindy, holding up a pickle.

"No," responded Amelia. As she pulled out a bag of chip crumbs she added, "I can salvage this. I think."

"So, about the journal assignment for English," began Cindy, "did you understand it?"

"Kind of," said Amelia. "Ms. Copnet said it was to help us figure ourselves out, right?"

"That's where I'm confused," said Cindy. "How is it supposed to help."

"She said that by writing down what we believed, we would be making a decision," responded Amelia. "Then, we would feel good or bad about that decision and we would be able to change our feeling or opinion."

"I get that. But if we already have an opinion, how is us writing it down going to change it?" asked Cindy.

Amelia just shrugged. She didn't feel like doing the assignment and would probably avoid it until the last minute. She finished her lunch and sat preoccupied until the bell rang. Cindy said, "See you later," and then left for class. Amelia was

slow about cleaning up her trash and was the last student to start walking toward the door to head inside.

It was then that she saw it. In the shadow of a tree at the edge of the schoolyard. It was the darker than black creature from the glowing lagoon. Fear and anxiety spread through Amelia as the creature slowly turned and evaporated into a puff of darkness.

What was going on? Now she was seeing things at school. This wasn't just a little trick of the light. The shadow creature had actually been standing in the schoolyard. Amelia had seen it.

Amelia's head was pounding, and she felt her chest tighten. She was having an anxiety attack. She stopped moving and began to breath in slowly to calm herself.

"It's your imagination. It's not real. Everything is alright. You are not going crazy. You are just talking to yourself after seeing an imaginary creature that was real, but that doesn't mean you are crazy. You aren't crazy."

Amelia looked around to make sure no one had seen her freaking out. That would be an additional pain she wasn't ready to deal with right now. It looked like she was alone.

Suddenly, that thought wasn't very comforting either, and she ran to get her books and get to her math class.

The bell rang, and Amelia sat listening. Her mind was

racing so fast that she almost missed the voice that startled her back to reality.

"Miss Splint, please come with me," said Doctor Bernaird.

Amelia felt her anxiety increase. Why was he pulling her out? She was ready to cry but held her composure as she followed him out into the hall.

"Why aren't you listening today?"

"I'm not feeling very good," responded Amelia numbly. "Sorry."

"Are you sick?" he asked, stepping back a little and covering up his mouth and nose.

"I think I might be."

"Well, rather than spreading it around, how about you go to the office so that you can go home and get better."

"Alright," muttered Amelia, trying to maintain her steady breathing while she talked to him.

There wasn't any comfort anywhere. It was possible her teacher was trying to be nice, but it came across as being mean. Amelia went back into the classroom and grabbed her bag.

Amelia was in a daze as she worked her way to the office. The receptionist tried calling Sarah to come pick up Amelia, but Sarah didn't answer.

"You don't look well," said the receptionist. "We can't get through to your guardian. Would you like to rest in the nurse's office?"

"No," whispered Amelia. "I need to head home. I can walk there."

"We really aren't supposed to let you just leave," said the receptionist.

"It's fine," said Amelia. "I'll have Sarah call when I get there."

"Alright, just go straight home," said the receptionist, furrowing her brow. "Do you need someone to walk with you?"

"No," said Amelia. "I'll be fine. I can make it alright."

She wasn't sure if she could, but she didn't want to be here anymore.

When Amelia left the school, a cool wind blew against her clammy skin. It was precisely the thing to help calm her. She looked at the beautiful leaves that were barely starting to show a glimpse of their fall wardrobe. She could see people cleaning up around their yards and gardens. There were folks out conversing across their fences and running errands. While she was lost in her own thoughts, the rest of the world was continuing merrily on. Maybe everything would be okay.

By the time Amelia reached the house, she thought

about how silly she was acting and how she had let her imagination get the best of her.

"There aren't any scary monsters out to get me. I am not going insane. What was I thinking? Well, at least I got out of some school. I mean, I am talking to myself again, but I'm sure lots of people talk to themselves."

Amelia grinned and then frowned, hoping that no one had seen her again as she arrived at her front porch. Amelia hoped Sarah wouldn't be upset that she had come home early. Amelia yelled that she was home once she got inside but didn't get a response. She went to check the garden to see if Sarah was outside. There wasn't any sign of her there either.

I guess she must have gone out on an errand, thought Amelia.

Amelia sat down on the couch in the living room to wait, but quickly got bored and went to her room. She was feeling better, but still jumpy. She went to Sarah's room to see if Sarah might be asleep, feeling silly that she hadn't thought of it first.

When Amelia opened the door, she could see the bed, curio cabinet, and the writing desk. Curiosity got the better of her and Amelia snuck over to see what Sarah had been writing. From the doorway, it looked like Sarah had been drawing something and making notes. Amelia's arm hairs

were standing on end, and she got the feeling that she was doing something she shouldn't by invading Sarah's privacy as she slowly walked toward the desk.

A loud clank from downstairs nearly made Amelia wet herself as she jumped in fear. She quickly left the room and shut the door. She walked downstairs as calmly and collected as she could, looking like she had casually come from her own room. She could see the mail that had been pushed onto the front hall through the loud mail slot on the front door, and as Amelia pulled a curtain aside and looked out the window, she could see the postman walking to the next home on his route.

"Great!" said Amelia, speaking out loud once more. "Now I can add paranoia to my list of problems."

She chuckled to herself nervously, turned, and went to sit on the couch in the living room. As she sat down she noticed that all the blinds were closed and that the room was dark. They had been so when she first got home, but she hadn't been thinking about it. Usually, Sarah liked having sunlight come into the house.

Amelia was about to get up and open the blinds when the room started to get brighter, seemingly on its own. Amelia looked at the blinds. They were still closed. The lights were still off. Where was the light coming from? Amelia was

worried about getting lost in her imagination again as she saw what looked like a circle of light appear in the middle of the room. The circle began to form a ring of continuously popping bubbles that spread out as it grew. The ring got larger, and larger, until it was as big as a person. Gradually the bubbles stopped popping and the remainder formed into a single strand that ran along the outside of what looked like some kind of portal. Sarah stepped through.

The world had gone silent. Time stood still. Then the screaming began. It took a second for Amelia to realize that it was coming from herself. Sarah looked surprised. That look was quickly replaced with panic and worry. Before Sarah could say anything, Amelia sprinted out of the room, out of the house, and down the street.

Her mind was zipping along faster than she could run to keep up with it. What was going on? She didn't know and couldn't think. Was Sarah really a witch like everyone had said? No. That wasn't it. Amelia knew that it wasn't that, but what was happening?

Amelia kept running until she was almost out of breath. She was in the farm areas now and out of town. She was running on one of the dirt roads that led up the canyon. She ran until she was ready to pass out and finally stopped as she reached the base of the first mountain. The dirt road

curved and continued up a valley into the mountains, but Amelia had reached her limit. She sat down on the dirt and tried to get some air into her lungs.

She still couldn't get any thoughts straight. Sarah couldn't have just appeared unless she was magical. Amelia held on to that faint hope for a moment and then had to let it go. There's no such thing as magic. So, what was going on? Amelia continued to think about it until she had finally caught her breath. She couldn't find answers, only more questions.

Amelia forced her body into action and walked the dirt road up the canyon. If Sarah wasn't magical, then it left one other option. Amelia didn't want to think about it. Yes, she had been seeing things. Yes, she had been sent home for it. But could her sanity be so far gone that she would imagine Sarah appearing in the living room rather than walking through the front door?

The answer was obvious. Amelia's mind must be breaking down. How could she go back and tell Sarah, or anyone else for that matter? She would be an outcast again. She would end up in hospitals and all sorts of weird places. Cindy wouldn't want to be her friend anymore. It was even scarier than the thought of Sarah being a witch. What would everyone think? Could she have a normal life, or would things continue to get worse?

As she kept walking, Amelia felt separated from the beautiful scenery. The stream next to the road gave off a gentle burbling sound, and Amelia saw birds, three deer, and a rabbit. She even saw a skunk as it wandered off to the side of the road further on.

Eventually, Amelia calmed down again. The numbness went away enough that she could think more clearly.

Twice in one day, thought Amelia, chuckling a little. I really am getting messed up. Since getting outside is the only thing to help, maybe I should just live out here.

Amelia stopped and sat down by the stream. She took off her shoes and socks and put her feet in the water. Maybe being crazy wasn't so bad.

She felt a strange sense of liberation as she consigned herself to her fate. The fear left for a moment, and she was at peace. It didn't last though. Amelia had a thought that made her feel sick. What had Sarah thought? She probably came in and saw Amelia freak out and run off. She was probably worried about Amelia. For all Amelia knew, Sarah could have already called the police and they were swarming the town looking for her.

Amelia looked around and had another realization. She had completely lost track of time. It was probably getting

late.

She quickly got her socks and shoes back on and started jogging toward town. By the time Amelia reached the base of the mountain, the sun had already gone over the top of the next mountain range and everything was starting to dim. When she finally got home, it was dark.

Amelia couldn't see either of the town's two police cars. She also didn't see anything amiss on the outside of the house, so she quietly went inside. She wasn't sure what to expect. She was ready for yelling or crying. She even thought that Sarah might run up and give her a big hug. Instead, she was left disoriented. As Amelia entered the kitchen, Sarah was just pulling the casserole out of the oven.

"It's almost ready," said Sarah. "How was your day?"

Amelia stared at Sarah dumbfounded. "W... what?" stuttered Amelia.

"How was your day?" asked Sarah.

Amelia sat at the table and was more confused than ever. Had Sarah seen Amelia when she ran off? Had Amelia really run off? Was it really dark outside? She was so confused, frustrated, and angry again that she couldn't keep things in. She couldn't form any words, and so she began to cry.

Sarah didn't say anything. She only walked over and

held Amelia. They sat together while Amelia cried.

This is almost like being held by Binky, thought Amelia. Then she cried all the more because of her feeling of losing control. She knew that Bartholomew wasn't real, and it only reinforced her feelings of helplessness.

Once Amelia was past the bawling stage, she moved into the sniffle and whimper stage of her crying. She was tired and wanted to sleep. Sleep would bring a new day and more clarity.

"I didn't want you to find out until we had gotten to know each other a little better. I wanted to make sure you were ready to learn first. Unfortunately, it looks like I have no choice but to start your training sooner than I expected," Sarah calmly said.

Amelia would have screamed, but she was too tired. Instead she curled up on the chair, began rocking back and forth, and started chanting something like a mantra to herself.

"I don't want to go insane. I don't want to go insane. I don't want to go insane. I want to be normal. I don't want to go insane. I don't want to go insane. I don't...."

Amelia was snapped out of her chant by Sarah's loud laughing.

"Insane? Just because you see one person pop out of thin air, you think you are going insane? Come now. You're

smarter than that."

"Smarter than…" began Amelia, feeling stunned. "Seriously! You… I… it…"

"Are you going to finish one of those?" asked Sarah.

"It's not just this one incident," said Amelia, now getting defensive. "I've been losing my sanity my whole life. I don't even know if this conversation we are having now is real. For all I know I'm up in my bedroom and lost in my imagination."

"Is that honestly what you think?" asked Sarah, incredulously. "You know better than that. At least you should by now."

"Really?" asked Amelia. "How can I trust you? Everyone in town knows that you're crazy too."

"Amelia," said Sarah, shaking her head, "having a special gift doesn't make either of us crazy, it makes us different. It is real, whether it should be or not. It doesn't mean you are delusional. It means that you are special.

"Look, even though mentally you think that this must all mean that you are crazy, how do you feel about it in your heart?"

Amelia had a difficult time getting her racing mind to slow down enough to think clearly. It was all so sudden. Amelia had been convincing herself for years that her friends

and adventures were imaginary. It was difficult to believe that she could change that point of view. She closed her eyes and tried to focus on calming down and letting go of the arguments in her head.

The more she pondered it, the more she realized that Sarah was right. This wasn't weird or crazy. Amelia had been doing things and going places her whole life. It felt natural. The only thing that made her feel like she was going crazy was that according to everyone else, it must be crazy. Deep down, she felt at peace about what she could do.

"So..." began Amelia, slowly opening her eyes. "Is this magic?"

"Ha!" Sarah started to blurt out laughing but caught herself. "No, it's not magic."

She had the cheerful note in her voice that Amelia was used to. Sarah was acting happy and normal again.

"Well, if it helps, at the beginning you can call it magic. You could also call it ESP, telekinesis, or any number of other things. The point is that it is not any of those things, but it has attributes of all of them."

"Huh?" said Amelia, her thoughts spinning out of control.

"Oh, boy." Sarah shook her head with a smile and continued. "There is no easy way to explain this, but I will do

my best. What you have happen is real. It also isn't magic. It's natural. Magic is another way for people to say that they don't understand how something works. Sciences like chemistry used to be considered magic simply because most people couldn't understand how they worked.

"According to many scientists, our gift isn't real because they currently don't have a way to quantify it. Even in science they give the effects of this gift different names, but none of them are completely accurate. Anything outside of the scope that they give it is considered to be impossible. Just because people say something isn't possible, or real, doesn't mean that it's not. Mankind is discovering new things all the time.

"At one point, people didn't understand how gravity worked. That didn't mean it didn't exist. It was something they couldn't see. It was only something they could feel. Later, they learned about objects and attraction. They can now explain how it works… a little. Well, this is the same.

"People inaccurately interpret parts of your ability and give it names. They don't yet have the knowledge to understand it as a whole. Eventually the rest of the world will catch up. But for now, don't worry about it. Other people's ignorance doesn't make your gift unnatural or make you crazy. It means that they don't know everything. That's why people

are still making new discoveries all the time and constantly proving their old ideas and beliefs wrong."

"Whoa!" said Amelia. "Just… just give me a minute."

Amelia's head was pounding. It was too much information. The emotional ups and downs of the day had completely drained her. She was fighting off another panic attack, and tears welled up. Amelia was hopeful but was almost scared to believe that what Sarah was telling her could be true.

Sarah was kind enough to finish making dinner while Amelia sat quietly whimpering. Amelia was trying to get used to the idea that she wasn't crazy. They ate in silence, and both helped to clean up after.

"I don't feel like going to school tomorrow," said Amelia, feeling weak.

"I don't blame you. You have a lot of new things that you are dealing with right now. Tomorrow is Friday. I'll call the school and let them know that you won't be able to attend."

"Thanks," said Amelia, stifling a yawn.

"You better get some rest," said Sarah, trying to cover her own sympathy yawn. "Before you go, there is something that you should know though. You and I aren't alone. There are many with our gift. For now, I say you could call it magic.

This is only to help make it easier to get your mind around it at the beginning. You won't call it that for long once you start to understand it. There are eternal rules, principles, and laws that govern this ability and everything else in nature. You can't do anything you want to with this ability. There are limits. As you learn more about it though, you will find ways that appear to defy these eternal laws."

"I don't understand," said Amelia, cutting Sarah off. "Can you explain it in a simpler way? I can't handle much more right now."

"I'm sorry," said Sarah, shaking her head. "I can try to explain it again."

"It's okay," said Amelia, giving Sarah a hug. "I'm exhausted, and this is a lot to learn all at once. I need to go to bed before we get into any more tonight."

"Alright," said Sarah. "There is one more thing I wanted to tell you before you go."

"What is it?" groaned Amelia, stopping on the bottom stairs.

"Among those who have this ability, it is known as 'The Great Inheritance.'"

CHAPTER NINE

Adonei

 A caterpillar was living on her teeth.

That, or her mouth had grown fur in the night. She had fallen asleep last night without even trying to get ready for bed.

Amelia finished blow drying her hair. The single, old, bathroom outlet had about ten adapters and various objects plugged into it, and Amelia did her best to unplug the hairdryer while trying not to start a fire. She then, gratefully, brushed her teeth until they felt smooth once more.

As she stepped out of the bathroom and went down the short hall to the kitchen, she noticed that everything looked gray. It was too early, and she was too tired. This morning's breakfast matched the color of the day. A bowl of oatmeal, plain. Amelia put in a pinch of salt and a dollop of butter, then rooted around in the cupboards until she found some honey and cinnamon to add. She sat and ate, trying to keep awake.

"How did you sleep?" asked Sarah, coming down the stairs with a large and full pack.

Amelia could only scowl in response. She spent most of the night crying and waking up panicked as she tried to come to terms with yesterday's revelations.

Amelia couldn't hold back one of the thoughts that had been pervasive throughout the night. She held back the biting remark she wanted to make and instead asked, "How did you know that I had this ability?"

"That's a good question," responded Sarah. "There is a lot to it, but the short answer is that there are individuals that identify and keep track of people with this gift. They can't find or keep track of everyone, and it is an imperfect ability, but it works for the most part."

"Okay," said Amelia, not wanting to start Sarah on another long-winded rant. The information was already going over her head. She didn't want to go anywhere. She didn't want to do anything. She only wanted the pain to go away and

her own racing mind to stop. She couldn't think of how to do that though. In the end, she decided to go along with Sarah and take in whatever she could. "So, does the place we are going have a name?"

"Yes," replied Sarah. "Its name is Adonei. It is also sometimes called 'The City of The Twins.' Its name and nickname both have a very long history."

Amelia could tell if she didn't say something that Sarah would proceed to go into that "long history," so she interjected.

"When will we be leaving?"

"Oh, um..." said Sarah, thoughtfully. "Let me call your school first to let them know you won't be coming in. After that, we can go."

Amelia felt disconnected somehow. The concept of "school" didn't feel real at the moment.

Amelia put her dishes in the sink while Sarah made the call, and then they both went into the living room. Sarah pulled a bottle of blowing bubbles out of her pocket. She took out the little bubble wand and blew. A single large bubble floated out and popped right in the center of the room. As it popped, it turned into many bubbles that started popping and multiplying. They continued to grow and expand until they formed a ring around a portal that had appeared in

the center.

"Well..." said Sarah, putting the bubble bottle back in her pocket, "this may not make sense to you, but hold my hand and trust me."

With that, Sarah took a dazed Amelia by the arm and they stepped through the portal. It took time for Amelia's eyes to adjust to the light. Once they did, it seemed like Amelia's vision came back with an intensity of color that was difficult to handle.

Amelia and Sarah were standing in a courtyard that was circular and at least a hundred meters wide. There were assorted red bricks and cobblestones laid into the ground in seemingly random circular patterns. Around the edges of the courtyard were ancient and giant trees. In the very center was a huge fountain with statues of people in various positions. Some were holding vases that had water pouring out. Some were in ballet poses with water shooting out of their mouths. Some were crying, others had spouts shooting out of their hands. They were all circled around two figures that stood in the center of the fountain. They were the largest and by far the grandest. While the rest of the fountain was carved from multiple colors of granite, the center two figures were carved from some kind white marble with gold veins running through it. They looked tall and regal. They each wore

resplendent robes and had long flowing hair. Amelia saw that they were staring at something and turned to see what it was.

From the courtyard, where many various portals and people were appearing and disappearing, a single pathway led to the city. The city was built on a hill and the statues' gazes rested on the very peak where a monolithic structure made from the same material as the statues was standing.

The bottom third was layered like a wedding cake, and the center rose like a giant spike sticking out of the city. A large crenellated wall that periodically had spires rising out of it, circled the structure. It was something that seemed too large and grand to actually exist.

This all would have been impressive enough, but from what Amelia could see from the courtyard the city itself made the building seem small. It was layer upon layer of architecture from every different culture and time period of the world. It was like the history of the world was compiled in one place. Amelia stopped herself and realized that she probably wasn't too far off from the truth.

"I never realized how many people would have our gift," said Amelia.

"Huh?" said Sarah looking up. She had been busy trying to get her bag straightened and make sure nothing was falling out. "Oh! Well, there still aren't that many. You see, the

city itself is large. But there aren't that many people living here."

"Then why are there so many buildings? Why would it be so big?"

"Well, the city was designed to house the growing number of people that are discovering their gift and was constructed with the future in mind. The beodet do the upkeep," replied Sarah. "They were one of the more ingenious creations of The Twins."

"The who?" interrupted Amelia.

"The Twins," said Sarah. "There's a statue right there of them," she said, pointing at the fountain in the middle of the courtyard. "Their names were Rafflesia and Boreal."

Amelia looked at the two central figures, before turning to Sarah and asking, "Where are we going?"

"Right," said Sarah. "Follow me."

They walked up the large path from the courtyard, and into the outskirts of the city. As soon as they got to the first road, there was a line of driverless horses and carriages to take them where they wanted to go. Sarah helped Amelia into the first available carriage, and spoke to the horse saying, "Please take us on the slow and scenic route to the peak." She placed something into a leather case hanging from the horse's side, and then got into the carriage herself.

"Let me guess, not a regular horse?" asked Amelia, as they started up the winding streets toward the tower.

"Nope. Much stronger, faster, and smarter," said Sarah, shifting in her seat until she became comfortable. "Would you like to hear about the Twins now?"

"Sure," responded Amelia. "If I can keep looking out the window while you talk."

"No problem," said Sarah, smiling. "They were discovered by a member of the Scythiet Learners and found to have abilities that were previously unknown."

"Who are the Scythiet Learners?" asked Amelia.

"It was a secret society that was formed of people with our abilities," responded Sarah.

As the carriage climbed, Amelia could now see that the courtyard they had come from was surrounded by a grove of enormous trees. The grove was surrounded on the sides and the back by farmland and small cottages as far as the eye could see.

To one side, was a mountain range that ran along the edge of the city and off into the distance. The mountains made the city look like it was made on a molehill. To the other side of the city, was the ocean. The continued climbing of the carriage revealed the docks and all the ships, boats, and vessels that were lined up at the base of the city.

"Unfortunately, they never understood how it worked," continued Sarah. "They could only keep records of the creatures that were created and keep track of the people that had the ability. They had the barrier of not being able to go into each other's paradigm spheres. They had to simply rely on the stories that people told."

"What?" asked Amelia, turning to Sarah. "What's a 'paradigm sphere'?" Something about it clicked for Amelia and drew her attention.

"It's the world that you create and can visit through your portal," responded Sarah. "I'll be teaching you more about it over the next few weeks."

Fantastic, thought Amelia. This was the missing piece. She would finally understand how she traveled to another world, and who her friends really were. Amelia wanted to learn all about it right now, but as Sarah had already moved on to more of her story Amelia patiently looked back out the window. She watched as they passed a group of ladies who were walking what could only generously be called dogs. One was scaly, one had feathers, and one seemed to be surrounded by a bubble of liquid.

As the carriage meandered through a small neighborhood, Amelia saw a group of kids have a water fight in one of the yards. Only, they didn't need squirt guns or

water balloons. The water flowed from all sorts of inventions and even coalesced out of the air into streams. As quick as the kids playing had appeared, they were also gone. Amelia, feeling overwhelmed, focused back on what Sarah was saying.

"Anyhow..." proceeded Sarah. "People couldn't visit each other's paradigm spheres, so that limited what they could learn. They did their best though. At the very least, they worked as an outreach program to help people with the ability to understand what was going on. That is, until The Twins came along."

Sarah stopped for a moment, put some odd coins in a slot of the carriage wall. She then pulled open a compartment that had water and snacks that she shared with Amelia as she continued to talk.

"The Learners found that not only could they visit The Twin's spheres, but that The Twins could make new spheres. It was a breakthrough that led to everything we have and know today. In 1849, they created the common spheres. And on the first day of January in 1850, this city was founded. The Twins called it 'Adonei.' People are still unable to go into another person's paradigm sphere, but once they have visited with someone else that has been here, they can come to the common spheres."

"So, I can come here anytime I want now?" asked

Amelia.

"Yup," responded Sarah, smiling.

Amelia grabbed and ate one of the cookies from the carriage compartment. It was a pleasant day, and the bouncing of the carriage was somehow soothing.

"You don't want to miss this," said Sarah, waking Amelia up.

Amelia rubbed her eyes and looked out of the carriage windows. They were nearly at the wall that surrounded the central building at the peak. Now that they were closer, Amelia could see that each of the towers rising out of the wall had a different banner at the top.

When they reached one of the gates leading through the wall, the carriage was stopped and searched by two creatures that looked like lion-headed beastmen in guard outfits. Sarah showed one of the guards a card, which it took and inspected as it looked at her. Satisfied, the guard handed it back, and they were allowed entry.

The carriage slowly went through the tunnel in the protective wall and entered the inner courtyard surrounding the central building. Now that she was here, Amelia started to appreciate the scale of the central building. It took them a long while to go from the gate to the edge of the lowest layer

of the structure, which was supported by large, fluted columns. The horse and carriage stopped at the base of the layer, which had stairs leading up to it on all sides.

Sarah thanked the horse and gave it a pat on the head as she and Amelia exited the carriage. Amelia looked up at the waterfalls flowing off the upper tier, and the trees hanging over the edge, while she followed Sarah up the stairs.

What Amelia was walking into was like a city in itself. She reasoned that the ceiling was probably thirty stories high, and this was only the lowest level of the massive three-tiered structure that was at the base of the large spike. There were roads, small buildings, fountains, parks, and statues running in all directions. Lights were scattered throughout, although Amelia couldn't tell what kind of lights they were. There was a large canal system that was built into the floor that had gondolas floating through them. There were also small carriages with miniature horses that were taking people to different places. It felt like a theme park.

A few people flew over Amelia's head, and she realized that they were on broomsticks.

"Hey!" said Amelia, pointing to the broom riders. "I thought we weren't witches."

CHAPTER TEN

Laroop

 Amelia continued to jump up and down, pointing in the direction of the people on brooms. Her eyes were wide, her eyebrows were raised, and she put on the smuggest "I told you so" smile she could make.

"We aren't," said Sarah. "They are doing it for show. It's the laroop."

Obviously Sarah thought that this explained everything. Unfortunately, Amelia still didn't understand.

"What's a…" began Amelia. However, Sarah caught on before Amelia continued.

"Invisible creatures that are kept as pets. They are extremely helpful."

Rather than press, Amelia let herself be satisfied with watching all the strangeness around her while they rode one of the small carriages up to the central building that became the spike of the larger structure.

They went through the entry arches and through two sets of double doors to get inside. It looked like a cross between a giant museum and a library. The walls were lined with shelves of books, and there were massive cases that housed artifacts of every shape and size.

"This is the collected knowledge of all the people with the gift throughout history. Technically, the city and this center started a century and a half ago, but we have collected information, specimen, and artifacts that date back tens of thousands of years. We have records and stories that run back almost five thousand years," said Sarah.

"Who is 'we'?" asked Amelia.

"The researchers here," said Sarah. "That's my job. I'm a researcher."

Things finally started to click for Amelia, and she listened in a daze as Sarah got more and more excited while they walked through the massive hall. Amelia could barely keep up as Sarah spoke faster and faster.

"...same expedition, and this artifact I found in Greece. It belonged to a man that had used his ability to create the replica of Mount Olympus in his paradigm sphere that caused all those stories to spread. This carpet was one that was used for flying. It was woven extra thick to support the people being carried on it. We found traces of the laroop in the fibers. It has helped confirm the progression of the laroop and trace them further back into history. Then, there is the history of the unicorn. As you can see by this skeleton that we discovered, it was a real creature. Actually, it was various creatures. The first was a one horned bull. It went through variations with different people. One person even created whales with a unicorn horn. They escaped into the world and have been running amok ever since. And then..."

Amelia hadn't seen this side of Sarah before. It was almost as if the real Sarah was breaking out of some restrictive cell she had been hiding in.

"Good, an elevator. I was worried we would have to take the stairs in this place," said Amelia, when they arrived at the sliding door that revealed a compartment inside.

"Kind of," said Sarah, smiling. "A little different though."

They got into the compartment with a few other people who were overloaded with papers and artifacts. There

were slots all over in the walls of the compartment, and Amelia watched Sarah and the others pull out what looked like key cards. Each person blew on the end of their card and then stuck them in one of the various slots. When the elevator reached the floor that a person wanted to go, their key card would pop out of the slot. They would pick it up off the floor and exit. Sarah and Amelia were the last ones on the elevator when Sarah's key card popped out.

"Floor one hundred and twenty-six, the head research office," said Sarah, stooping to pick up her keycard. "It also acts as a security device. If you aren't supposed to be here, you get booted out at the bottom floor."

After a short pause, the doors opened. They stepped off and into a waiting room that had chairs lining the walls and a large desk at the end where a receptionist was sitting. Sarah led Amelia up to the plump and happy-looking lady sitting behind the desk and announced that she was here to deliver her latest research. The receptionist wrote a quick note on a piece of paper and threw it into the air where a wind seemed to catch it and carry it through a vent and off to whoever was supposed to receive it.

"It's a small variety of laroop," whispered Sarah quietly. "Very useful."

"Would you like a chocolate while you wait?" asked

the kind receptionist.

"Yes, please," said Amelia, who had just realized how hungry she was.

She and Sarah both took a chocolate from the bowl on the counter and sat down to wait. The receptionist returned to her knitting that she had hidden behind the counter. Finally, after what felt like ages, someone came to get them. It was a short and shriveled old man who smelled like books and dust.

He was wearing a dark suit and a pair of gold-rimmed glasses. He was bald on top, but had short, silvery hair around the sides of his head, and a neatly trimmed goatee. His appearance was accentuated by a very large nose and ears. His smile was inviting, and Amelia had to fight a strange urge to reach out and pet him.

"Sarah, so good to see you again. It's been months, hasn't it? Any luck with the research?" he said, eyeing her bag longingly.

"Yes," said Sarah, smiling. "I've had some wonderful breakthroughs. By the way, this is Amelia," she said, gesturing.

"Wonderful," said the little man, looking like he was about to explode with excitement. "I heard you were going to be taking care of someone. It's nice to know that you finally get a little company. I told you it would be good for you." He

turned to Amelia and shook her hand. "My name is Jasper Bobbleknob. I'm the head of the research and studies. It's an absolute pleasure to meet you."

"Jasper is the de facto leader of Adonei," said Sarah. "Adonei was founded on learning, and so the head researcher is in charge."

"Yes, and it's a pain too," said Jasper, shaking his head. "I simply want to do my own work, but I spend most of my time trying to deal with the mundane workings of the town."

"Do you have time now," asked Sarah.

"For you, I'll make time," said Jasper, smiling. "Where are my manners? Did you have lunch plans today?"

"No," said Sarah.

"Great," said Jasper. "You can eat with me."

Amelia followed them down the hall and into an old office, only half listening to the banter between Sarah and Jasper as they went.

They sat down, and Sarah began to pull things out of her bag to show Jasper. Amelia was just starting to doze off again when a tall, thin woman with an apron came to get them and took them to a room that had an overly long dining table with matching chairs, and a large chandelier overhead.

Lunch, a mix of sandwiches and charcuterie, was brought out by two women who were dressed in black and

white maid uniforms. They looked almost human except that they had very feline features. Amelia could even see a tail sticking out from under one of their dresses.

Jasper turned to one of the feline women standing by and beckoned her over.

"Have any of you eaten yet?" he asked kindly.

"No, not yet," she softly purred back.

"Invite everyone in, including Betty, Alice, John, and Janice. Janice made more food than we can eat ourselves, and everyone is probably hungry. Besides," said Jasper, pointing at Amelia, "it would probably do her good to meet more folks and get used to the place."

Fourteen people and creatures made their way in and sat down around the large table. Jasper offered a prayer and they began to eat. There were a lot of conversations going on, but Amelia was not involved in any of them. She was wrapped up in everything that she had learned today. She did have something nagging her though, and so she spoke up.

"Sarah?"

Sarah was lost in a conversation with Jasper and didn't hear. So, Amelia spoke up even louder.

"Sarah!"

"Oh, sorry. What is it Amelia?" responded Sarah.

"I still don't understand the laroop," said Amelia.

Sarah looked thoughtfully for a moment and then turned to Jasper.

"Jasper, you're good at explaining things. Would you tell the story to Amelia?"

"I would be happy to," said Jasper, scratching his bald head and scrunching up his face. "Now, where to begin?"

He thought about it for a moment, and then leaned forward in his chair. "I guess we should begin at around the start of the seventeenth century, when they got a name to identify them. The name 'laroop' was created by a gentleman named Zharen Paloka who discovered that he had the ability to see things that are invisible to the normal human eye. Because of that gift, along with his ability to go to his paradigm sphere, he thought he had become a spirit medium," said Jasper, moving his hands animatedly while he spoke. "He thought that he was seeing ghosts and going to the afterlife. He soon discovered that they weren't ghosts at all. They were sentient creatures. Now, he didn't invent them. He only named them. The laroop had been around almost as far back as we have information. Many people with the gift had contact with them, but no one from the Scythiet Learners had ever had contact with them until Zharen Paloka."

"But what are they?" asked Amelia. "I mean, how can something alive be invisible?"

"Easy," interjected Sarah. "They are made of refined elements that are invisible to the human eye. The elements they are made of also allow them to pass through physical objects. Much like water through a mesh. However, if they want to, they can concentrate their body parts enough to physically touch and move objects."

Amelia was still confused. She didn't understand how a living creature could exist and be invisible. Then again, she didn't know that people could have her abilities until yesterday.

"This has all been very interesting to study," said Sarah. "If you can just get your head wrapped around the idea that everything is material, even the unseen elements, then it makes it easier to understand the research. Our elemental table is eightfold the size of the one you have at school. Our table only includes the elements we have learned to measure, let alone the ones that we are still trying to explain. I mean, if the rest of the world knew…"

"You're rambling again," said Amelia. She looked over to see Jasper grinning at Sarah after being called out.

"Anyway," continued Jasper, trying to recapture the previous train of thought. "After learning to communicate with them, Zharen found that they weren't ghosts, but were instead a creature made of refined material. They had been

123

used to carry people on carpets, carry people on brooms, guard treasure, and do many other things. To support his starving family, he talked the laroop into helping him to create the illusion of telekinesis. He would do shows and appear to make objects move. Eventually, his fame brought members of the Scythiet Learners to his performance. After they explained to him about their society, they discovered that he also had a paradigm sphere.

"The Learners taught Zharen about his ability. With the knowledge he gained from the Learners, and with some advice and information from the existing laroop, Zharen went into his sphere with new vigor and created various new laroop for different functions. The contact with Zharen allowed the Scythiet Learners to finally understand all the cases of witches and such that they had previously not understood. It also helped them to learn more about the elements."

"We have learned more since then," said Sarah. "But some things are still the same as they were for Zharen. The laroop are our friends. It is almost a pet and master relationship, like taking in a dog. The laroop are here to help. In return, we provide them with love and attention."

"Great, I'll have to get me one," said Amelia, trying to stop Sarah before she started giving a longer explanation.

Under her breath she then muttered, "Get me some laroop, get me a broom, put on a pointy hat, and scare folks in a little town. No wonder there are rumors."

CHAPTER ELEVEN

Formaldehyde

 Amelia watched the morbid slow-motion ballet of flesh as pieces of decay and death flew into the air. Their foam core boards were scattered, and the dissected creatures with them. It happened so suddenly that Amelia couldn't fully take it in. Her table had been knocked to the side, and the source of the strange calamity smiled with a now empty specimen jar.

"Whoops," said Jessica with a wink that the teacher couldn't see.

"She did that on purpose!" hollered Cindy.

Cindy's outburst surprised Amelia more than getting

covered in the specimen fluid. Cindy never got angry and yelled.

"Now, now," said Mr. Opal, "I'm sure she didn't mean to. It was an accident. Wasn't it, Jessica?"

"Oh, yes," said Jessica, with feigned remorse. "I really am sorry. I don't know how I could have lost my balance like that."

"It was not an accident!" shouted Cindy. "It was deliberate! We were just finishing our anatomy charts and she ruined them!"

Amelia looked down at the table and floor to see what could be salvaged. The simple answer was, not much. Pieces of worm, frog, snake, and mouse were everywhere.

"Now look at them," said Cindy.

She looked like she was about ready to cry. Amelia felt sorry for her but didn't know what to do.

"I'm sorry," said Mr. Opal. "If it helps, I will give you and Amelia another week to redo the mouse after I give you a new one. I've seen and can give you credit for three of the ones you have finished, even though you don't have them to turn in anymore."

Amelia went from feeling exhausted and distant, to feeling furious. Didn't Mr. Opal understand how much care and effort she and Cindy had put into their charts and into

dissecting and properly labeling everything? It was bad enough to have the other students attacking them. But when the teachers didn't show any appreciation for their hard work, it was enough to make Amelia want to quit. It wasn't fair.

Amelia and Cindy had to spend the rest of class cleaning up the mess. Their project was ruined, and they got stuck with janitorial duties. The worst part was that despite a quick scrub in the bathroom, they now had frog juice and guts in their clothing and had to smell like formaldehyde and rot the rest of the day.

Things didn't get better as the day progressed through the rest of the morning classes. All Amelia could rely on was her partner in stink.

"I've never heard you yell before," said Amelia, when they finally sat down for lunch. "Are you okay?"

"Yeah," responded Cindy. "I had a run-in with Jessica, Becky, and the rest of the gang on Friday while you were gone."

"What happened?"

Cindy looked too embarrassed to answer, but Amelia kept prodding and bugging her until she finally talked.

"They were teasing me," Cindy began sheepishly. "They said that you had left because you didn't like me. They said that I was a nuisance and that you had gotten fed up with

me and didn't want to talk to me."

"I didn't leave because I was angry at you," said Amelia.

"I know," said Cindy. "It's only that I wasn't sure. You didn't walk home with me Thursday, and then you never came on Friday. You left and simply disappeared. I tried calling you over the weekend, and nobody picked up. You never called me, and so I was worried about you. It's also that... I haven't had a real friend in a long time. Not since elementary school. I was worried that I had scared you off because I'm so weird."

"You're better than that," said Amelia. "I used to get frustrated because you would keep me from fighting, but now I respect you for the same reason. You're strong enough to walk away and not give in to their baiting."

"Really?" asked Cindy.

"Yes, really," said Amelia. "I'm sorry for not calling you to let you know what happened. To be honest, I've never had a good friend at school either. They always hurt me in the end. So, I'm not sure what to do."

"It's okay," said Cindy, smiling at her. "We'll learn together, if that's okay with you."

"Sounds great," said Amelia, smiling in return.

Amelia tried to take a bite of her sandwich but ended

up gagging and not being able to get past her own smell. Cindy had a similar problem, and they eventually abandoned eating. When the bell rang, Amelia went to her math class.

Amelia felt a twinge of anxiety. She couldn't figure out why she was feeling anxious until she suddenly remembered why she left school on Thursday. She had the realization that the creature of darkness wasn't in her imagination. It was real. This thought sent Amelia into a panic attack. With no immediate indication of danger, she had to work on consciously focusing on her breathing to calm down. She would have to ask Sarah about it later. For now, she would go on as normal.

The teacher put the daily question up on the board. Amelia tried very hard to be the first one to answer. It didn't matter though. Nobody cared how much she worked. They just expected it.

"Amelia got it right again," said Doctor Bernaird lazily, while he rested his head against the open window.

To Amelia's frustration, he wasn't even hiding the fact that he was just trying to get fresh air. Amelia hung her head and hoped that the rest of the day would go quickly.

After her math class, Amelia went to choir and ended up with similar problems.

"Quit trying to show off. We already told you that

you're no good," hissed Becky. "All you're doing is throwing our section out of balance. Shut up and lip sync so you don't get in the way."

"It's hard to breathe," commented a senior girl. "Go take a shower already."

"Yeah, you and your singing both stink," said Becky.

She and the other girls chuckled at the last comment. Amelia stifled a couple of choice remarks that she wanted to share with all of them. It was no good talking back to Becky or anyone else. Somehow, they would get away with it and Amelia would be caught.

As Amelia continued to sing, she imagined Becky's head on a frog's body. She thought of how funny it would be if she was hopping around from lily pad to lily pad saying, "Is there a prince anywhere to kiss me and cure me of my zits?"

Amelia's imagination at least allowed her to make it through the rest of class. Afterward, she went to find Cindy so they could walk home together.

"So, what do we need to do to get the mouse finished?" asked Amelia.

"Well, we already did it once," responded Cindy. "I think if we do the same organization for the chart, it shouldn't be too bad. We can do the dissection much more quickly this time."

"You really get into this, don't you?" said Amelia.

"A bit," admitted Cindy. "Actually, when I get done with high school I want to be a scientist. The problem is that I am not sure exactly which field I want to get into. I've thought about geology, chemistry, biology, paleontology, and a lot of others. I just can't make up my mind. I know that I need to specialize eventually, but it's all very cool. What do you want to do?"

"I haven't talked to anyone about this before, but I've thought about art a little," began Amelia. "Kind of like you and science, I'm not sure what area though. I know most people talk about becoming doctors, or lawyers, or things like that, but I like the thought of creating things. I haven't done much, and I don't know if I can even get a job with it, but I have been sort of feeling like it's a direction I want to check out."

"That's great," said Cindy. "Well, this is where I need to turn off. Do you think we can finally hang out after school sometime? I'm sorry we haven't been able to yet. My parents keep telling me that I can and then end up making me help out instead."

"Of course," said Amelia. "We definitely need to. If you get free time, and let me know, I'll just have to ask Sarah."

"Alright," said Cindy. "I'll see you tomorrow."

"See you," responded Amelia, automatically.

Amelia was happy. She thought again about how wonderful it was to finally have a real friend.

Amelia felt a sharp pang of guilt in her chest. This wasn't her first real friend. Her other friends weren't imaginary. She had been so caught up in her own life that she had totally forgotten about them.

They had crossed her mind very quickly a couple of times over the weekend, but never for very long. Amelia had been too wrapped up in everything new she was learning about. It was finally sinking in that she really was gifted instead of crazy. Amelia promised herself she'd find and talk to them the next chance she got. She would apologize and be a much better friend from now on.

What would they say though? She was afraid they couldn't forgive her after the way she had left the last time. She wasn't sure what to do.

Amelia arrived home to find Sarah sitting in the living room, crocheting patiently.

"I was wondering when you were going to get here," said Sarah, looking up from her work. "Are you ready to go?"

"I guess so," said Amelia. "Where are we going today?"

"You'll see," said Sarah secretively, before pausing with a look of shock. "What happened to you?"

"Don't ask," said Amelia, rolling her eyes. "Just give me a few minutes to get showered and changed."

"All right. Hurry up though."

After getting cleaned up and heading back into the living room, Amelia saw the now familiar sight of Sarah's bubbly portal opening. Once it was done expanding, they stepped through and onto a large field.

This field looked like something out of a painting. It was full of wildflowers and tall green grass. Amelia saw tall, snow-capped mountains surrounding them. The sky was a bright blue.

"Where are we?" asked Amelia.

She didn't get a response. Upon their arrival, Sarah had started walking across the meadow and toward a stream. She was now quite a distance away from Amelia. Amelia had been so entranced that she hadn't even noticed. She called after Sarah and ran to catch up.

"I said..." began Amelia, now that she was close to Sarah, "where are we?"

"Well," said Sarah, with an excited smile. "If you must know, we are in the region of Felatin. We are in one of the smaller common spheres. It is a sphere that I have been using

a lot to do research."

"What kind of research?"

"I can't talk about it right now," said Sarah, looking around. "But I will tell you when we get to our destination."

"Why didn't you just open your portal directly there?"

"I have trouble making it work underground or underwater," said Sarah. "I'm not as precise as some people. It appears where I am most comfortable with it appearing."

Amelia was about to ask what Sarah meant, but she never got the chance to begin. Sarah had stopped at a stone by the stream and whispered something. There was a deep rumble that startled Amelia and caused her to back away a few steps. The stream, and the land around it, transformed. The section in the center of the stream lifted to reveal a doorway. The stream itself seemed to now run up one side of the doorway and back down the other.

"Let's go," said Sarah, motioning to Amelia. "It only stays open for a short while."

Amelia quickly followed Sarah, and they headed down a dark staircase. When they had gotten partway down, the opening closed behind them. Amelia couldn't see anything as the darkness surrounded them, but the cool moist air, the echoes, and the sound of dripping water made Amelia feel like they were in a cave. Amelia had been in a lot of caves on

adventures with her friends.

Another pang of guilt. First about her old friends, and then about Cindy.

"Sarah," said Amelia, hesitantly, "I have a question, if you don't mind."

"What can I do for you?" asked Sarah, pulling out a small glowing stone to light the path.

"How do you tell other people about your abilities… without sounding crazy?"

"I don't," responded Sarah. "Telling a Dormant is trouble."

"A what?" asked Amelia, stepping around a puddle that had formed on one of the steps.

"You haven't heard that term before?" asked Sarah. "Even while we were in Adonei?"

"No. Is it bad?"

"It isn't," said Sarah. "It simply refers to someone that doesn't have our gift. It isn't derogatory though. Everyone has the potential. That is why they are called 'Dormant.' It is just not being used and is locked away someplace inside of them. We don't fully understand why, but some people are born with access to these abilities, while others are not. Anyway, someone born with this gift is called a 'Learner.' It comes from the Scythiet Learners."

"So, we are Learners, and people without the gift are Dormants?"

"Right," said Sarah. "And, the place you keep calling the 'real world' is actually called the 'Dormant World.'"

"All right," said Amelia, feeling confused again. "Can you answer my question now? I have a friend that I want to share things with. I wasn't sure if there were any rules against it, or if it would be okay."

"It depends," said Sarah. "It isn't illegal or anything. There have been a lot of parents that have learned that their children have abilities. They trust them and believe in them. Some people tell their husbands and wives about it, and they believe them. It depends on the people, and the relationship. It's not like they can go into the common spheres or anything."

Sarah paused for a bit before continuing. "Things don't always work out though. In my case, I was engaged. I thought that our love was strong enough for him to understand. To my shock and dismay, he became the foremost person to try to get me put into an asylum and only my parents helped to keep me out. He told everyone awful lies about me, spreading unsavory rumors throughout Pickleton. That is why I have never married and had children of my own. I felt hurt and became very wary of other people

137

for a long time. Telling or not telling someone something is entirely up to you. Just make sure that you think it through fully before you make a decision."

That was heavy, thought Amelia. She still didn't know what to do though. She followed close by Sarah, took her hand, and gave it a squeeze of support.

When they arrived at the bottom of the stairs, there was a large stone blocking the passage.

"Torick? Jake? I told you I would be back again today," said Sarah. "I need you to open the entrance if you would."

Amelia watched as the stone began to shift and turn until they were able to pass next to it.

"Laroop?" asked Amelia.

"Yup," said Sarah, turning back to look at the stone. "Make sure you close it tight. I'll meet you inside once you are done."

"Can they really go through solid rock?" asked Amelia, trying in vain to see the invisible creatures as the stone moved back to block the passage.

"Yes," said Sarah. "As I said before, they are made of a refined material. To us, the rock looks solid. To them, it is like walking through water."

They arrived at a large wooden door that was set into

the stone. It looked like something Amelia would imagine in a fantasy dungeon. Sarah turned the knob and opened it.

"I really hope you don't have a dragon that likes the taste of human flesh inside," said Amelia.

"No, it prefers pork cutlets and kale," said Sarah, smiling.

Amelia couldn't tell if Sarah was teasing or not.

CHAPTER TWELVE
Laboratory

 Wrought iron chandeliers, a grand fireplace with a blazing fire, white plaster, stone, rough-hewn wood, and a raised ceiling with giant wood rafters. It looked more like the inside of an English cottage than what Amelia imagined the inside of this underground structure would look like.

Amelia took a drink from her glass of milk and continued to look around.

"Over there in the step-down is the forge and my work tables," continued Sarah. "Through the door there is the library, and the other door leads to the kitchen."

"You have a secret lab?" asked Amelia. "And that isn't a kitchen. I peeked in while you were grabbing the milk. It looks like an apothecary."

"That's a big word for you," said Sarah, eyebrows raised.

"I watch movies."

"It's multi-purpose," responded Sarah. "There are a lot of unique things that have come from people's paradigm spheres that need to be studied."

"Is that why we're here?' asked Amelia.

"Not today," said Sarah. "I just wanted to share what I do with you and start talking about your paradigm sphere. Let me get the sandwiches first."

Amelia jumped as she heard the giant stone in the passageway moving again.

"He's here," said Sarah. "Guess I'll make an extra sandwich."

Sarah went into the kitchen and Amelia watched for the wooden door to open. Instead, a small flap of wood on the bottom of the door swung into the room and Amelia saw a very small, purple creature step through. It locked eyes with Amelia and then proceeded to climb the three large wooden steps from the entrance. It was about the size and shape of a small cat, except it moved more like the smaller monkeys that

Amelia had once seen at the zoo. She tried to call to it, but it quickly ran off toward Sarah and was gone before Amelia could even get more than a squeak out. Amelia could hear the stone doorway closing once again and she was left to wait by herself.

Sarah came back with a platter that had three peanut butter and jelly sandwiches, some beef jerky, and a smaller glass of milk.

"I'm sorry," said Sarah. "It's the best I had. I am usually too busy to eat lunch and so I only keep snacks around."

"It's fine," said Amelia. "More importantly…"

"I know you have a lot of questions still," said Sarah, cutting Amelia off. "We have a limited amount of time tonight though, and I need to begin your instruction or else we will never get to it. First, you need to understand a few things about paradigm spheres. Second, you need to understand the research that I have been doing. Third… what is it Amelia?"

Amelia was now standing on her chair and waving both arms like she was in school and had to get urgent permission to use the bathroom.

"I know you have stuff to tell me, but I have a few questions that I need answered before I can pay attention

very well," said Amelia.

"And they are?" asked Sarah, after a short pause from Amelia.

"What was that thing that came inside a little bit ago?"

"Oh!" said Sarah. "That was Enion. He helps me with my research. He was the first creature I met when I entered my paradigm sphere. He became my best friend."

"Okay," said Amelia, feeling another stab of guilt. "I have other questions, but I guess they can wait."

"Great!" said Sarah. "Remember that this won't be easy to explain. Bear with me please."

Sarah got a drink of milk and then cleared her throat importantly.

"A paradigm sphere is an extension of you, or simply, it is an extension and creation of both your conscious and unconscious mind."

"Huh?" said Amelia, immediately confused.

"Basically, it is something that you create both on purpose and by accident. When you want something to happen, it can. However, things also can happen because deep down, something inside you wants it to happen."

"Yet again..." said Amelia. "Can you explain it in a way that I can understand?"

"Okay," said Sarah, clearing her throat to try once

more. "Have you ever made something happen while you were in your own sphere?"

"Yes."

"Good. That would be a conscious creation. Now, have you ever had something happen that you didn't think about before it happened, such as finding a new place or a new creature that you didn't try to make?"

"I guess," responded Amelia, unsure about the question.

"Well, there you go," said Sarah, triumphantly. "That would be an unconscious creation. When you purposefully cause something to happen in your sphere, then you are creating things consciously. When things just seem to happen as a coincidence of what you are thinking of outside of your sphere, you are creating things unconsciously. There is nothing that is created in your paradigm sphere that you don't make. The exception to this being whatever the sentient creatures in your sphere build or make after they are created and begin to act autonomously. One of the groups in my sphere, a long time ago, built a large tower. Initially I thought it was my creation because of a book I had been reading, but they informed me that…"

"Rambling…" interjected Amelia.

"Basically, it is a place in which you have control," said

Sarah.

"Wait! That can't be right," said Amelia. "I don't have complete control over my sphere."

"Of course you don't," said Sarah. "While you may gain some mastery of your abilities, you will never be omnipotent."

"Then..." started Amelia, "where are the spheres at? How does our ability allow us to make them, and how do we know..."

"I don't have all the answers," said Sarah. "I can only tell you what I know. Everyone has the inborn ability to create. Those with the Great Inheritance simply have a more potent and powerful version of that ability. You have a place that your subconscious mind knew how to create when you were either scared, stressed, alone, or bored. We don't know if it happens immediately, or if it is developed over a long period. That sphere is where you're conscious and unconscious mind can be safe enough, and comfortable enough, to work in harmony and use the special gift that you have.

"That's why it doesn't work in the Dormant World. Even if you consciously want something to happen, your subconscious mind is hiding and protecting you and your gift. On the other hand, things that are created in the paradigm

spheres can then come into the Dormant World through the passage that you create. As you start consciously directing your ability, your skills will be severely limited in the common spheres as well and you will see an overall drop in ability at first."

"Saturday you said that I couldn't use my abilities in the Dormant World," said Amelia, cutting off what she felt was already diving too deep.

"Correct," responded Sarah.

"Is that why I'm able to do things in my paradigm sphere that I can't do in the Dormant World?"

"Exactly," said Sarah. "You will struggle in the common spheres as well until you can…"

"No, no, no," interrupted Amelia, remembering choir earlier that day. "I mean, like, I can sing better, dance better, and talk better than I can in the Dormant World. Does that mean that I've been making myself more talented in my paradigm sphere and can't really do it in the real world?"

Sarah let out a loud laugh that caught Amelia by surprise.

"Don't be silly," Sarah said with a few residual chuckles.

Amelia knew that Sarah was trying to be reassuring, but she felt attacked.

"Sorry," said Sarah. "I am not laughing at you. I had the same misconception when I first discovered my ability. I spent a full month trying to make myself as tall as the other girls in my grade and was frustrated for years after because I couldn't. Looking back now, I have to laugh at my effort."

"Well, why can't you?" asked Amelia. "You make it sound like we can create anything with enough training."

"Not anything," said Sarah. "There are limits and rules. In this case, it took me a long time to understand why. In the end, I realized that it was because our subconscious knows that it is better if we are happy with who we are. It is also the case of not being able to create something out of nothing. For your skills, you have to develop those on your own. It takes practice to develop your abilities, using your gift is the same. You have to put in the study and time to develop a sort of muscle memory."

"So then why am I not as talented in the real world?" asked Amelia.

"Dormant World," corrected Sarah. "The spheres are real worlds as well."

"Fine then," said Amelia, "why am I not as talented in the Dormant World?"

"It is all about your audience," Sarah calmly explained. "In your sphere, everything is quiet and happy to listen to

you. Likely, your creations happily cheer for you when you perform. It helps to give you instant gratification about your ability. Outside of your sphere, people don't always pay attention to the talent in those around them. In many cases, someone that is a star, and someone that isn't, is not determined by the skill. It's more a case of being in the right place at the right time. The best singer in the world with no audience is still the best singer in the world. The difference is that they don't get the praise to be able to feel like others appreciate their talent. So, all you need to do is realize that any skills you have are your skills. You worked for them and you developed the talent on your own. All you need is the right audience."

"But changing your body isn't a skill," said Amelia. "Some athletes use steroids to make their muscles bigger. Why would this be different? Why couldn't you make yourself taller?"

The small purple creature named Enion came over, stealthily grabbed one of the sandwiches while keeping an eye on Amelia, and then sat in front of the fire and began eating it.

"For the same reason you shouldn't use drugs," responded Sarah. "The changes and growth are unhealthy and can cause serious side effects. Your mind and body won't allow it. You can obviously change things through the natural process of exercising and eating right, but you can't do anything that is unnatural."

"Really? Aren't you leaving out some details?" asked the creature in what Amelia thought was a very soft, quiet, and extremely intelligent voice. "What about medical alterations?"

"Well, we can't get into all the nuances right now," said Sarah. "I am trying to lay out the basics at the moment."

"When are you going to tell her about the enemy?"

"Enemy?" asked Amelia.

Sarah scowled at Enion.

"During the time of The Twins, there was a sort of a..." began Sarah. "It was a, um..."

"It was a war," said Enion. "If you are going to tell her about it, then the reasonable thing to do is to be honest about it. Calling it a disagreement wouldn't do it justice. It was an all-out bloody war."

"Yes," snapped Sarah, looking very disgruntled. "If you enjoy talking about it so much, then you go ahead and tell her."

Sarah sat back, grabbed a piece of jerky, and took an angry bite. She then proceeded to chew in a grumpy silence. This was a side of her that Amelia hadn't seen before.

"You have to understand," began Enion, licking some peanut butter off his paws. "Sarah has difficulty with this. After discovering the goodness in herself, she has trouble seeing anything but the good in others. But, and let me be very clear on this, there is evil in the hearts of certain others. Even Sarah has to admit this fact."

"But most are good," said a grumpy Sarah defiantly.

"Yes," said Enion. "Most are good. In fact, most everyone has good in them, and even good people can do terrible things for seemingly good reasons. I am not talking about them. There are forces at work that are driven, not out of good intentions, but for purely selfish reasons. This war that took place was driven by some of their twisted reasoning. It was about power and who would possess it. Although Sarah sees your ability as a fascination and a gift, there are those that see it as a right and a source for dominion."

Enion stretched his legs out and yawned a little half purr that was mixed with something apelike. As he stretched, Amelia noticed that his paws were more like little padded monkey hands that had individual fingers. They uncurled fully while he stretched. Finally, he sat up and grabbed his sandwich before talking.

"The battles raged between those that wanted to learn and those that wanted to rule. Those that wanted to rule killed anyone else with the gift so that they alone would possess it. In the end, it was the Learners that won. The Twins had disappeared along with countless others. All are assumed dead. The progress that had been made was slowed almost to a halt for a while. Peace came back, but it wasn't to last."

Sarah interjected, "There are still people that want the power for their own and have similar ideas as the people from the great war. Some use their power in terrible ways to create things that should never be created, and to do things that should never be done. I don't like to dwell on it, but there are those individuals whose minds have been so twisted by fear, hate, envy, and other things that they can use their gift to twist their own appearance, like I said before that we are unable to do. Their subconscious has bowed down to the will of their misdirected conscious."

Amelia decided that she no longer had an appetite and put the piece of the sandwich she had been eating back down on the platter.

"So, should I be scared?" asked Amelia hesitantly.

"No, of course not," said Sarah.

"Then explain your hidden lab to her," said Enion.

Sarah shot him a warning glare. Enion glared right back. There was a tense moment, and then Sarah began to

speak.

"You just need to be cautious. In Adonei and most other large cities there aren't many problems."

"If you stay out of the dark districts," added Enion.

"Because," continued Sarah, "there are trained protection forces that patrol and take care of any of those problems in the cities. There are also protector patrols that control things that escape into the Dormant World. There have been a lot of problems with wild creations and, even worse, people who have gone into the Dormant World to do horrible things. A very small number of those same people who have twisted their minds don't seem to have the same limitation that we do of not using our abilities outside of the spheres. These individuals are kept in check by other FRLs. There have been no major incidents in the last sixty years. Everything is much more strictly monitored, controlled, and contained now with the help of the laroop, shiviets, denkles, and nerwillies."

"So, are we in danger or not?" asked Amelia.

"Outside of the main cities in the spheres there can sometimes be problems. There isn't anything to worry about. It is only a precaution. You simply have to be safe and learn to defend yourself. That will be part of your training. We are not still in the war like Enion makes it out to be."

"Though there have been rumors," began Enion.

"Okay, we're done with this conversation for now," said Sarah, to Amelia's dismay. "Enion, help me clean up."

"Fine," said Enion, sniffing Amelia as he walked by. "By the way, is no one going to mention the smell in here?"

Sarah looked at Amelia and Amelia sniffed herself.

"What?" said Amelia. "I tried to get it all off. Honest."

Sarah took the dishes and the leftover food to the kitchen. Enion slowly followed. He hung back far enough to make eye contact with Amelia and mouthed the words, "Don't leave her side when you travel with her."

Amelia couldn't understand much of what was being said through the now-closed door, but it sounded like they were having a heated argument. Amelia didn't have to hear the words. She caught the gist. Sarah was trying to shelter Amelia, and Enion didn't think she should be sheltered.

The unspoken danger reminded her of something. The shadow creature, and a name that she could no longer remember that was written in the lagoon. It was probably better if Sarah didn't hear about that quite yet. Amelia would keep her eyes open and follow Enion's advice.

With the angry noises changing to laughter from the kitchen, it didn't seem like much of a threat right now

anyway. Amelia allowed herself a moment of levity as she imagined how cute Enion would look riding Raskiel's back. The knot of guilt in Amelia's stomach continued growing.

CHAPTER THIRTEEN
Azolla Bears

 "You wanna have a sleepover next week?" asked Amelia. "You know, for Halloween."

Cindy looked up, surprised.

"I mean, if you don't want to or if you have other plans, I would underst..."

"Are you kidding?" said Cindy. "That would be great! What are we gonna do? Scary movie night? Trick-or-treating? Ghost stories? Pranks? Scaring kids? What?"

"I don't really have anything planned," admitted Amelia. "I haven't even asked Sarah if it's okay yet. I just thought it would be a good idea."

"It's a great idea," said Cindy. "You get permission tonight, and we'll have a little over a week to plan it. This is gonna be so much fun."

"Sshhhh," whispered Amelia, as Ms. Copnet stood up again at the front of the classroom.

"You all seem to be done with the worksheet, so we can continue. For the next two weeks, you will work with a partner. You will spend all your time during class discussing your journals with that partner. The point of this assignment is to share your views with someone who has not heard them before. Through this exercise, I hope you will learn how to speak about things that are important to you in ways that you haven't been able to. Although you may have disagreements and differing points of view, I expect you all to treat each other's ideas with respect."

Amelia gave a thumbs up to Cindy, who returned the same. Ms. Copnet obviously caught the exchange as she continued with, "I will be assigning the partners. Cindy, you will work with Jeffery. Amelia, you will work with Spencer. Bailey, you will…"

The teacher continued, but Amelia didn't care to listen further. This was impossible. Yes, Spencer was quiet and had never done anything outright to hurt Amelia or Cindy, but he

was still part of Becky's group.

Amelia shifted her desk mindlessly, and then she and Spencer proceeded to sit in silence during the rest of the class period despite many promptings from Ms. Copnet.

Amelia was so furious that she simply zoned out the rest of the day. She was tired anyway. Sarah had been keeping her busy every evening with visiting the common spheres and going through training to learn to control her ability. She didn't want to waste time on a stupid journal assignment, or any of her other homework for that matter.

"Can I have Cindy over for a sleepover on Halloween?" asked Amelia, arriving home after school. "She thinks that she can finally get out of helping her parents."

"Of course. That would be great," said Sarah, smiling. "About time you got a friend. Now hurry and get ready."

"Rude," said Amelia, smiling on the outside at the innocent teasing. Meanwhile it caused a pain in her chest and stomach again.

She kept planning to visit her own sphere and talk to her friends, but the weeks went by. The trips to Adonei and the common spheres became convenient enough excuses that Amelia convinced herself that she was too busy to return. Deep down, she was scared of what they would say. They might not even like her anymore. The longer she avoided it,

the harder it became to face.

"Where to tonight?" asked Amelia, setting down her bag. "Back to the lab, or to the outskirts of Adonei again?"

"The Grieving Fields," said Sarah. "It's in Azolla. One of the smaller common spheres."

"Sounds… um, depressing."

"It was, but it isn't anymore. Now it is peaceful."

"What happened?" asked Amelia.

"There was a great battle there. It was one of the largest during the war," Sarah began slowly. "Millions were killed. Only a small number were human like us. The rest were created creatures. It raged for a short four days, but in the end, there was a heavy toll. There are artifacts that were created, as well as healing remedies, and other products of great learning that were used during the battles. The knowledge that was used to create them was lost during the great war when all learning was set back, but the artifacts still remain."

"So you collect them to learn from them," said Amelia.

"Right. And now it is time that we better get going if we are going to succeed tonight."

Sarah put on her large backpack, pulled out the bubble blower, and opened her portal. They stepped through

and onto a large grassy field. It was a beautiful and serene place. Amelia couldn't imagine there ever having been anything violent happening here. It did have something odd about it, however. There were no trees, or bushes. There were also no rocks, hills, or mountains. It was flat and covered with grass as far as the eye could see. Except, as Amelia looked closer, she noticed that very large sections of the grass were moving.

"What's going on?" asked a startled Amelia.

"What do you mean?" responded Sarah, who had now pulled a large map out of her backpack and was sitting down to read it.

"The whole field is shifting," said Amelia. "Also, why are you looking at a map. There's nothing to see or use as a landmark."

"You have a lot to learn," said Sarah, with a mischievous grin. "I thought you were more creative than this. Remember, looks are often misleading. You need to learn to understand how things are actually working. Look closer at how the ground is shifting."

As Amelia did so, she noticed that it wasn't randomly shifting as she had originally thought. The sections of ground were shifting in very specific patterns.

"You see?" said Sarah. "If you follow the patterns,

you can find where you are going. And..." she looked at the map once more. "We go this way."

They began walking as they followed Sarah's map.

"Have you been practicing?" asked Sarah, after making them turn to the right on another section of shifting grass.

"Yes," said Amelia. "I've gotten better. It now only takes me a minute to create a mushroom kind of thing. It takes about two minutes to make a worm-ish creature, but it didn't move. I also created a frog-like thing last night while you were in the trade tent and busy talking to that dog-headed man, but it didn't turn out the way I wanted it to."

"What? That's great. Why didn't you show me when I came out?"

"Well," said Amelia. "It was supposed to be a frog, but it wasn't really right, and it also ended up having a head that was sort of mousy."

"Oh," said Sarah. "You'll get it eventually. Keep practicing. By the way, where is it now?"

"I don't know. It flew away."

"Flew away?"

"And carried off one of the crates that was on the back of the wagon parked behind the tent," confessed Amelia, while trying not to make eye contact.

"One of those crates that was the size of you?"

"Yup."

"I see. Well... we'll just leave it there then."

"Yup," replied Amelia again. "So, how much longer till we get there?"

"Only a bit further," said Sarah. "By the way, I am actually very proud of you. Even though you couldn't make exactly what you wanted, you still made a living creature. Early on, people generally either have nothing happen when they are trying to consciously create something, or else they create the form without any life."

"Huh?"

"Let me give you an example. You can create a worm, right?"

"Kind of," said Amelia.

"Is it alive?" asked Sarah.

"Once in a while," replied Amelia.

"Most people can create the form, but not the life," said Sarah. "They get the muscles, organs, bones, and everything else, but there is no life. There is no soul. It takes most people a long time to learn that. Some never do. Those that aren't able to give life, usually use their gift to create inanimate things such as metal, or stone. They usually become craftsmen and focus on creating objects that give

them more powers than they currently have. Others, with some life-giving abilities, are adept at creating plants. They create trees, grass, flowers, vegetables, herbs, and other things. They generally use their skills in creating things for medicines and what you would call potions and such. There are many ways to use this gift. However, the most difficult is bringing life to creatures. You have a knack for it."

"Thanks," said Amelia, feeling a little embarrassed.

Amelia was distracted and almost ran into Sarah, who had stopped suddenly.

"Oh! We're here," said Sarah, surprising Amelia.

"How can you tell?" asked Amelia, under her breath.

She could see nothing but the same grass stretching off in every direction. She didn't understand how they were anyplace different from anywhere they had just been.

"Now you get to learn the secret of the Grieving Fields," said Sarah with a smile.

She pulled a bottle out of her backpack and poured it on herself and Amelia. Amelia was going to say something about getting drenched, but quickly noticed that she wasn't wet in the least. In fact, any perspiration she had started to disappear. She also found that she was breathing less heavily despite the recent exercise.

"What's happening?" asked Amelia.

"It's Oxysprout," said Sarah, as if it explained everything. "I poured thousands of them on you. They are small plants that attach themselves to the first semi-dry object they come in contact with. It will help you underwater. That's why I needed the map and we had to walk a bit. I can arrive close to my destination, but never quite where I want to."

"But there isn't any wat..." Amelia began, before getting cut off by an extremely loud whistle from Sarah.

Two large water creatures that looked like bears pushed their way up from between shifting sections of grass. Their heads were elongated and almost dolphin-like. Their paws were giant and webbed. A strange seaweed seemed to be growing in place of the thick coat that bears usually wore.

"Hello, Speck. Hello, Lin. How are you two doing?" said Sarah. "And there's Durin," she continued as a smaller one of the creatures climbed its way up and through the grass.

Amelia had expected them to talk, but then realized it was like Sarah was speaking to a couple of horses, or dogs. Amelia watched Sarah playfully give them hugs and scratch behind their ears. After a short while of getting used to them, Amelia walked over and tried petting the smallest one while Sarah was busy petting and talking to the other two.

For a brief moment, Amelia was worried about being

163

bitten, but the little creature closed its eyes and growled in pleasure. She had expected the seaweed-like coat to feel like a plant, but it was more like soft fur.

"What are these?" asked Amelia, continuing to pet the smallest of the creatures.

"For lack of a better name, we call them Azolla bears," replied Sarah. "One of the researchers back in Adonei created them and helped train them for me to use to get around in this sphere. Little Durin there was born last year. So, now there are three."

Amelia would have liked to continue talking about the bears, but they were in a hurry. With prompting from Sarah, Amelia climbed onto the back of the Azolla bear called Speck. The large bears pulled back sections of the shifting ground and dove down into the water. It was how Amelia had imagined flying. Because of the Oxysprout, it felt like she had wind rushing past her as she and Sarah rode the Azolla bears deeper. She could see everything clearly and felt as dry as she had before they entered.

The bears continued to descend, and Amelia looked back toward the surface of the water. She could now see that there were stalks going up to giant leaves floating on the surface. It wasn't shifting grass that they had been walking on. It was furry leaves that were shifting on top of each other.

The stems from the leaves went down and attached to large bulbous plants that simply floated in the water and had roots shooting out in all directions. As they rode the bears past the house-sized plants, Amelia started to see other things. There were mountains and valleys. There were large, ruined buildings. There were underwater plants that had grown wild. Among the many creatures Amelia was seeing, there were bright blue fish, long green and orange serpents, and something that looked like a skinny manatee with horns. There was a whole other world beneath the leaves.

CHAPTER FOURTEEN

Tracy's Pendant

A group of humanlike creatures called and waved hello to Sarah and Amelia as they continued their descent. Amelia thought they were beautiful. They had webbed hands and feet, as well as slightly elongated features. They had an elegance about them as they swam and played around in the water.

"The Derwets," said Sarah. "Great family. They've helped me to find a lot of artifacts that I couldn't have found otherwise. Two of them are out on an assignment for me now. Their grandparents came from someone's paradigm sphere shortly after the great war. They've grown into their own community and have mixed with many of the other citizens of Azolla."

Amelia kept her eyes open and tried to take in all the new life and creatures that she had never seen before. Shortly after, they went through an underwater forest that opened to reveal their destination. It looked like it used to be a giant castle but now it was mostly rubble. Piles of armor, weapons, artifacts, and trash were scattered around.

"Why isn't everything rusted?" asked Amelia, as she was dismounting her bear.

"This area has preservative qualities," said Sarah. "Artifacts that we collect are brought here to be restored before we study them. You see, most of the battle was fought up on the surface, but it ranged everywhere. Water, surface, and even sky. After the battle, everything fell through and came down into the water. This is mainly due to the fact that the giant burga plants go dormant in the winter and their leaves die and sink into the water. Anyway, since that time, Learners have returned to find things and study them to regain some of the lost knowledge."

"Doesn't anyone come and steal the stuff here?" asked Amelia.

"They try," said Sarah. "However, there are many things that guard this restoration site from unauthorized

people and creatures. It may look open, but it is quite safe."

"Great. Anything in particular we are looking for?"

"No," responded Sarah. "But we do have the potential for a lot of new artifacts to discover. You see, the local merweck colony has recently evacuated their home."

"The what?"

"Merwecks," said Sarah, rubbing her forehead. "Mermaid-type creatures that have crablike arms and the temperament of squirrels. They collect anything shiny and hide it in their caves. They live in large colonies that are similar to anthills."

"Oh," said Amelia.

"Anyway," continued Sarah, "there were five major colonies at the time of the great war. Three were destroyed during the ensuing chaos. Of the remaining two, one died out about twenty years later. It has already been searched through. That is where we found many of the artifacts we have from the great battle. The final one is still inhabited. The merwecks are not friendly and are usually extremely protective of their treasures. Lately though, they have become more docile and have been leaving their homes."

Sarah looked distracted for a moment, but quickly started talking again.

"We finally have the chance to explore and see what is

stored there. The two Derwets on assignment are supposed to be bringing a new load of artifacts for me to evaluate today."

As they waited, Amelia asked permission to look at all the things piled around. It was weird. She felt like she was both walking and swimming at the same time. She found many interesting things, that Sarah assured her were junk. Amelia even had fun trying on some of the armor that was piled up. All in all though, it was a rather boring wait.

Just when Amelia had created a new game of throwing stones into an upturned helmet, made all the more difficult when the water shifted, two creatures swam frantically toward Sarah.

"Good," said Sarah. "They're here."

"Sorry for taking so long," said the older looking one of them in a bubble-like voice. "It was too big of a haul. Rather than make you wait longer. We decided to set it at my house and figured that it would be faster to just bring you over. I'm sure Elga would be happy to have an excuse to see you as well."

"Amelia, this is Nyawa and his eldest son Egwey," said Sarah. "Nyawa, this is Amelia."

After bows and handshakes, Amelia and Sarah climbed up on the bears and began to follow Nyawa and

Egwey. On their way, they passed through a village containing different structures with various Derwet families and other mermaid-type creatures. It wasn't long before they got to the stone building that was Nyawa Derwet's home. It was surrounded by what looked like an underwater farm.

Amelia could hear yelling. As they swam to the ground, a scream pierced through the water.

"Mom!" shouted Egwey.

Nyawa and Egwey immediately took off to the front of the structure, grabbing tools as they went. Amelia and Sarah followed them around the side of the building.

"Creonocens," said Sarah, with a cold tone in her voice.

Amelia saw a multilegged creature with a lobster-like tail fighting Nyawa. At its core was something humanlike, but it was distorted and twisted.

There was a gilled creature, which otherwise looked human, standing a short distance behind the fighting. He wore dark clothing and could have almost passed through a crowd unnoticed if he had been wearing a hood. He was strangely cold though, his features chiseled and emotionless.

On the ground behind Nyawa was Egwey helping wrap large leaves around the bleeding arm of what must be his mother.

Sarah hopped off Lin and made movements in the water that were much more acrobatic than an older woman with a full pack would have been able to make on dry land. Rock formations started shooting out of the ground at the two Creonocens. They turned their attention toward Sarah. As quickly as Sarah made the formations, they broke apart and reformed as jagged projectiles that shot back toward Sarah and Amelia. Right before they hit, they sprouted tails and swam away as a school of fish.

Amelia watched the fish swim by and noticed Egwey heading to the village. A now-bleeding Nyawa stood protecting his wife.

With Sarah's next movements, water around the Creonocens froze solid. It only lasted a moment, and then the ice separated and started turning into groups of long-fanged sea serpents. As these neared, they changed into streams of bubbles that floated past Amelia.

Amelia climbed off Speck and watched in amazement at the apparent ballet between Sarah and the Creonocen in the dark clothes. For each movement, there was a countermovement. Swords, then fish, then underwater fire streams, then rocks, and so on.

Durin stayed by Amelia while the other two Azolla bears went after the multilegged Creonocen.

The bears kept him at bay, while Sarah exchanged blows with the gilled one. The Creonocens had the advantage. They were starting to press it when Derwets and other creatures from the village arrived, spears and tools in hand.

When it became clear that the two Creonocens and their twisted creations were outmatched, they tried to escape. The gilled one called for a dragon-like creature, mounted it, and left. The multilegged Creonocen pulled out a bottle of green liquid and broke it as it followed, swimming away like a fleeing crawdad.

The crowd would have pursued if not for this. In horror, Amelia saw that anything the green liquid touched immediately withered and died. It was killing all the crops. Acting quickly, Sarah stretched out her arms. Bubbles flowed out, surrounding the area, and pushed the liquid back together into a sphere the size of a basketball. There it froze and transformed into a dark green stone.

"That is dangerous stuff. I've been able to change it, but that stone will be deadly poison to anything it touches. It will need to be disposed of," said Sarah to the Derwets.

Egwey went over to the pile of objects that had been scattered by the Creonocens. It looked like the whole thing had at one time been together in a large net, but it was now torn open and dumped out. Egwey pulled out an old and

rusted shield from the mass. He gave it to two of the older Derwets from the village. They used it like a scoop to pick up the stone without touching it. Then they carried it off, all the while balancing it so that it wouldn't touch living material.

Amelia was so distracted, that she didn't notice that Sarah had collapsed. She finally figured out something was wrong when one of the female Derwets swam up and grabbed Sarah. Amelia turned to see her floating body and then helped to carry her into the home.

The home was mainly stone, with many beds made of a woven long grass. They carried Sarah in and laid her down on one. Amelia thought it was strange because Sarah floated slightly above the bed whenever she breathed in, and Amelia had to remind herself that they were still underwater.

The villagers came in and out, helping to patch up everyone. Nyawa had been hurt the worst, but after getting stitches and given a healing salve he looked like he would be in the clear. Nyawa's wife Elga also had her arm stitched up. It had looked worse than it was. During this process, the group discussed setting up a guard system around the farm for the next few weeks and went into other details about keeping a better watch over the village and surrounding area.

Amelia was anxious the whole time. It took over an hour before Sarah finally woke up. By then, most of the

Derwets had returned to the village.

"How is everyone?" asked Sarah. "How bad was it?"

"We are fine," said Nyawa.

"Of course we are," said Elga, with a smile. "We are made of tougher stuff than that."

"I am so sorry," said Sarah. "I had no idea that Creonocens would come to bother you here. I am so very sorry for bringing this to your family."

"What kind of creatures are Creonocens?" whispered Amelia.

"They aren't creatures," said Sarah. "They are Learners, like us. Dark class Learners. Enion tried to get me to tell you about them, but I didn't listen to him. I didn't think there would be any problems."

"Those were human?"

"Yes," said Sarah, looking depressed. "I have no idea what line of thought could help them justify their actions, or allow them to alter themselves like that."

"It doesn't matter," said Elga. "It's better if you don't understand. You are made of tougher stuff too. Besides, cheer up! My Nyawa has brought things for you. Smile and look it over. Fight off the bad by focusing on the good. My husband does good work. Don't shame him by pitying instead of appreciating it."

"I will try," said Sarah. "We will look into getting some shiviets from the restoration site stationed over here. That way..."

"No," said Nyawa, cutting off Sarah. "We can take care of our own families. We don't need others to watch us. They can do what they are here to do."

"Alright," conceded Sarah. "If you ever change your mind though…"

"We will let you know," finished Nyawa. "We are grateful for your caring."

Sarah still had such a depressed look that the tiniest one of the many children Nyawa and Elga had swam up to comfort her. Amelia wanted to feel bad for Sarah, but had a hard time with it because of how sweet the sight was.

"You okay?" asked the little Derwet. "I can give you kiss to make you better."

"Thanks, Omea. That would be nice," said Sarah.

She leaned down and got a kiss on the forehead.

"You happy now?" asked Omea.

"Yes. I'm happy now," said Sarah, with a forced smile.

"Good."

Omea then gave Sarah a big hug. Sarah gasped in surprise.

"What is it? What's wrong?" asked Amelia. "Are you

feeling lightheaded?"

"No," said Sarah. "Something wonderful."

"What is it?" asked Amelia.

"May I see that?" asked Sarah, pointing at something that was in the little child's hand.

"Okay," said Omea. "It's my pretty."

The little child handed it to Sarah and there was a moment of silence as she examined it. It looked to Amelia like a little, silver, heart-shaped locket. Sarah opened it up. Inside was a tangle of extremely tiny and intricate clockwork pieces that were moving. Sarah looked up at Amelia.

"Look at this," said Sarah, with a quiet but excited voice. "It's still in perfect condition. I would expect nothing less for something of this importance, if it is what I believe it to be. Tracy was a genius with some of her creations. Not even a spot of tarnish or oxidation."

"What is it?" asked Amelia.

"I am not positive, but I think that this is an artifact that Tracy Sparkwen carried. It was lost during the battle. It was a pendant that was created to allow people to speak with many of the unseen creations, such as the laroop."

"Can't you speak with the laroop now?" asked Amelia, surprised.

"Partially," said Sarah, studying the object carefully.

"Some of the laroop, and only in limited ways. Not everyone can speak to, or understand, them. This object would allow that. The problem is that we weren't sure if it even still existed. Jasper found an account about it many years ago. He did the research and found that it was lost here since Tracy no longer had it when she returned after the battle. Unfortunately, she didn't live long enough to recreate it. Jasper could only find a single photograph of Tracy wearing it to help us with the identification. This is one of the items on my short list of things to keep an eye out for."

Sarah was as happy as Amelia had ever seen her, but Omea soon started crying that her toy had been taken away. Elga tried to calm her, with little success. Finally, Sarah had to barter with Omea to get what she wanted. She kept the pendant, and Omea was given the pair of colorful socks that Sarah had been wearing. Omea now had two new pretties instead of one.

When they left, Nyawa and Egwey said that they would get the rest of the artifacts to the restoration site. Sarah thanked them profusely. She also gave a round of hugs to all the children and was strongly embraced by Elga. Two of the villagers with spears escorted Sarah and Amelia as they rode the Azolla bears up to the surface.

CHAPTER FIFTEEN

Evening Walk

 The ship was empty and anchored in the harbor of Raskiel's island again. There was no one in sight, and it was eerily silent. Every time that Amelia had tried to force herself to finally visit her paradigm sphere and her friends in the last week, the ship had been the same. It was tearing her apart. Couldn't they appreciate how much she wanted to apologize? She had already tried going to the island over the last few days, and they hadn't been there either. She didn't want to try again tonight. She was too drained.

Amelia's doorway appeared, and she stepped into her

bedroom. She sat down at her desk and finished the last of her homework before going into the hall and quietly knocking on Sarah's bedroom door.

"I know I saw you a little at dinner, but can I come in?" said Amelia.

"Sure," came the reply from Sarah.

Amelia slowly opened the door and saw Sarah sitting at her desk with dozens of drawings and diagrams scattered all over. Sarah was frantically scribbling all the individual parts that she had found in the pendant. Amelia felt awkward for disturbing Sarah, but she went in and sat on the bed to watch what Sarah was doing.

"Have you been able to figure out how it works?" asked Amelia.

"No!" grumbled Sarah. "I've had to resort to studying the internal mechanisms for any clues. I'll probably have to go back to my lab to do further tests. I can't even get it to start working here."

"What do you mean it doesn't work?" asked Amelia.

"The mechanical pieces are working, but the actual functionality isn't there," said Sarah. "It's like a disk player that spins but doesn't put out any video or sound. It's very frustrating. You see, it isn't just mechanical or electric. This has organic and elemental components as well. A lot of what

is making it run isn't visible to the human eye."

"The refined materials you told me about, like the laroop?" asked Amelia.

"Yes, exactly," said Sarah, leaning back in her chair and stretching. "It would make sense. Especially if this is used to communicate with those types of creatures. The worst part is that this might not even be the real pendant. It might just be a look-alike that matches the one in the photo of Tracy. I'll have to run a lot more tests before I can be certain. I may also need to come up with some new approaches. I'm just hitting a wall with how much I can figure out. I need some fresh air to get new ideas."

Sarah stretched once more and then started to pick up the papers that had been scattered across the floor during the sketching process. Amelia stood up and helped pick up the last of the mess.

"Do you want to go for a walk?" asked Sarah. "Unless you have something else planned."

"No. A walk would be great," replied Amelia. "I only wanted to spend some time with you."

"You sure you wouldn't rather be with your boyfriend?" asked Sarah, grinning.

Amelia plopped the papers unceremoniously onto Sarah's desk.

"I tell you one thing, and now you're going to tease me for it? Seriously? This is why I can't tell people anything."

Sarah was still grinning, and said, "But you said he was cute."

"I said that I thought he was kind of cute," corrected Amelia. "He's still one of Becky's gang members, and I don't trust him. It's just that…"

"Just that, what?" coaxed Sarah.

"It's just that he's been kind of nice to talk to in class, now that he is talking a little," said Amelia, feeling oddly bashful. "Anyway, I didn't tell you so that you could make fun of me. Can we just go for a walk already."

Sarah's continued grin was just infuriating.

Amelia stormed downstairs and put her shoes on. Sarah came downstairs and sat down on the couch to tie her shoes.

"It's your fault that I'm going to flunk and have to repeat a grade," said Amelia. "I've been scrambling the last few days to finally get caught up in the evenings, now that you are too busy doing your research for us to go anywhere."

"Did you get caught up?" asked Sarah.

"Just barely," replied Amelia.

"No harm then," said Sarah. "Did you get your practice in yet?"

"No," said Amelia. "I told you that I've been spending all of my time getting homework done."

"Regardless, I want you to make sure to practice a little every day. Go into your sphere for a half hour after dinner or something to practice. It's the only way."

"Are we going to go or not?" asked Amelia.

"We'll go, we'll go," said Sarah, standing up.

The evening was lovely. The autumn air was cool but was still tolerable with a light sweater.

As they walked around Pickleton, they enjoyed seeing all the gardens that were filled to the brim with vegetables. The leaves on all the trees had turned their fall colors. There was also a heavenly aroma that came from a mix of freshly cut grass, and the smell of barbecue. They occasionally passed other people who were out walking around in the cool air or working in their yards.

"Sometimes," began Sarah, "the Dormant World can be more wonderful than anything you could create on your own."

Amelia couldn't disagree. The walk was making her feel very calm. This small town was every bit as beautiful and miraculous as any of the fantastic places that she had visited. It was common, and so she occasionally took for granted how special it was. She imagined that one of the creatures from the paradigm spheres would stand in awe if it were to visit here.

"Sarah?"

"Yes?"

"Why did you take me in?" asked Amelia, slowly. "I mean, was it just because I have this gift?"

"Of course not," said Sarah, looking shocked. "The fact that you have a special gift was an unexpected surprise. It is great that I have the opportunity to teach someone about their skills, but I would have taken you in even if you had been a Dormant. I had been looking at the foster program for almost a year. I've told you before that I've been alone for a long time. I needed someone to care for and show love to. It wasn't until after you started to disappear in the evenings that I asked someone to confirm that you had the gift. If you hadn't been going to your paradigm sphere, then I was worried that you were sneaking out or running away at night."

"Alright," said Amelia. "You've just been so focused on making me practice all the time, I wonder if that isn't what's really important to you."

Sarah stopped, turned, and gave Amelia a big hug.

"I'm sorry if I've made you feel that way," said Sarah. "I guess I'm just excited to share this with someone."

She pulled away and looked Amelia in the eyes before

saying, "If I'm pushing too hard, just let me know. I care about you. Not your ability."

"Okay," said Amelia, before giving Sarah another hug and continuing their walk. "Sarah?"

"Yes?"

"How do we make these things? I thought that there were rules about how things could and couldn't work in nature. Even the other day, when we were in Adonei, I saw a walking pile of stones. How can a pile of stones come to life? It isn't natural."

"You are asking two questions," said Sarah. "But I will be happy to answer both. Let's start heading toward the canyon so that we won't be overheard."

They walked down the same road that Amelia had run down the night that she found out Sarah's secret. It had gotten dark, but the moon was bright out and so they had no trouble seeing where they were going. The additional chill in the air was not unwelcome either.

"To begin with," said Sarah, once they were out in the farmland. "I will answer your second question. We don't break the natural laws when we create things. You are right. A stone creature can't exist, that I know of yet. A creature with skin that looks like stone, can. In this case, the creature you saw in Adonei was probably just a denkle."

Amelia had heard the name before but wasn't sure where.

"A denkle," continued Sarah, "appears to be a walking pile of stones. The stones are more like a shield, or clothing. They are actual stones, not the creature itself. The denkle is like the laroop. It is a creature that is made of refined materials and can't regularly be seen. It wears stones. As it grows, it switches its stones for larger ones. In that respect, it is very similar to a hermit crab."

Sarah yawned, and then continued talking. "Our gift doesn't break natural laws. We have instead found creative ways of following the natural laws to do things that seem impossible. As I've told you before, it is all about seeing things in a different way. Sorry," said Sarah, suddenly. "I need a break."

They had reached the base of the canyon and Sarah sat down on a large rock that was on the side of the road.

"I'm not as in shape as I used to be."

"It's alright," said Amelia.

"We can keep talking while we sit though," said Sarah. "Where were we. Oh, yes! How do we create?"

Sarah leaned back on her arms and took a deep breath. Amelia sat down next to Sarah and got comfortable.

"I guess the best way to explain it, is to give you an

example of how the Dormants can create," said Sarah.

"I thought Dormants couldn't create like us," said Amelia. "You mean they can?"

"Yes," said Sarah. "They create by having children. People don't consciously know how to cause a child to develop. They don't control each and every stage. Deep inside, somewhere, is the knowledge. The egg gets fertilized. Life is created. The cells start to split and grow. Soon, there is a small beating heart. Then the child gets larger and starts to kick and move. Eventually, it is large enough and developed enough to leave the womb and continue developing on its own. The mother doesn't know how to create a central nervous system any more than the developing child does. Nor do they know how to create bones, or muscle. Yet the child is born anyway. It is an instinctive knowledge that is held quietly in the body, mind, and spirit. Our ability is the same way. That is why it is called 'The Great Inheritance.' It is a knowledge that everyone has inherited. We just have a more advanced and externally usable form of that creative ability."

Sarah stood up and stretched again.

"In the same way," continued Sarah, as if she hadn't stopped, "we can create things without knowing the full extent of how they are formed. Our minds, bodies, and spirits have the knowledge necessary to handle many of the details. Somehow, we can control materials that are both seen and unseen, in order to create. For us, it is more about learning to focus and control what you can while helping guide your unconscious mind to handle the rest. The more you study and understand, as well as practice, the better effect you will be able to achieve."

"I'm ready to head back now," said Amelia. "I have to get some sleep so that me and Cindy…"

"Cindy and I," corrected Sarah.

"So that Cindy and I," said Amelia, imitating royalty, "can abscond with the neighborhood candy to our sleepover tomorrow."

"That's right," said Sarah, snapping her fingers. "I had completely forgotten. We will need to get you all set up for it before we go to bed. I can't believe I still haven't put up the Halloween decorations yet this year. I've been too distracted with my work. Let's hurry back."

As they began walking again, Sarah leaned in and asked, "Vocabulary word this week?"

"Ten points, if it's on the test tomorrow," responded Amelia smiling.

Upon arriving home, they quickly cleaned the house and set out Halloween decorations. Amelia made sure that Sarah wrote a note to herself to pick up candy, popcorn, and

a scary movie for them to watch. After they were all done, they got ready for bed.

While Amelia happily turned off the front porch light, she looked into the darkness outside and saw something darker than the night moving across the road. It was gone before Amelia could confirm that it was really there.

That was the second time that day, and the fifth time in the last week. Still, not wanting to bother an already busy Sarah, Amelia chose to ignore it and simply went upstairs.

When Amelia finally got into her bed, she could barely move. She began drifting off almost immediately. Right before falling completely asleep, Amelia was only vaguely aware of the shadowy figure watching her from the corner of the room. She remembered nothing about the nighttime visitor when she awoke the next morning.

CHAPTER SIXTEEN
Ghost Stories

"Bwah, ha, ha, ha, ha!"

Amelia was chuckling as well, but it was nothing to Cindy's reaction. Cindy stopped for a moment to take in some air, and then started laughing again.

"No more, ha, ha, ha. No more, snicker, I'm going to wet myself if I can't… stop.. ha… laughing," said Cindy, clutching her sides.

Before Amelia and Cindy stood Sarah, dressed in full green grease paint makeup, a long black dress, a black pointy hat, a fake nose with a giant wart on it, and square-toe black shoes with a giant gold buckle on each.

"I thought you might like it," said Sarah, grinning happily.

"I love it," said Amelia, who was wearing the same second-hand pirate costume that she had gotten the year before. She stooped down to help lift a still giggling and gasping Cindy off the floor. Cindy was in a beautiful Victorian dress.

"This isn't going to help your image around town," said Amelia.

"Exactly," said Sarah. "That's what makes this so funny."

This set Cindy off again, and Amelia held on to her as they went out the front door.

"We'll be back after we get candy," said Amelia.

It was a clear night, and there were children running everywhere. Amelia and Cindy proceeded to systematically go through the small town to maximize their collection efforts. They avoided the two houses where they knew most of the high schoolers were having parties and made good time through the rest of the houses. After a couple hours, the younger kids were all gone, and lights were going out on front porches. It was time to return home.

Something caught Amelia's attention. Down one of the side roads, she swore that there had been something. The

same shadow, or just her imagination? She didn't know and didn't want to wait around to find out.

"We better hurry home," said Amelia, as she picked up the pace.

"Yeah, we still have a movie and ghost stories to get through tonight," agreed Cindy, ignorant of Amelia's motivations.

They arrived home and found Sarah waiting for them in the living room. She had already taken off her costume and cleaned up her makeup. She was in her pajamas and ready for the slumber party.

"The television is set up in here," said Sarah.

She had brought the little television with the built-in player out of the kitchen and put it in the living room so that they could all sit on the couch for the movie. She even had all the snacks and drinks set up for them so that they could start watching sooner. Amelia was particularly proud of the two kinds of fudge that she and Sarah had made right after school.

"I don't imagine that we'll have many more trick or treaters tonight," Sarah continued. "But I will handle it if we do. You two go get cleaned up so that you won't hurt yourselves if you fall asleep watching the movie."

Sarah was pointing at the big sword that was stuck in

Amelia's belt for the pirate costume.

They quickly changed into their pajamas, got some pillows and blankets, and settled in for the movie. It was an old black and white horror film. It was so poorly done that it was difficult to be scared.

"You can see the man in the back holding up that foam spider," said Cindy.

"That's nothing compared to the actress that is supposed to be an Egyptian queen. She's wearing sneakers," replied Amelia, amidst chuckles.

"The special effects were so revolutionary when it came out that I never realized it wouldn't hold up," said Sarah. "If the man from the future hadn't started choking when he gave his arrival speech, it would have been better."

"Yeah, but the dry ice fog from his cardboard spaceship was just too much," chuckled Amelia.

"I have no idea how this scared me as a little girl," said Sarah.

"I don't know," said Cindy, with a serious tone to her voice. "The fear of undead zombies from the future going to the past, causing worldwide destruction, and setting us up to be vulnerable to the Martian spider migration in the year two thousand and fifty feels like it could be a very legitimate thing."

There was a short silence before Cindy couldn't keep a straight face any longer. They all burst out laughing. They ate snacks, poked fun at the movie, and laughed all the way through.

Once the movie ended, they set up sleeping bags for Cindy and Amelia on the floor. Then, all three of them sat down to tell ghost stories.

"I'll start," said Amelia. "There was a lady driving home one night when a car pulled up behind her and…"

"Back seat, with a hook," said Cindy, cutting Amelia off. "Now for a real one. There was a man that used to visit town selling meat pies. He wasn't…"

"Wife was in the pie," said Amelia, smiling as she cut off Cindy. "Even I know that one."

Cindy gave a smug, wrinkle-nosed grin in return, and they both laughed.

"Girls," said Sarah. "Apparently you need something that you haven't heard a thousand times."

"Fine," said Amelia. "You're up."

"This is the story of Polly and Jane," began Sarah, in a very quiet voice. "Once, a very long time ago, in a village not too far away, two girls were born within a few weeks of each other. They grew up next door to each other, and soon became close friends. They shared everything. They told each

other everything. They were closer than even two sisters could have been. They supported each other and loved each other."

Sarah leaned back in the couch and eased into the next part of the story.

"As they grew up, they eventually started to look for work and had to begin spending time apart. That is the way of life. Jane was able to take over her mother's store, and Polly was forced to travel to a neighboring city to seek work as a seamstress. They stayed in close contact. They would write daily because their friendship was still so very strong. Jane would write and tell Polly of all her financial success and happiness. Polly would write back and tell Jane of all the joy she was finding in her life, even though she was forced to endure constant hardships. Then came a letter one day that notified Jane that Polly was going to be visiting her with a surprise. Jane was excited. She closed shop and prepared for the arrival of her dear friend. She was expecting a wonderful gift that her friend had probably found for her.

"As Jane looked down the main road of the village, she could see Polly. Only, Polly was not alone. It was then that Jane realized that Polly had fallen in love. Jane remembered that Polly had written her about some young man that she was enjoying time with. Jane hadn't understood that it was so serious. That was the reason that Polly had come. She came to make introductions and to tell her good friend Jane all about what she couldn't fit into her letters. She was engaged to be married. Polly was poor but happy because the one thing she did have was love. They spent a wonderful afternoon chatting and getting caught up. Finally, late in the evening, Polly decided to go visit a few other people in the village that she had known growing up. Polly's gentleman stayed at Jane's house because he said that he was tired from the trip. Jane also stayed behind at the house to prepare for dinner. While Jane was busy making preparations, the man did something that was unforgivable. He stole a kiss.

"Through no fault of Jane's, she discovered that Polly's gentleman was not one that would remain faithful. Due to her feelings of guilt for being on the receiving end of the kiss, Jane could not warn her friend. Until this time, they had shared everything. Now, when honesty was required the most, Jane had a secret that she would not share. If Jane had been honest, her friend would have been sad for a moment, but would have been happier in the long run. Their friendship and trust would have grown even stronger.

"Though she didn't fully admit it to herself at the time, Jane had something else causing her guilt to be intensified. During their time apart, Jane had become more interested in her own well-being and had begun to worry that she would have to take care of her friend that had gotten the poorer lot in life. It wasn't much, but it was the beginning of her selfishness. To cover that selfishness, and the guilt she was feeling, she kept the secret of the kiss and wished Polly well as they left the next day.

"For the next few years, they kept in touch. Polly had moved further and further away due to her husband's interests. She shared everything. All the love and joy that she had found. Then later, concerns about her husband. Her life became even more difficult. Jane, who felt ever-growing guilt for not having been honest with the friend of her childhood, felt her love wax cold. Her concern turned to revulsion. She didn't want to deal with her friend's problems. She also didn't want to appear heartless and wrote out of obligation instead of love. She wrote about the day's events and what was happening with the town. Her replies became more about the news than about herself.

"Finally, the dreaded letter came. Jane learned of her friend's most dire circumstances. Polly had been beaten and left for the worst. Her husband no longer felt a need for her and had apparently been unfaithful for a long time. He left her alone in a foreign land and in a terrible physical condition. She was writing to her friend Jane from what would become

196

her deathbed. Jane had been so prosperous, that she could have easily gone to her friend's side, brought her back, and nursed her to health. By this point though, her affections had become so withdrawn that she no longer felt able to do anything. Nor did she have a desire to. She just wanted her guilt and shame to disappear, and so it came to be that she ignored the letter. After a few more arrived, they stopped altogether.

"Jane felt like her troubles had finally gone. She could continue her prosperous life. That is," said Sarah, leaning forward and making her voice very still and even more quiet. "Until one fateful night. Jane woke up, hearing a voice. She couldn't understand it at first, but soon realized that it was the voice of her friend.

"The first night, she couldn't understand what the voice was saying. But soon, after many nights, she could make out the word that the voice was calling out. 'Why?' She began to hear it more and more clearly every night. 'Why? Why? Why?' It became a haunting voice that followed her from dusk to dawn. Soon, she began to see a ghostly visage out of the corners of her eyes during the day. While she was at the millinery shop, the figure was just slipping by and out of sight. As she walked home, she almost caught a glimpse of it, but then it was gone. She was confused as to what it could be.

"Jane didn't have long to wait until she found out. One night as she awoke to the question 'why?' once more, she saw the pale and sickly figure of her friend sitting on the end of the bed. 'Why? Why? Why were you not there for me?' Came the questions from Polly's ghost. 'Had we not always been the closest of friends? What is it that kept you from helping me during my most difficult hour? Why? Why? Why?'

"Even with all this, Jane still couldn't bring herself to tell her oldest friend the reason. She had wrapped herself in so much guilt for the secrets that she couldn't share. She had set herself up for a life of being alone and absorbed. Although she could point back to the kiss as the catalyst, by this point she knew full well that it had started before then. Despite this knowledge, she had no answer to give Polly. She wouldn't reverse the damage, or even attempt to provide her friend with the slightest peace in death. Without answer, Jane lay back down and pretended that she couldn't hear or see the ghost of her friend.

"This continued the same every night after. Jane would wake up and always find Polly sitting at the end of the bed and asking, 'why?' It continued for months. Through it all, Jane's guilt built up even stronger. Not remorse, that would have driven her to make a change and bring her and her friend a resolution, just the ever-tightening guilt. Even more than being frightened of the disturbing image of her former friend, Jane's own guilt and confusion was driving her to ruin.

"Finally, one night, when everything became too much to bear, Jane wound her way up the hill that stood in the middle of the local cemetery. The whole way up, she was followed by the ghost of her friend with continued assaults of 'why?' At the top of the hill, where there stood a great old oak, Jane could stand the question 'why?' no longer. Using a rope, she finally decided to put it to an end. Although she was no longer part of the mortal realm, she didn't succeed. Even now, on late nights in that tiny village, people going through the cemetery can still hear two faint voices being carried on the wind. Both of them asking, 'why?'"

Amelia lay there and let the story sink in. After a few moments, Sarah said that it was time for bed. Both Amelia and Cindy agreed. They had gotten their fill of ghost stories anyway. After all, there was no way that Amelia or Cindy could top what they had just heard. There was also the fact that Amelia was now once again lost in thought over all the shadows that she had seen. It got her thinking about how important being open in a friendship was. She was confused and unsure about what to do.

So, she did what she knew how to. She got ready for bed. They brushed and flossed their teeth, did their nightly scripture and prayer, and Sarah went up to sleep in her bedroom. Amelia and Cindy crawled into their sleeping bags and lay in silence on the floor.

After lying there for a while, Amelia decided that now was the time to open up to Cindy about everything. She was worried but decided that it would be the right thing to do.

"Cindy," started Amelia, feeling her chest pounding with anxiety.

"Yeah, Amelia?" replied Cindy.

"Thanks for being my friend," said Amelia.

"Ditto."

Amelia didn't know where to go from here but felt like she better say something.

"After the story, I decided that I want to be open and honest with you," said Amelia, hesitantly.

Cindy rolled onto her side and propped herself up on her elbow so that they were facing each other. This didn't help Amelia talk. In fact, it made it more difficult. She tried, but had trouble knowing where to begin.

"What do you mean?" asked Cindy, after a while.

"I have a secret," said Amelia. "I feel like I have to share it if we are really going to be friends."

Amelia was expecting a comment, but Cindy was quiet and attentive. Amelia could see that she was trying to listen and be a good friend. That helped give Amelia a little more courage to say what she felt like she needed to.

"The stories about Sarah, well, they aren't entirely untrue," said Amelia. "She has a special gift. I have it too."

She paused and waited for a response. When none came, Amelia began again.

"We have the ability to create things and make things happen. Every night, we travel to other worlds and places and go on adventures. We went to a gigantic city, and then to an underwater continent where we were attacked by dark and evil people called Creonocens. I even have my own world that I created and have lots of friends there. Only, I didn't know that they were real until recently and now I can't find them. Not since the shadow creature appeared."

There was still silence from Cindy. Amelia was feeling extremely vulnerable by sharing. She wasn't sure what to do. All she could think of was to continue talking.

"Let me start from the beginning. When I was a kid, I found a door that allows me to go places. I thought I was crazy. I would go on adventures with friends that I made when I was exploring. Once I moved here though, things went weird and I started to be attacked by a creature that was

darker than shadow. It invaded the safest places in my world. Afterward, I found out Sarah's secret because I came home early on the Thursday I had to leave school. I left because I saw the creature at school, and it made me feel like I was going crazy. When I got home, I found Sarah coming out of a portal, and found out that she had the same gift that I do. Since then, I realized the things in my world are not imaginary. They are real. Which means that so is the shadowy creature that has been following me. Tonight, I saw it when we were coming back from trick-or-treating. Even now, it could be outside lurking around in the dark. I'm not sure if it is the same creature. I just know that somewhere, something is out there."

She waited for Cindy to say something. Whatever Amelia expected, Cindy's response wasn't it. Cindy started laughing, and congratulating Amelia.

"That was great," said Cindy. "That was almost scarier than Sarah's story. How long did it take you to come up with that?"

Amelia realized her mistake. She had picked the worst possible time to tell her secret to Cindy.

"No!" said Amelia, more forcefully than she intended. "I'm serious. I'm trying to tell you everything. It isn't a ghost story. It's the truth."

"Right," faltered Cindy. "Stop trying to get me. It was good, but I'm not going to fall for something that obviously can't be real."

"No!" replied Amelia. "I'm not trying to 'get you.' I know it's bad timing, but I am trying to be honest."

"Look," said Cindy, stretching. "I'm sorry I didn't get scared or buy into the story. I know that must be what you wanted. But I'm tired and ready to sleep. Just leave me alone already."

"I'm not trying to trick you," said Amelia, getting angry. "I'm serious. Why won't you listen to me? I thought we were friends."

"I thought so too," replied Cindy, her voice cracking. "But real friends aren't mean to each other, and they don't lie or try to trick each other. Enough is enough."

She turned away from Amelia and stopped responding.

"I'm not lying!" said Amelia. "Why won't you believe me. Huh? Why? I thought you would understand."

Amelia tried for a while longer to get a response from Cindy, but finally rolled over and attempted to sleep as well. Cindy wasn't moving and wasn't talking. Amelia felt hurt. She had opened up completely but was not believed. She felt angry and resentful. She sank into her thoughts as they

203

spiraled out of control.

Why did I even try to be honest? How could I be so stupid as to believe that someone could actually be my friend and show me trust? Every time I share something, I get hurt. How could I let this happen again?

Amelia screamed in her mind. Raging, and raging at her choice.

Amelia couldn't sleep much that night. She tossed and turned angrily. It was a very long and miserable night.

The next morning Cindy got up, packed her things, and left without a word. Amelia was awake but didn't move or say anything. She was so hurt and angry, after a night of dwelling on her thoughts, that she was glad that Cindy had left. Who needed a friend that wouldn't be a true friend?

Amelia finally got out of bed when Sarah came down to start cooking breakfast.

"I heard loud voices last night," said Sarah, concerned. "What's wrong?"

"You were right," said Amelia, through clenched teeth. "I shouldn't have told anything to a Dormant."

Amelia couldn't handle talking anymore. She ran upstairs to her room and locked the door. She just wanted to be left alone. No one cared anyway. Amelia hated the world.

Nobody could love her or have faith in her, so she didn't want to pretend anymore and didn't want to be around Sarah either. All Amelia wanted was to disappear.

CHAPTER SEVENTEEN
The Chase Festival

 Much to her chagrin, Amelia woke up again and realized that the world hadn't, in fact, blown up during her absence. From the way her body refused to move though, there was a small chance that she had fused with her mattress and quilt.

Another knock at the door woke her out of the sleep she was trying to drift into. The door opening just drove it home.

"If you are here to try and cheer me up or tell me things will be alright, I don't want to hear it," sulked Amelia.

"I wasn't going to bother," said Sarah, grinning.

This disinterest was new, and mildly perked Amelia's attention. At the very least, she sat up.

"Actually," said Sarah. "I was going to continue your education."

"I don't feel like it," said Amelia, flopping back down on her bed, and making sure that the disappointment was very evident in her voice.

"I, of course, have an ulterior motive," said Sarah. "I'm trying to distract you from your problems. Even giving you that knowledge, I think it will work."

Although she refused to give Sarah any satisfaction by showing outward signs of interest, Amelia could almost feel her ear bending as she consciously willed it to listen more closely to what Sarah had to say.

"You see," whispered Sarah. "I am going to share a discovery with you that only a few people know about. To keep down the charlatans, it isn't something that all the Learners get to hear about. It is the basis behind all of our progress over the last thirty-five years."

Amelia lay quietly and waited. After a moment, Sarah stood up.

"Well, I guess if you don't want to hear it..." Sarah began.

That did the trick. Amelia quickly sat up and said

"No! Wait!" She could see the smile still sitting on Sarah's face. Sarah had won their little battle of the wills. Amelia knew it but didn't care. She was more interested in what Sarah had to say.

"Well," said Sarah, sitting back down on the edge of Amelia's bed. "Thirty-five years ago, we figured out a special part of The Great Inheritance that we didn't previously know about. It was the discovery of individual gifts and abilities."

Amelia was disappointed again.

"You already told me about this," groaned Amelia. "I already know that different people have different levels of abilities."

She flopped once again on her bed, but Sarah had apparently not given up yet.

"You misunderstand me," said Sarah, with a cheerful sneakiness in her voice. "I am not talking about levels of skill with using creative powers in The Great Inheritance. I am talking about completely separate and distinct gifts in addition to the general ability to create."

Sarah's distractions weren't working. Amelia's mind was already wandering back to Cindy and the long, painful night she had just gone through. Her chest ached with anger and loneliness. She just wanted to be left alone.

"Let me try simplifying it again," said Sarah.

"Everyone that has the gift of The Great Inheritance has various levels of the ability to create."

"Yeah," drolled Amelia, trying to now get Sarah to leave her alone. "Some can only create inorganic objects. Some can create life."

"Well, does everyone have the ability to see and talk to the laroop?" asked Sarah.

"No," replied Amelia, still not sure where Sarah was taking the conversation.

"Can you sense who is a Learner and who is a Dormant?" asked Sarah.

"No," replied Amelia again, tired of the stream of questions.

"There are some people that can. I asked one such person about you, shortly after you moved in. That is how I discovered that you were a Learner," said Sarah. "Anyway, there are additional and individual gifts and abilities that come along with The Great Inheritance. We didn't fully understand this until thirty-five years ago when we found a man that had the ability to see what the gifts of others were. He could meet with another Learner and tell them what gifts they had. Because of his ability, we learned about the gifts. It caused everything to start to make sense."

"What do you mean?" asked Amelia, rolling to face

Sarah.

"It helped us to see things in a different light. We thought that anything that happened was done by using the creative ability of The Great Inheritance. We were only looking for what trick was used to accomplish certain things, such as how The Twins could take Dormants into their sphere. Now we know that it was an individual gift they had. It wasn't that they were using a trick of creating, it was that they had the gift of being able to let anyone into their sphere."

Amelia still didn't understand. She rolled onto her back and put her arm over her eyes. She just wanted to stop hurting.

"Do you remember the story you heard about Zharen Paloka?" asked Sarah.

"Not really," said Amelia, not even trying to remember.

"He was the gentleman that used the laroop to support his family. He had the ability to see and speak to the laroop," said Sarah. "The Learners of the time simply thought that he had advanced so far in his creative abilities that he could almost feel the created creatures. With an understanding of the gifts, we can now review the story of Zharen and see that he actually could see these creatures that were made of refined materials. He had the gift that allowed him to see those things, and the gift to communicate with them."

"How many different individual abilities are there?" asked Amelia.

"Thousands that we know about," said Sarah. "Some seem so small as to not be noticed. Others are huge. We have been discovering more and more, but we are still being surprised all the time. It is all about seeing things in new ways."

Amelia was tired of hearing that last sentence.

"So, what are my gifts?" asked Amelia.

"Unfortunately," began Sarah. "I don't know. The man that had the ability to tell you, passed away well before you were born. I guess you will have to discover it on your own, like everyone else."

"What would I even look for?"

"Anything that can't be explained by the creative side of your gift," said Sarah. "To even start to tell you the various gifts and ranges of abilities would not only take forever but would also be fruitless. You will find out when it becomes important. Otherwise, you may go through life and never realize that you even have any additional gifts. Who can tell? The important thing is that now that you understand it, you

can use that knowledge to see things in a different way. If nothing else, it gives you something interesting to think about."

With that, Sarah stood up and started to leave.

"What are your gifts?" asked Amelia.

Sarah stopped and thought about it for a short while before responding. Amelia waited with her eyes still covered.

"I am not sure about all of them," Sarah finally said. "I do have one special one that is individual to me. I have the ability to see how things work. If I spend enough time with an object, I can eventually understand the function of it. Aside from this pendant, it usually doesn't take very long. Anyway, that is my gift. You just need to keep watching for yours."

"Alright," said Amelia.

"By the way," said Sarah, her tone changing slightly. "I love you. I hope this has helped and that you can start to feel better. If you need anything, let me know. I'm here for you. I will be working in my room again, but I will drop everything if you need something from me."

Sarah turned to go but stopped at the door.

"One last thing," said Sarah. "Did you want to go to a festival with me tonight?"

"Don't be weird," said Amelia, pulling her quilt over

her head and rolling away from Sarah. "There isn't a festival until next Friday."

"Not in Pickleton, no," said Sarah, with that sneaky cheerfulness in her voice again. "Adonei has one that is starting tonight."

Sarah shut the door and left. The thought of the festival took Amelia's sleepy mind and started it racing again.

She got out of bed and went to see if Sarah was really going to take her. Amelia latched on to the opportunity to focus on something other than her friendless state. She couldn't shake the pain in her chest, or the emptiness she felt, but a distraction would help keep her moving.

Hours later, they arrived near the fountain of The Twins. Amelia was expecting it to be dark like it was in Pickleton when they left. Just like her sphere, she kept forgetting that it was always a couple of hours earlier in Adonei than it was in Pickleton.

"Great," said Sarah. "We're in time to get there before it begins."

"Before what begins?" asked Amelia, looking around. "I don't see any decorations or anything. Are you sure there is a festival today?"

"Of course, there is," said Sarah. "You don't think they would spoil it by making it obvious do you?"

Amelia was confused, but shrugged and kept pace with Sarah. They walked up to the road and caught a horse-drawn carriage.

"Please take us to the Learner's Spire," Sarah told the horse. "We want to be there in time for the opening speech."

They rode at an accelerated pace up the hill to the peak of Adonei where Amelia had gone on her first visit. When they arrived at one of the gates leading in, the lion-headed beastmen stopped them to inform them that the carriage wouldn't be allowed inside. They got out and were inspected quickly before being allowed in. Once inside, Amelia saw why the carriage was not allowed. The area was packed with people and creatures of every shape and size.

Amelia felt confused again. There were no food stands, no vendors, no games. Aside from the large crowd, there was nothing that would give the impression that there was a festival. Because of the crowd, they couldn't get any closer to the main building. They were forced to wait on the outskirts, near the outer wall. It took about twenty minutes until the sky started to go dark. When it did, the crowd hushed and became very quiet. Occasionally, a child could be heard crying or a creature grunting, but it was otherwise very still.

"What's going on?" asked Amelia, who was frustrated

and feeling the pain in her chest get stronger.

"Oh, he loves to perform at these events," said Sarah, almost to herself.

"Who?" asked Amelia.

But she never heard a response. There was a giant explosion of cheering right at that moment. Amelia looked up to the sky where Sarah was staring. There was, what appeared to be, a giant fireball plummeting straight toward the crowd from the top of the spire. As it got closer, Amelia realized that it was the shriveled old man who was the leader of Adonei. He was riding on a giant open book. A wall of flame was wrapping all around him, sparkles appearing in his wake, and fireworks shooting off in all directions.

"Isn't he going to crash?" yelled back Amelia.

"No," hollered Sarah. "Just watch."

Sure enough, right before hitting the ground, Jasper stopped. The wall of flame that was wrapping around him spread out over the heads of the crowd like a tidal wave. As it passed and disappeared, strings of lanterns appeared overhead, stretching from the lower circular section of the tower to the outer wall. Giant panels appeared along the outer walls, and at various places in the building. Jasper could be seen on the panels as he and the book slowly lowered the final portion of the way to the ground. The book then shrank

215

and disappeared into one of Jasper's pockets. He was standing on a pillar that had risen in front of the steps leading under the first section of the tower. As he spoke, his voice was clear to everyone present. It was as if he was speaking to them in a casual conversation from only a few feet away.

"Thank you all for gathering here today," came Jasper's cheerful voice. "I assume you are here for learning? I would love to share some of the wonderful things that we have been discovering. No? Well, alright then. Your loss. I guess we will just have to begin."

Amelia watched as he raised his arms. Six golden orbs materialized above the crowd. As they did, there were showers of sparks. Brightly colored birds flew out and over the crowd with each new set of sparks as the orbs got bigger.

"Showoff," said Sarah, admiringly. "Although anyone that has the gift quickly learns that the basis of the gift is more than simply making things, and that it is literally learning to control all the seen and unseen elements around us, it is still amazing to see someone that can control and create so much at the same time. The focus and energy required is enormous. Very few others would be able to pull this off."

Amelia strained to hear Sarah, while even more jets of flames and sparks appeared around the orbs. Clouds

appeared, and it began to rain and lightning in little circles around the golden orbs. The orbs started to glow, the rain died away, and rainbows could be seen in the last of the falling mist. All this happened while thousands of butterflies flowed out of the remainder of the clouds that surrounded the orbs until there was nothing left but the large orbs floating above the crowd. The crowd fell silent once more. A rattle above could be heard. Resplendently, the orbs cracked open and from their respective orbs, six silver birds flew down to a stand that had appeared next to Jasper.

"Those are rainbow falcons," yelled Sarah. "They have the ability to change their appearance."

Amelia could barely hear her over the screams and cheers that had erupted upon the sight of the birds.

"I hope you will all enjoy this year's Chase Festival," said Jasper, sounding like he was only a few feet away. "Every year, I have the honor of starting things off. It is one of the many festivals that we celebrate. Due to the sport, it is one that I truly enjoy. For those of you that are new this year, and there are always many newcomers, I would like to explain the rules to you."

Jasper cleared his throat importantly and continued. "The goal of this festival is to catch the falcons. The first group to do so, wins a very generous prize. The second group

wins a slightly less generous prize. The rest continue so on and so forth. The remainder that don't catch a falcon, won't receive a prize. Remember, the falcons are tricky and hide in many shapes. The key is to use your creative skills and abilities to find it. No attacking other teams. You will just be racing and searching. There are referees throughout the city that will be watching.

"First group to reach a falcon gets a chance to search and then capture it. If they are unsuccessful, then the next group to reach the falcon will get a chance. If you try to interfere while another group is trying to catch it, then you will get a penalty. As for the start, no leaving the courtyard and starting the chase until after the whistle is blown. Anyone leaving early will be sent back and held in penalty for ten minutes. Any other fouls or rule breaking will be an additional ten-minute penalty.

"After the falcons are caught, the food and the merrymaking will begin. Last year the falcons were caught in the first twelve minutes. Three years ago, the final falcon wasn't caught for five days. In the event that the chase goes long, there will be small treats provided to help tide people over until the main festival. We don't want anyone passing out from hunger like they did in the festival that we had eight years ago. We learned our lesson then. Now, let's get ready for

the event!"

Amelia watched in amazement as the chase began. Jasper raised his arm and the rainbow falcons started taking off and formed themselves into a circling pattern above him. They kept going higher and higher until they were almost out of sight in the sky. When Jasper lowered his arm, a loud whistle sounded, and Amelia saw the six falcons flew in different directions leaving brightly colored rainbow streaks in their wake. Immediately, a few hundred people who were the closest to the platform, were off after them. Some on flying horses, some on brooms, some seemingly able to fly with their arms outstretched, and some in flaming balls of fire or other such flashy things. All of them were disappearing at speeds that astounded Amelia. After the initial explosive exit, the panels that had previously shown Jasper were now displaying images of the action.

Amelia and Sarah walked around the courtyard and watched the screens as it progressed. One group was following a rainbow trail as close as possible without actually being able to catch the falcon. The falcon swooped down into a small alley in the city and disappeared. The group landed in the alley and immediately started to create thousands of ant-like insects that swarmed all the surrounding buildings in search of the falcon. One of the pillars shifted. In its place,

the falcon appeared and took off. The ants disappeared and the group was off after the falcon again.

There was a new group that had reached the falcon while it was in midair, and the first group was forced to stay back and watch if the new group would be successful or not. This new group was traveling in great balls of fire. They looked like five meteors that were darting around the falcon and trying to capture it. Amelia thought that they had a good plan too. Three were zooming around in large circles to keep the falcon pinned into a specific area of sky. The other two were darting into the center with nets and trying to catch it. With all the fire from the group, and the rainbow from the silver bird, it looked like an elaborate light show.

There were many other groups that were taking their turns at trying to catch the falcons. One group of two ladies that were riding on winged dolphins were fast enough to be the first ones to reach their falcon each time it got away from them. Other groups couldn't even catch up to the falcon after it took off before the two ladies had reached it again.

At a few points, Amelia would hear a loud whistle, and a group would be brought back to the courtyard in a giant cage that was held by flying elephants.

"Rotten cheaters," Jasper called out to them. "This will teach you. Follow the rules next time."

It continued, and each time a falcon was caught the panels would change to follow the remaining falcons. Finally, the two ladies who were riding on winged dolphins caught the last falcon, and all the panels went dark.

The contestants returned to the courtyard and Jasper appeared on the panels.

"One hour, four minutes, and twenty-three seconds," said Jasper looking at his golden pocket watch. "Not the best record, but definitely a good run. It was a great game. Everyone did well. In general, it was much cleaner than last year. Except for the Spindle Strouts," continued Jasper, as he looked down at a group of four boys that were still in a giant cage and reveling in the attention. "Who after five penalties are still in their sixth ten-minute penalty for the next two minutes. I'll be speaking to your father the next time I get a chance to visit. I would have thought that the scolding he gave you last year would have taught you a lesson on playing fair.

"Anyway, I'm pleased to announce the winners," said Jasper, with one last glare at the Strout boys, who now started to look very scared at the mention of their father. "First place goes to the Pentafires."

There was cheering, and Amelia recognized the group of five people that had been riding in fireballs. Jasper

congratulated them and handed them their prize. He continued to do so for the rest of the winners. In second place were the Stone Shrinkers, then the Critter Crusaders, the Blodgets, the Rainbow Chasers, and finally the Dillywonk Sisters.

There were many other groups that didn't even see the falcons after the initial exit, and many more that had seen them but hadn't caught them. It had been quite the event. Amelia had seen so many amazing things that she was fired up to try practicing her abilities, but that would have to wait until another time. Right now, she was just going to enjoy the festival.

"Let the celebration begin," came Jasper's voice.

Upon his pronouncement, it was like someone had turned on a light switch and the night sky lit up. Amelia followed Sarah and the rest of the crowd out of the gate, past the lion-headed beastmen, and found that the empty streets were now full. Lanterns, floating lights, and fireworks made it seem like daytime had returned.

Amelia and Sarah started down the road from the gate, and Amelia was overwhelmed instantly. There was a line for an ice slide that went from the peak, all the way down to the docks. In the distance, carnival lights on rides seemed to be surrounding the city.

"Is that lady selling living snake wigs?" asked Amelia, trying to take in the overwhelming variety of food stands, vendors, and games in front of her.

"Looks like," responded Sarah. "I already have them in two species at home if you want to borrow one for a night out."

Again, Amelia couldn't tell if Sarah was joking or not.

CHAPTER EIGHTEEN

Butterflies

 "Are you sure it will make me glow?" asked Amelia.

"That's what the vendor said," responded Sarah. "We can try it together. On the count of three. One, two, three."

Amelia gulped down the slimy orange drink. It wasn't disgusting, but it didn't taste great either. They waited and watched to see what would happen. After a few moments, their fingernails began to glow slightly.

"That's it?" asked Amelia, holding up her hands.

"Apparently," said Sarah. "What do you want to try next?"

For Amelia, the orange drink was the closest thing to food she had taken in since the movie snacks the night before. Amelia's growling stomach informed her that it was now ready to be put back to use after being neglected for so long.

They opted for a stand that was selling doner kebab sandwiches, which Amelia had never heard of before. Sarah assured her that she would love it. The stand was nestled between a lady selling beetle-shaped jewelry, and a man who was running a fishing game that, according to the sign, had hybrid reptilian fish that were created just for the game.

"I thought that the city wasn't very full," said Amelia, looking at the crowds that seemed to be getting larger.

"It isn't normally," said Sarah, taking a bite of her food and then speaking through a partial mouthful. "But when there is a festival, Learners from everywhere arrive. Most aren't here for the actual chase portion of the festival. There simply isn't enough room in the tower courtyard. However, they do tend to show up once the food and games begin."

They ate their food while continuing to walk the streets. There were a series of artist booths, a shooting alley game stand, and a fortune teller that Amelia went to first. Amid protests, Sarah followed Amelia through a haunted

house. They even went on one of the aerial roller coaster rides. By the time they got rainbow-colored drinks that refracted real rainbows, Sarah looked exhausted.

"Are you okay?" asked Amelia.

"Yeah, we just need to find somewhere to sit for a bit," said Sarah. "I think I know a place that will work."

Amelia followed Sarah down winding streets and back alleys until they had gotten far enough away from the crowd that the noise died down.

"Where are these buildings from?" asked Amelia.

"It's Japanese architecture," responded Sarah. "There's a nice spot just up ahead, if someone else isn't already there."

They began to climb narrow stone steps that went between the houses and wound their way past small shrines and a graveyard. To Amelia, it all felt very old. The moss-covered granite statues and stairs were heavily weathered.

They sat down on a granite block that was on a landing between the steps leading up the hill and the entrance to one of the shrines. Amelia and Sarah didn't talk. They quietly sat and enjoyed the calm. Amelia leaned back against the stone wall and the tension began to lift from her muscles, at least until she caught sight of something that made them stiffen again.

The darker than black shadow had appeared. It was

sitting on the corner of the rooftop below them, right next to a fish-shaped statue on the roof tiles. Amelia didn't move. She didn't know what to do or say. She could hear other footsteps coming from the alley below. It was the one that they had come through a few minutes before. She looked back from the alley, to the rooftop. The shadow was not gone as she expected. Instead, it was now flying toward her and Sarah at a frightening speed. Sarah was sitting with her eyes closed and looked like she was falling asleep. When Amelia looked back, the shadow with the sword was almost on them.

Then it happened. Amelia reacted almost without thinking. A large granite barrier appeared in front of her, blocking the creature. The wall behind her gave way and created a hole. Then, the entire section of ground they were sitting on slid back into the wall. The granite barrier she created slid backward and covered the entrance. Once in place, it began to change and became transparent. Amelia instinctively knew that it was now like a one-way mirror. She realized that somewhere in her mind she had planned it that way. She could see out, but anything outside would only see a wall of granite that blended in with the rest of the wall they had gone into.

"Impressive," said Sarah, opening her eyes. "But what was that all about?"

"Shhhh!" said Amelia, quieting Sarah.

Amelia was tense and was looking to see where the shadow creature had gone. She couldn't see it anywhere. Instead, there were two figures that appeared from the alley below. Both Amelia and Sarah recognized them at the same time, and Sarah sat forward. Creonocens. One of them was the gilled Creonocen from Azolla. He no longer had gills, but there was no mistake about who he was. The new Creonocen was larger and had purple mottled skin that looked bruised. Amelia and Sarah stayed very quiet.

"I know they came this way," hissed the purple faced Creonocen. "We have to find what they did with the pendant."

The formerly gilled one nodded silently, and the two men went up the hill quickly. Amelia was worried that their new hiding spot would be found. After a few minutes of not hearing anything, she finally relaxed.

"That was close," said Sarah. "How did you know that they were coming?"

Amelia didn't want to tell Sarah about the shadow creature. She had already lost Cindy, and she didn't want to scare Sarah away too. Instead, she shrugged. Sarah had to help open their way out because Amelia wasn't exactly sure how she had done what she did.

They walked quickly back toward the lights and crowds of the festival.

"We need to let Jasper know," whispered Sarah. "The reason we can't catch Learners that have become Creonocens is because it is hard to tell them apart from other Learners. You have to catch them doing something to figure out who they are. The severely mutated ones, that can't change their appearance back to normal, stay out of the cities. The rest can be difficult to identify. We can at least warn them about these two and see where things go from there."

Once they reached the crowd, Sarah and Amelia split up. Amelia was put on a gondola lift that had been set up to ferry large numbers of people quickly from the festival around the summit to the portal yard. Sarah headed back to the spire to find Jasper.

As soon as Amelia arrived at the fountain, her door appeared on the side of one of the giant trees that lined the edge of the portal yard. She stepped through and into her bedroom. As Amelia went down into the kitchen, she saw that it was already after midnight. She got a drink and then sat down at the table to wait for Sarah to return.

Amelia couldn't calm down. She felt more and more anxiety until Sarah finally arrived through her portal in the living room two hours later.

"It's all taken care of," said Sarah. "The guards were able to catch them a short distance away from where we saw them. The worst part is that one of them is a researcher at the Learner's spire. He had been stealing information from the inside. That is how they knew about the pendant.

"Anyway, some things have changed. Monday, the pendant will go to the Learner's spire. I must continue my work there under a close guard. Jasper will send out announcements about the great discovery and will notify everyone that it is being researched in the capital. The Creonocens will then no longer be after us to find the pendant. Until then, we will be guarded. Don't worry. We will be more than safe enough."

Sarah's statement did nothing to comfort Amelia.

"As an extra precaution, we need to adjust your training," said Sarah. "I don't want to risk you being unprepared in the future."

"So, I get to learn to fight?" asked Amelia, picking up on what was left unspoken.

"You already know how to do that," said Sarah. "You need to learn to better control your ability to protect yourself and others, but only if the situation arises. For now, you need to go to bed."

"Church tomorrow?" asked Amelia. "Can't we sleep

in this week?"

"Nope," said Sarah. "Now, let's get ready for bed."

Amelia was struggling with very mixed feelings. She was happy that they were safe but was still confused about the shadow creature that had attacked them. Her chest was still aching over the evening before, and her head was now throbbing again.

Amelia woke up the next morning, screaming. Sunlight was pouring into the room, and she couldn't get oriented. It was morning. But it had just been nighttime.

Sarah came running into her room.

"What's wrong, Amelia?" asked Sarah. "What happened?"

Amelia didn't know how to answer. She was still confused. It had all felt so real to her. It started with that shadow attacking them at the festival, but then she had fallen through a hole in the ground and was back in her home as a child. She saw her father confronting an evil man that she had long since blocked from her memory. There was the shadow again. It was scaring her, and so she ran into her room and hid under her bed. There was screaming that started in the room she had just come from. She wanted to stay and help her family but was too scared of the shadow creature. She

should have stayed. The guilt of being a coward welled up inside of her, and she started to scream and cry. When she had finally gotten the courage to go back out into the other room, she no longer had a family. Amelia was alone again, and she began to scream louder. That was when she had woken up.

"I saw my family again," said Amelia, through tears. "I was back at the night that they were, when they..."

Sarah held Amelia and rocked back and forth to comfort her. Amelia cried until her supply of tears was exhausted. When the pain subsided enough, Amelia unclenched from the fetal position and Sarah went downstairs to get them breakfast. Amelia didn't have an appetite, but she knew that staying alone with her thoughts would only make things worse right now. She got ready for the day. Even with the panic, Amelia needed to go to church.

Amelia felt like the routine would help. It did, and she felt much more at peace by the end of the service. Still exhausted, after coming home and having lunch Amelia took a nap. She was back in that same night with her family. Amelia woke up screaming.

"What's happening to me?" cried Amelia when Sarah came into the room. "Why am I remembering all of this now?"

"I'm not sure," said Sarah. "Something must have triggered it. It will pass. I am here and I love you. You will make it through this."

They spent the rest of the afternoon together. Amelia still couldn't talk about what had happened in her childhood. It was too painful. Amelia was grateful for Sarah's company and love. She wished that she was still able to call Cindy. Cindy would understand her problems. Amelia had to correct her thoughts. No, she wouldn't. Cindy wouldn't have believed her. That was why they weren't friends anymore.

With the same memories flooding her dreams during the night, those feelings lasted into the next day. She went to school but felt alone. It was especially difficult during her biology class because she was assigned the seat next to Cindy. They didn't talk. Both worked on projects individually. Their proximity made the pain even more poignant.

During English, Amelia was stuck sitting next to her assigned partner, Spencer. They were supposed to be talking about their journal assignment, but Amelia was silent and lost in thought. She almost jumped out of her chair with surprise when she felt something touch her hand. Amelia flushed a little when she realized that it was Spencer's hand.

"Are you alright?" asked Spencer, with his quiet voice.

"You haven't seemed happy today. Did something happen between you and Cindy? You two haven't been hanging out the way you normally do."

Amelia pulled away at the mention of Cindy. She didn't want to talk about it. Amelia realized that there was a cute boy who was trying to comfort her though. She desperately wanted someone to talk to, but she was scared of saying something to Spencer.

As class continued, Spencer began speaking once more.

"S-s-so, my mother yelled at me this weekend," said Spencer. "I can't get things right around her. Everything I do isn't enough. I feel like I'll never be able to measure up to what she wants me to be."

It was strange to Amelia to hear Spencer sharing something. She could see that he was waiting for a response. She didn't want to leave him feeling vulnerable like this.

"I had a bit of a thing with Cindy this weekend too," said Amelia, quietly. "I think I did all of the yelling though."

Why was she telling Spencer this? Didn't she hate him?

"I tried telling her about my past and she wouldn't believe me or accept me," continued Amelia. "I have been having flashbacks about when my family passed away."

Too much information. Why was she still talking? She looked at Spencer's eyes, and her mouth just kept moving on its own. Wasn't talking about this supposed to hurt?

"It has been bringing back all of my guilt for not being able to somehow prevent it from happening."

"Why would Cindy not be able to believe that?" asked Spencer.

Why? Amelia couldn't tell him everything. She wanted to tell him something though. She fished around in her mind for a few moments, and then latched onto the shadow creature. Why did she have to tell him anything though?

"I told her about a darker than black creature," said Amelia.

It was exhilarating for some reason. Spencer didn't pull away. He simply listened intently. Amelia couldn't help but continue.

"Promise you won't make fun of me?" asked Amelia.

"Promise," said Spencer.

"When I remember the night I lost my family, I keep seeing a dark creature that scares me away from where it happens. I am so frightened that I can't go out to stop it or do anything about it."

"And Cindy didn't believe that the creature could have scared you away?" asked Spencer.

"Something like that," said Amelia, looking down at the floor.

"I gu-guess that whatever you remember, it is yours. Other people shouldn't have a right to decide if it is real or not. Only you would know," Spencer mused.

Amelia's heart leaped. He believed her. He really believed her. He wasn't attacking. He wasn't abusive. He just listened.

Neither of them knew what to say after that. When the bell finally rang and Amelia started to get up to go, Spencer stopped her.

"You know that there is a festival on Friday, right?" asked Spencer.

"Uh-huh," said Amelia. "The Pickle Festival."

"Yeah, well, you aren't going with anyone, are you?" asked Spencer, looking down at his shoes.

"Probably just Sarah," said Amelia, not quite understanding the line of questions.

"W-w-well, w-would you like to go with me?" asked Spencer, looking up at Amelia.

Amelia felt her face go red hot and knew that she must be blushing.

"Yes. That would be great," said Amelia, watching Spencer's worried look vanish into a big cheesy grin.

236

"C-cool!" said Spencer, clumsily. "I'll pick you up after school on Friday then?"

"That would be great," said Amelia, suddenly feeling very dizzy and off balance. This was a new type of anxiety. It was oddly one that she didn't want to leave immediately. "I will see you Friday… and tomorrow. I guess tomorrow, and every day this week up until Friday. But I will definitely see you Friday as well."

Despite the cringe-worthy ending of their conversation, Amelia felt like she was floating. Somehow everything was wonderful and hopeful. Even when the bad memories and worries tried to bother her, her mind didn't have enough room to let them in.

Amelia had one all-consuming thought that was taking over. It was sending endless streams of butterflies to churn her stomach. Amelia was going to the Pickle Festival with Spencer.

CHAPTER NINETEEN
Reunion

The next couple of days were happy ones. Even though Cindy still wouldn't talk to her, Amelia couldn't stop the giddiness she felt. Spencer didn't hang out with Becky's group anymore. This fueled their cruelty, but Amelia didn't care. English class made it all worthwhile. She could sit down and talk with Spencer. It brought out all sorts of warm and wonderful new feelings.

On Wednesday night, Amelia arrived home to find a note from Sarah.

Dear Amelia,

I had to go to Adonei again to continue research on the pendant. I won't be around this evening until late. There is something for you to warm up in the fridge. Love you. Get your homework done. Also, don't forget to practice what we have been working on. Have a good evening.

Love,
Sarah

Sure enough, as she checked the fridge, there was a plate of food that had another plate on top as a cover. It had a note stuck to it that said "Amelia." Amelia closed the fridge and set her homework out on the table.

She had no idea what to do about her English homework. Things were going well with Spencer. In fact, they were now doing a lot of talking during their English class. They never actually got around to talking about their opinions for the journal assignment. At the moment, Amelia couldn't even remember what they did talk about. She simply smiled as she remembered how it felt to be around him.

Amelia spent the next couple of hours trying to get her homework done but was very unproductive. She couldn't get her mind off Spencer. Finally, she decided it was dinner time. She warmed up her meal in the microwave and sat down to eat. Even while trying to eat dinner, her thoughts drifted back to Spencer. After a moment of thinking about him, Amelia realized that she was dripping mashed potatoes and gravy onto her papers and had to clean things up. She finally gave in to the fact that she wouldn't be able to get much accomplished with her journal.

Amelia quickly finished eating dinner and went to her room. A trip to her sphere would allow her to get some practice on her defensive skills, and it would be better than sitting around accomplishing nothing.

Stepping through her doorway, Amelia saw that Bartholomew's ship was no longer anchored off Raskiel's island. It was, instead, anchored outside of the glowing lagoon. There was still no one on the ship though.

"Open," said Amelia, looking at the cliff face and pulling her hands apart.

The cliffs didn't move. Sarah had warned her about this.

No friends, no abilities, no answers. All Amelia could do was keep working on the exercise that Sarah had given her. She concentrated and began breathing steadily. As she focused, she pictured what she wanted to do.

"A stone wall. A stone wall. A stone wall," Amelia chanted to herself.

As this is what she had done naturally when she felt threatened on the night of the Chase Festival, Sarah decided to start Amelia's defensive training with it. Amelia focused with all her energy and tried to produce the granite wall that she had used as a shield against the shadow creature.

Unfortunately, it was no good. She could produce a small granite block, but that was it. It was better than she had been doing. When she had tried the day before, she was barely able to produce a small piece of granite. Monday night she was able to produce a stone, but not the strong granite that she was able to do on the night of the festival. At one point she did get a wall-sized shape, but the gelatinous material collapsed quickly. At least this rough granite block was an improvement.

Amelia continued practicing, and she saw improvements quicker than she expected. After an hour, she could still only produce a partial wall. Well, if five oddly shaped stones could be considered a wall. It took far too long to create and wasn't very sturdy. It toppled onto the deck, scarring and denting the wood.

"Do you know how long it took me to polish and wax that?" came an angry voice.

Amelia turned around with both shock and excitement.

"Binky! You're back," said Amelia, running to the small, stocky, and wet figure that was pulling itself onto the ship.

There were hugs, and even more shouts of joy as Ohma, Amy, and Raskiel climbed aboard. Raskiel was last because he was busy tying up the rowboat, and his paws always made knot tying difficult. The joy and rejoicing soon turned to shock and sorrow.

"What happened to all of you?" asked Amelia. "Why are you all bruised and cut up? Amy, is your arm broken?"

"No, no," said Raskiel. "It's a sprain. We're all right. Just glad to see you again."

"Yes," said Bartholomew. "How are you doing?"

"Have you been happy?" asked Amy.

"We have experienced pangs of longing in your absence," said Ohma.

Now that she had them here, Amelia's eyes started welling with tears.

"I guess you aren't happy," said Amy, looking down. "Are you going to leave again?"

"No!" blurted out Amelia, finding her voice. "I'm back for good. I am not crazy, and you are all real."

"What changed?" asked Bartholomew.

"I found out that Sarah has the same abilities as me.

There are other people with the same abilities. What we can do and the things we can create are real. They are not imaginary."

"Well, that explains a few things," said Raskiel.

"What it doesn't explain," said Amelia, scowling, "is where you have been. I've been coming to find you and have been worried sick. I kept finding the ship at Raskiel's island, but with no sign of anybody anywhere."

Everyone fell silent and tried not to make eye contact.

"Are you that mad at me still?" said Amelia, starting to cry. "I'm really sorry for leaving so suddenly last time. I am also sorry for being so mean and for saying you weren't real. I didn't know. I was messed up and I'm sorry."

Amelia was quickly embraced by multiple sets of arms.

"Don't be sorry," growled Raskiel. "Lift your head up and move on."

"Yeah!" agreed Amy.

Ohma didn't say anything. He looked like he was in bliss in the group hug. When they let go, Ohma kept trying to get Amy to hug him again.

"Now that you're back," began Bartholomew, wiping away his sympathy tears. "Where are we going tonight?"

Amelia hadn't thought about going anywhere. She was

simply coming to practice. Being reunited with her friends was unexpected.

"Well," thought Amelia out loud. "Were you guys trying to get into the lagoon? Maybe we should go in there."

There was a silence again. Rather than worry about it, Amelia stepped forward to the front of the ship, did her usual hand gesture, and yelled "open." Once again, nothing happened.

"I'm sorry," said Amelia. "I can't fully explain why, but the things that I used to do aren't working anymore. Sarah told me that my conscious mind and subconscious mind would be at war with each other as I continue to learn to control my ability."

"So," said Raskiel. "Any place that you have to use your ability will be off limits for the trip tonight."

"I guess," said Amelia. "Where can we go? I'm not even completely sure what is part of my ability and what isn't."

"We should go to the fire valleys," said Amy.

"Too dangerous," said Bartholomew. "You would have been roasted last time if it weren't for Amelia."

"The underwater gallery," suggested Amy.

"No," said Amelia. "I already worked that one out. I'm the one that makes the bubble helmets, not the crystal

garden. Without them, we can't breathe underwater."

"The fish farms should be resplendent," said Ohma.

"Same problem, you dundering thesaurus," said Bartholomew, adding in the last part under his breath.

They continued, arguing back and forth over someplace safe that they could all go on an adventure. Amelia was touched that they cared about her enough to want her to be safe, but she was getting frustrated when she realized how much she couldn't do.

"Isn't there anyplace that we can go to?" Amelia finally asked in exasperation.

"What about the grassy meadows?" asked Amy.

"That would be too dangerous for..." started Raskiel, but Amelia cut him off.

"That would be perfect," said Amelia. "At the very least, it will give me a chance to work on my defensive wall."

"Yeah," said Bartholomew. "If you can get it up in time to keep from being trampled by the boarung."

"Precisely," said Amelia, grinning slyly. "At least it should be fun."

Amelia hadn't been overly creative with the naming of her islands when she was younger, and their destination was exactly how it sounded. A small strip of sand and rock that quickly transitioned to fields of grass and flowers. It was a

pretty, rolling landscape. The group loaded into the rowboat and headed to shore, watching closely for signs of the boarung. They landed and proceeded to stay alert while walking along the grassy fields. That's when they spotted it, the creature that looked like a cross between a baby elephant and a giant boar.

"You sure you want to do this?" asked Bartholomew in a whisper.

"Yup," said Amelia.

"Alright," said Bartholomew. "Then let's get going. We'll provide support."

Amelia approached the boarung and started yelling at it. As it charged her, she tried to create the granite wall. When nothing appeared, Bartholomew, Amy, and Ohma acted as rodeo clowns to distract it from its charge.

Amelia got its attention twice more and failed to produce anything. On her fourth try, she was able to create a small block that caused the boarung to trip as it charged. The boarung, deciding that it was tired of being harassed, wandered away.

They set out to find another boarung, and it didn't take them long. It took Amelia two tries this time before she got the small block to show up. The boarung dodged the block and ended up needing to be tackled by Raskiel, who

had been staying near Amelia.

The practice continued, and by the time they had gone through six boarung, Amelia could create a block after only a few seconds. It wasn't the wall she wanted, but it was a good start.

"I need a break," said Bartholomew, panting. "I can't keep running like this."

"What if we went to the fountain?" asked Amelia.

Bartholomew groaned at this, and Raskiel started wagging a now extended tail so much that his body shook.

Raskiel bounded into the front of the group and was followed by Ohma and Amy. Bartholomew started walking next to Amelia, and Amelia leaned over to talk in a whisper that only he could hear.

"Why are you all bruised and cut up, and where have you been?"

"I can't tell you," said Bartholomew, through gritted teeth. "I want to. Believe me, I really want to."

"Why can't you tell me?" asked Amelia.

"Because," said Bartholomew, "we made a vow. We swore that in exchange for something, that we wouldn't reveal the secrets."

"In exchange for what?" said Amelia. "Who did you make the vow to? What secrets?"

"Do you trust me?" asked Bartholomew, stopping and looking directly at Amelia.

"Of course."

"I'm not able to talk about it because I made a promise. Can you let it be for now and just trust me?"

"Yeah," said Amelia. "If I have to. But something that can get you to be silent and hold your tongue. It must be a powerful secret."

"Really?" said Bartholomew, rolling his eyes at Amelia's jab.

CHAPTER TWENTY

Mud Kingdom

 It was a menagerie of living stuffed animals. At least that is how it appeared. Bartholomew and Amelia continued to follow the other three to a large fountain that emptied into a pool. With no boarung in sight, they walked up to the other creatures that were bounding and playing around the edges of the water. Amelia looked at the various forms of bunnies, mice, deer, koalas, foxes, small bears, and other furry animals. They looked like their counterparts in the Dormant World, but were smaller, fuzzier, and friendlier.

Amelia sat down and picked up one of the bunnies to

hold and pet. Bartholomew sat next to her and lay down for a nap.

Raskiel seemed to be having the most fun. His transformation made him look like a giant puppy. He growled playfully and chased the small fuzzy creatures around. As he chased them, his fur color changed to match that of his prey. He would catch them gently in his mouth, let them go, and then the chase would begin all over again as he targeted a new fuzzy creature.

Ohma didn't have the same luck with Amy. He kept trying to chase her, and she would pretend to be a fuzzy animal and run away. The fact that Amy could fly didn't make it easier for Ohma to catch her either. It made Amelia and Bartholomew giggle at the sight. Amy had some difficulty flying because of her arm and ended up sitting on the top of the fountain.

Ohma couldn't reach her, and his continued efforts ended up causing him to fall into the fountain. This made Amelia and Bartholomew laugh even more. When Ohma came out soaking, he started to laugh too.

"I think we could all use some pampering time," said Amelia. "We should go to the island of mud and soak in the hot bubbling mud pots until I have to go."

"No, we should not!" yelled Bartholomew.

Amelia was startled. Amy and Ohma laughed.

"What's going on?" asked Amelia. "I thought you liked the mud baths. You used to want to go all the time."

"I just don't, okay," said Bartholomew, defensively.

"His lordship would not acquiesce a return to his former kingdom," said Ohma, between fits of laughter.

"His what?" asked Amelia, confused.

"His kingdom," replied Amy, floating down off the fountain. "He was a king."

"After you left last time, he moved onto the island of mud. He said that he didn't want to be in his ship until he had discovered the meaning of life," said Raskiel, joining them. "He made himself a crown out of mud and sat meditating in the mud pots."

Amelia could hear Ohma snickering and Amy laughing along.

"The problem was that he had forgotten about the mole colonies," continued Raskiel, his shoulders shaking with hidden giggles.

"It wasn't exactly like that," shouted Bartholomew, going red with embarrassment. "I didn't make the crown. I was trying to relax in the mud pots and clear my head. The bald mole tribe just kind of elected me as their leader."

"The bald moles?" asked Amelia, now having to hold

in her own giggles. "Not the hairy moles? With both of them constantly in battle over the island, and the mud pots in the center being neutral territory, I'm surprised you weren't scouted by the other side."

"Well, you know the moles, Amelia," said Raskiel, putting on a show to further embarrass Bartholomew. "The moles are in constant battle for dominion of the island. They are too harmless to fight though. With the mud being so easy to dig, and their diet of boiled, soft, roots, it makes sense that they don't have any claws or teeth."

"Yes, Raskiel," said Amelia, playing along. "But while harmless, they do have the battle campaign drive of Napoleon."

"Exactly," continued Raskiel. "So, picture this. Binky over here was wearing nothing but a giant dried mud crown and a pair of blue and purple swimming trunks that had by this time been covered in mud, and was leading an army of bald moles on a five-day campaign against the hairy moles. They basically crawled and bumped into each other nonstop until the day was over. Every night they would go home to their side of the island and sleep until the battle the next day. Finally, on the fifth day, they were all too tired, and fell asleep out on the mud flats."

"Poor things," said Amy.

"Up until this point, Binky had been leading them by standing on the edge of a mud pot and shouting out strategic commands for how to capture and destroy the enemy," said Raskiel. "After they finally woke up again on the afternoon of the fifth day they decided that he was a lousy commander, called a temporary truce between the bald moles and the hairy moles, and they told him that he was banished from their island."

"He was inexorably evicted from amongst their personages," said Ohma.

"Last time I talk to you guys about anything that happens," growled Bartholomew. He then turned to Amelia sheepishly and said, "I had some things to work out, so I took up command as a diversion to help me feel better. Now, I can't go back."

Amelia was nearly busting with laughter. She wanted to say something comforting, but with Bartholomew's serious and sad expression, it made it even more difficult not to laugh. It took a little bit, but she finally found the words.

"It's not like they can enforce your banishment," said Amelia, wiping tears of laughter off her cheeks.

"I know," said Bartholomew. "I just want to wait a while longer so that they won't be mad at me anymore. I hope they forget about what happened."

"They're so wrapped up in their little battles, that I'm sure they've already forgotten," said Amelia trying to be comforting, and trying to suppress giggles at the same time.

"If not," said Raskiel, "maybe they would be willing to take you back as their king if you can show them a new and better victory plan."

"Really?" asked Bartholomew, perking up. Bartholomew quickly frowned when he saw the renewed laughter. "Oh, I see. Ha, ha, you mangy…"

"Be nice," said Amelia, still trying to control her laughter. "You have to see the humor in this, right?"

"Yeah, I guess, but I'm not gonna put up with it from old hairy there," said Bartholomew, pointing an accusatory finger at Raskiel.

Amy flew down from her perch, and Ohma sat next to her. They quietly whispered back and forth. Done with teasing, Raskiel began chasing after the fuzzy creatures again.

"As silly as things got, I do have something I've been thinking about," said Bartholomew. "I started to think seriously about it right after you left last time."

"What is it, Binky?" said Amelia, and then quickly corrected herself after seeing Bartholomew's frown. "I mean Bartholomew. I do need to start using your proper name. I'll be better."

"It's alright," said Bartholomew, with a sigh. "I don't mind it that much. Anyway, I was just wondering who I am. I mean, you supposedly created me. So, where was I before you made me? What would have happened if you hadn't made me? What happens when you stop believing in me? Would I simply disappear? I don't know. I sort of had a, um, a bit of a breakdown after you left, and was trying to find answers."

"I don't know either," said Amelia, trying to stifle another giggle. "I wonder those same things myself. Especially after my family died, I had a lot of the same questions. Don't you remember? I wondered what the point of life was. I wondered if I had any value. I wondered what had happened to my family after they had died. I still sometimes wonder what will happen to me. Will I see them again? I believe that I will, but what if I'm wrong. Will I just become nothing? I don't know yet."

Ohma and Amy chased after Raskiel as an impromptu game of tag began.

"I did hear something once though, and it feels right," continued Amelia quietly as she stared into the water. "It was long and wordy, but the gist is that if you keep doing your best, good things will happen. I don't know if we need to have all the answers. I think that for now, we just do what we can with what we have."

"So," said Bartholomew. "You really believe that things will work out in the end?"

"I think so," said Amelia. "Maybe."

They sat in silence, looking at the water. Glowing insects started to appear and were reflected, dancing above the surface as everything got darker. A wind began blowing, and the air cooled. Many of the small animals huddled together and fell asleep.

"One more thing," said Bartholomew. "Did I ever tell you about my life before I met you?"

"No," said Amelia. "I assumed you were created when I first discovered my door. I mean, Sarah told me that I had unconsciously created everything here, but I didn't think about when it must have actually begun. You weren't created when I first found my doorway?"

"No," said Bartholomew. "I know that you created me, but the more I tried to understand how I came to be, I realized that I started to be aware of my existence sometime before you appeared. The passage of time didn't make sense to me then, so I am not sure exactly how long it was. I'm guessing that it was about the time that you were becoming aware of your own existence. I don't know whether I was born, or how it happened. I was just here. I slowly learned to walk and talk. There were others then. A lot of creations that

were all living on a single island. I don't know what happened to them. I vaguely remember Raskiel. I believe he was there, but I don't know about the rest."

Bartholomew stood quietly and looked like he was trying to remember something. Amelia didn't know what to say. She listened and waited. Bartholomew began speaking again.

"After the last incident when you took off, I started to question a lot of things. I tried to remember how it had all started. It was difficult to feel like I was imaginary. Memories have been slowly coming back ever since. It was like I've forgotten things, and now they are starting to wake up as I'm looking for them."

"Like what?" asked Amelia.

"Like remembering that I had to learn to eat and talk. I didn't automatically know how to do them. It was a slow process. All of us on that island learned together. Over time, the island itself grew. As it got larger and started to change, it started to split off and separate into new islands. Thinking back to what you have told me about your childhood in the past, and what you just said about unconsciously creating everything, I think that it was all happening while you were learning and growing."

"What do you mean?" asked Amelia.

"Well," said Bartholomew, "when did you start liking pirates?"

"I don't know," said Amelia. "I guess the summer before my door appeared, after my sister read me a book about them."

"And I had my ship appear before I met you," said Bartholomew. "I somehow knew about pirates and started seeing myself as one. What other things were you interested in before you met me?"

Amelia was starting to understand.

"Cats, snow, flowers, fire, fish, oceans, singing, and lots of other things," said Amelia.

"And we have an island that split off that has cats," said Bartholomew. "The moving ice sculptures appeared. The flowers and grassy fields of this island appeared and split off. The fire creatures appeared. One day, the water was filled with fish. I am guessing that the fish appeared after your trip to the aquariums that you took with your family."

"So, I was creating my paradigm sphere before I even knew about it?" asked Amelia.

"I think so," said Bartholomew. "It doesn't fully explain what is going to happen to me, or why I am here, but I think I'm okay with that now. I just want to live a good life and see what happens."

"I'm in the same boat," said Amelia.

They were quiet again, both lost in memories. Amelia knew that she needed to head home soon, but she couldn't bring herself to do it just yet. It was nice to be back with her oldest friend.

"I love you," whispered Amelia. "My king of the mud pots."

CHAPTER TWENTY-ONE

The Pickle Festival

 The sun was setting as Amelia got to the top of the ride. The cage she and Spencer were sitting in flipped over and shot down to the bottom. Amelia grabbed on to Spencer and screamed in terror and delight. They went through another loop, and the ride stopped at the bottom to let them out.

"Are you sure it's okay?" asked Spencer. "She seemed pretty upset."

"Sarah is fine," Amelia assured him. "She just had a meeting come up tonight and was mad that she couldn't make it."

"B-but she said that she would call the cops if you weren't home by ten," said Spencer.

"Don't worry about it," said Amelia. "I'm more surprised that your mom let you come."

"Me too," said Spencer, looking at his feet. "She was against it, but I got my dad to say yes. I'll definitely have extra chores tomorrow though."

"Oooh, bumper cars," said Amelia. "Let's do those next."

She grabbed Spencer's hand and started walking. As she did so, Amelia noticed someone with a black mask covering the top half of their face and wearing all-black clothing standing behind the lemonade booth. The individual frowned and walked away when they saw her.

She got in her car, and as soon as the light turned green, Amelia was off and ramming anyone she could. Spencer had apparently gotten a defective car and ended up mostly spinning in a circle. Amelia had to help him walk when they left.

"You gonna be okay?" asked Amelia.

"I think so," Spencer responded. "Let's not do the spinning rides just yet. I nearly threw up last year, and with how my stomach feels now I wouldn't make it."

"What if we did some of the carnival games?"

"That would work," said Spencer.

This time, he held Amelia's hand and pulled her toward a baseball pitching booth. On the way, Amelia saw something unusual. Another dark figure ran behind one of the rides.

At the booth, Amelia couldn't help but laugh. Spencer wasn't very good at throwing, and his baseballs completely missed the stacked metal milk bottles. When Amelia tried, she toppled three of them and won a small purple plush rabbit, which she gave to a blushing Spencer.

The dart game that they tried next had the reverse outcome, and Spencer gave Amelia a pink version of the same plush rabbit he had received. Amelia, on the other hand, nearly stabbed the booth attendant with her first shot, and they decided to continue on before she could throw any more.

"Are you hungry yet?" asked Spencer.

"Yes," responded Amelia.

"I'll get us something if you can save us a spot at the picnic tables," said Spencer.

Amelia sat down at the first open table she could find in the hardware store's parking lot. Her feet were grateful. There was a Dixieland jazz band playing up on a stage that had been set up next to the store entrance, and people would

stop occasionally to listen or eat. A cute older couple had started dancing to the music and didn't seem to care what else was happening around them. A few times, Amelia saw people in dark clothing running by at the edges of the rides and behind booths.

"Here they are," said Spencer, distracting Amelia from her thoughts. "I got you a footlong hot dog and root beer."

He set down the handfuls of food he was balancing with the drinks.

Amelia picked up the hotdog and took a giant bite. She looked up, realizing what she had just done, and quietly tried to finish the bite off without looking like a carnivorous squirrel.

Between the upbeat music, the food, and the company, Amelia was immensely enjoying herself. Even though this was smaller, in some ways Amelia liked this festival better than the one in Adonei. With the sight of another figure clothed in black, Amelia was reminded how the festival in Adonei had ended, and she became much more conscious of her environment as panic gripped her.

The date was no longer about enjoying time with Spencer. It now felt like it was about survival. The things that Amelia had been enjoying were now the things that were heightening her panic. The pottery booth, the cheese vendor,

and even the local bank's booth were all extra places that could be hiding danger.

While Amelia did see two more dark figures, nothing had happened. No one looked aggressive. Everyone was just going about enjoying their evening, except for one little boy who was crying after wetting himself. He was quickly whisked away by his parents.

Amelia was overreacting, and it was spoiling her time with Spencer. She knew that she had to get things together or it would ruin everything. Amelia and Spencer rummaged through the library's used book sale. She made a conscious decision to ignore the dark-clothed figures, and it started to make a difference.

Spencer led Amelia over to the carousel. Holding hands on the ride and staring at each other was so wonderful that they went on it twice. Afterward, they bought cotton candy and ate it while riding on the Ferris wheel that was in the center of Main Street.

During the ride, Amelia felt something warm across her shoulders and back. She looked at Spencer, who was lightly whistling as he pretended not to notice that his arm was now behind her. Amelia's heart jumped at this escalation, and she leaned into him. His arm relaxed, and he pulled her closer. When the ride ended, they grudgingly left.

"Is there somewhere more quiet we can go to?" asked Amelia.

"We could go to the park," responded Spencer, blushing.

They walked between the library and the courthouse to the little park that sat behind them. It was instantly darker than Main Street had been, and there were far fewer people, mostly couples, that were wandering slowly through.

Amelia didn't know what to say. Apparently, Spencer didn't either. Instead, they walked hand in hand saying nothing at all.

A small breeze picked up and Amelia noticed the cool air. She was wearing the same hooded sweater that she had worn to school earlier that day, but it wasn't doing as well as it had been before. Instinctively she moved in closer to Spencer for warmth, and he put his arm around her again.

They found a nice bench under a tree next to the stream. It was dark, and Amelia felt a little strange being so near to Spencer. Her heart was beating so much faster than normal. She could feel her breath coming a little faster and shallower than it normally would. Her face was flush, and she no longer felt cold.

Unsure of herself, she moved her head closer to his. They stared into each other's eyes. Slowly, as if time was

stalling, Amelia and Spencer got closer and closer. Amelia closed her eyes as she moved the last few inches toward him.

Splash!

Amelia pulled back with a surprised yell. She was covered in a cold liquid that smelled like dill. She looked at Spencer who appeared just as surprised. He had gotten a little of the liquid on himself, but Amelia had taken the brunt of it.

She turned and saw Becky. Jessica and a few others were coming out of the shadows from behind the tree. Becky was carrying an empty bucket that was labeled "Pickles." They were all dressed in black and were taking off their masks and hoods.

"We were wondering how long it would take you to get here," said Jessica, in a cold voice. "We almost missed the whole festival waiting."

"What?" asked Becky, angrily. "Did you really think tonight would be some great romantic evening? You loser."

Amelia was in shock. She couldn't move. She was covered in pickle brine and was freezing. Everything had gone from wonderful to terrible in less than a second. Once she was finally able to move again, all she could do was stare at Spencer.

He stood up and gave Becky an angry look.

"He told us about the spooky ghost that haunts you," continued Becky, with venom in her voice. "The one that scared you away and made you let your family die."

"Did you see it again today?" asked Jessica, sarcastically.

"I'll bet that she saw it a few times tonight," said Bobby, the freckle-faced boy.

Billy, Clyde, and two other kids that Amelia didn't recognize, snickered at the last remark. They must have all been trying to scare her throughout the carnival. Amelia was absolutely horror struck at what they had done and what they were saying.

"Spencer set this up perfectly," said Becky, with the venom in her voice getting stronger. "He got your hopes up and led you right to us for the finishing touch."

Amelia looked imploringly at Spencer. The usually shy and quiet Spencer exploded in response.

"That's a lie," began Spencer. "I n-never..."

But it was too late. Amelia couldn't listen anymore. She had nearly gotten her very first kiss, and it had been ruined in the most cruel and unusual way possible. Despite her belief to the opposite, Amelia did what she usually did when she found something too horrible to handle. She ran.

Laughter exploded from the group behind her.

Amelia ran through the little stream, away from the festival. It was a dark night, and she wasn't sure where she was going. She only knew that she had to get away. The salty brine stung her eyes, and the tears flowed.

She ran a few blocks, but quickly had to slow down. Although her heart was racing, and her adrenaline was pumping, Amelia was freezing. She was soaking wet, and it was turning into a particularly cold night. She stopped and crouched, rubbing her shoulders to create some heat. She didn't know where she was going, she just needed to get away. Amelia pushed through the cold and forced her legs to move. Bit by bit, she got farther out of town.

Halfway along the little road that headed to the canyon, Amelia was finally forced to stop entirely. The moon was shining through the break in the clouds and lit her path, but the wind that was blowing made Amelia even colder. Her teeth were chattering, and her hands and feet were stinging.

"You should turn back," came a whisper of a voice. "If you don't, your health could be in jeopardy."

Amelia looked around, startled. A new chill came from inside and added to the cold she already felt. A short distance away was the darker-than-shadow creature. Strangely, Amelia was not frightened the way she normally would be. She had been through so much emotional pain that she was

now physically numb.

"What's it to you?" asked Amelia. "If you're going to kill me, then just do it. I don't care anymore. Whatever happens, it can't be worse than things are right now."

Amelia stood shivering in the road. She was too hurt to feel scared. Instead, she now felt angry. She was beginning to feel partially alive. She could even feel her heart again as she stood, defying death. She welcomed the opportunity for a fight and an argument. At least it would take away the lack of sensation.

The creature laughed a quiet, whispering laugh.

"Kill you?" came the same whispering voice. "Kill you? Oh, if you only knew. I am not here for that purpose. I am here to offer a warning."

"If you aren't going to kill me, then what could you warn me about?" asked Amelia, her anger rising.

"Your friends," whispered the creature. "They have been searching for me. You must make them stop, or else their safety can't be guaranteed."

Amelia was confused. What friends? Who would even know about the creature? Certainly, Cindy and Sarah wouldn't be looking. It took only a moment before Amelia remembered her friends from her sphere. They had been bruised and cut, with no explanations. This is what they had

been hiding from her. It must be.

"Why would they be searching for you?" asked Amelia, her speech starting to slur.

The shadowy creature was not forthcoming with answers. Amelia could not make out any features of its face, but she could tell that it was turning its head and looking around for a moment. Looking back at Amelia, it pointed a long finger that had darkness billowing off.

"Stop them, or they will suffer worse than death," it said, in a slightly harsher whispering voice. "They will also bring your slow destruction and demise. Though you may not fear death now, you may soon welcome it as an alternative to what lies before you."

The creature started to have massive amounts of darkness pour off it. Like a candle being blown out, the creature vanished, leaving only a light trail of evaporating darkness. Its final words came right as the last puff dissipated. "You are running out of time. Find them now."

With the creature gone, the pain returned to Amelia's toes and fingers. Her adrenaline rush went away, and her body convulsed uncontrollably with shivering. Amelia had trouble keeping her balance. She tried to walk, but the cold was too much. The wind had gotten stronger. It was making her even colder than before.

Amelia stumbled along a short distance before collapsing. She didn't feel cold anymore, and the shivering stopped. It became difficult to think. It was then Amelia realized that she might be in real trouble. She needed to get to someplace warm, and she needed answers.

In response to her heart's desperate plea, her doorway appeared a few feet away along the side of the road, mounted into the ground as a stand-alone structure. She forced her body to move through the open door, and she fell onto the deck of the Mistress.

She was instantly surrounded, and a hand touched her face.

"Grab a blanket," yelled Bartholomew.

Ohma disappeared, and Amy held Amelia. Raskiel snuggled his big furry body against Amelia to get her warmed up faster. When Ohma reappeared, he had a blanket that Bartholomew took and laid over Amelia's legs.

Amelia tried her best not to scream in agony as sensation came back into her limbs, and along with them a stream of stabs that felt like her insides were turning her flesh into a pin cushion. Her friends continued to bring her body temperature up.

"You'll be okay," said Bartholomew.

"Is the hug helping?" asked Amy.

"A most unfortuitous circumstance," said Ohma, pacing nervously. "Mayhap we shall find a better clime for the maiden."

Amelia couldn't respond until the pain finally started to subside.

"I know why you are all hurt," said Amelia, indicating Amy's arm. "You've been after the shadow creature. It told me."

"Did it do this?" asked Bartholomew, his voice rising in anger.

"No," admitted Amelia. "This was my own fault for not going home when I should have."

"What exactly did it say?" growled Raskiel.

"It said that you were searching for it and that if you continued, we would all be destroyed."

"We must be getting closer then," said Raskiel, to himself. "It's scared."

Amelia was finally feeling warmer and the pain was subsiding.

"So, now you can tell me where you've been going," said Amelia. "We can do this together."

"No," said Raskiel. "You are too vulnerable. You don't have any control of your ability."

"We still have an oath to keep," said Bartholomew,

through gritted teeth.

"To who?" asked Amelia. "I know what you are doing, and I can help. I just need to know what is going on. Can't you tell me?"

"We can't say," said Bartholomew, exchanging a meaningful glance with Raskiel. "We are still here for you though. Are you okay?"

"I'm fine," said Amelia, succinctly.

She wasn't fine. She was frustrated again. No one was going to say anything. Amelia forced herself to stand. She walked over to the door that had appeared in the wall of the ship and opened to her bedroom. She went through without saying goodbye.

CHAPTER TWENTY-TWO

Full Range Learner

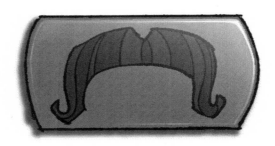

 It was repugnant. It sat upside down, on its head, mocking her. The pocket-sized pink plush rabbit that Spencer had given her, and which she had thrown across her room the night before when she got home. The horrid thing seemed to be glaring unblinking at her in retribution.

Amelia lay back down on her pillow. Her body ached, and it hurt to move, but she was oddly calm.

The loneliness, despair, and agony she brought home with her the night before had been debilitating. She had somehow found the strength to get showered and put her clothes in the washing machine, but Amelia couldn't force herself to stay up until Sarah got back.

This morning though, it was different. Amelia wasn't waiting for the next disaster. It was almost like a weight had been removed. There was nothing she could do that could make anything worse, and that was liberating in a way. Things would probably continue to fall apart around her, as they'd done before, but Amelia was now just a spectator in the process.

Amelia pulled her homework onto the bed. May as well finish it off, she thought. She needed something to get her moving. Her tears had run out, and she had been oversleeping since Halloween. Now, she suddenly had a renewed energy and needed to use it for something. After propping herself up with a couple of extra pillows, Amelia began to write.

I hate everything. I feel unappreciated and worthless. No one tells me anything. They keep me in the dark and tell me lies. Why won't anyone be open and honest with me? Why won't anyone show me love?

Amelia didn't have any answers to those questions, but she started writing more about it anyway.

This is a dumb assignment. I know that not everyone tells me lies. Sarah is trying to talk to me but doesn't trust me to understand everything. It's all my supposed friends that lie to me. I know Sarah loves me, but I have trouble feeling loved. Why am I feeling so numb? I hate this. What now?

Amelia was stuck. She looked at the handout the teacher had given her at the beginning of the assignment.

Yes, she was writing about her beliefs, thoughts, and feelings. Yes, she knew that she had to get it finished before Christmas vacation. Amelia kept scanning the paper. She had seen a line that was supposed to help. With continued scanning, she found it.

If you get stuck, don't worry. Pretend that you are answering a question or concern as if someone else had written it, and you were trying to help them. Try to forget that it is your own.

It sounded stupid. How could she pretend that it was someone else? Who else would have such psychotic problems and issues? How many other people had her abilities? Even though she felt silly, she pretended that there was an alternate Amelia that she was trying to support. It wasn't easy.

Don't feel worthless. It isn't your fault that everyone else is a twit. Especially those mean people that try to hurt you on purpose.

She wasn't sure if this was the right direction, but at least it made her feel a little better. Amelia continued to write.

Just because they are horrible, doesn't mean that you are. You are a good person that tries to help people. You make mistakes, but you aren't trying to do anything bad. You are trying to do your best. If they tell you lies, it isn't your fault. They are telling you lies because they don't know how to be honest. It isn't because you did anything wrong. Do you want their love? If they are going to be mean and not show you love, then they don't deserve to love you. You are a good person and it is a privilege for them to be able to be near you. You don't have to lessen yourself to have them near you. You deserve better.

Amelia wasn't sure about most of it, but she really did

feel like she deserved to be treated better and to have people be honest with her. She wasn't sure what else she should write.

After pumping herself up with all the writing of what she deserved, Amelia put her journal away and was planning to storm back to the ship to tell her friends how she felt. She was interrupted by a knock on the bedroom door.

"Yes, Sarah?" asked Amelia.

"It's lunchtime, and you still haven't gotten up for the day. Is everything okay?"

"Yeah, I was just extra tired. I'll be down in a bit," responded Amelia.

"Alright," said Sarah. "We have a visitor that you didn't get to meet last night. I want to introduce you to him."

After trying unsuccessfully to write more, Amelia gave in to her curiosity and went downstairs. Her legs were shaky at first, but she managed to brace herself enough to get moving and achieve a fairly normal gait. She didn't want to invite unwanted questions.

"Really?" came Sarah's cheerful voice. "I never expected that old Nancy would have ever done something like that. I thought she was still trying to make a floating cottage to live in."

"Yes, really," came a man's voice. "She was asking me

last week to help move the last of her venomous watchdog plants around the outskirts of her little garden. She's gone paranoid with the rumors of late."

"That's all they are," said Sarah. "Rumors. You remember the one from two years ago when everyone thought that Adonei was going to disappear and we would all wake up and find that we were part of a large trance. It's all nonsense."

"I know that," came the voice again. "But this time it could be something serious. We have been finding more and more of the dark class Learners. The fact that we are finding them means that they are becoming more active."

"Ever since that incident forty years ago, they haven't been an organized group," said Sarah. "Just a bunch of renegade Learners that have issues to deal with. It's not like..."

Sarah stopped mid-sentence when Amelia entered the kitchen. Amelia gripped the back of the chair closest to her. Her natural reaction to scream didn't happen. She was panicked, but she was all screamed out. Her newfound peace was just taking this new development in stride.

"Sarah," said Amelia, as even toned and calm as she could. "Why is there a Creonocen in our home?"

The dishes flying through the air and the floating sponge over the sink could be explained away by laroop, but

the man orchestrating the strange ballet was also producing steaming water and bubbles from the air above his hands. At Amelia's question, he turned quickly, and the floating items fell to the sink and floor with clanks, clatters, and crashes.

"Where are they at?" he asked, rushing past Amelia and up the stairs before she could respond.

His footsteps pounded as he ran around on the floor above. Doors were opened and more thudding footsteps could be heard. Amelia braced herself and stood still. His heavy footsteps came down the stairs behind her.

"I couldn't find anything, Sarah," he said. "Amelia, was it? Right. Amelia, where exactly did you see them."

Confused at the question, Amelia turned and lifted her finger to point back at the man. He spun to look at the staircase once more.

Finally, the man turned to face Sarah and said, "Does she know what a Creonocen is, or does she have a different meaning for the word? Help me out here, what am I missing?"

"I don't know," responded Sarah. "Amelia, what do you mean?"

"I thought he was using his gift to do the dishes," said Amelia, hesitantly now.

"Of course, it's much faster that way," he said.

"But we are in the Dormant World," said Amelia.

"He's an FRL," said Sarah, as if that explained everything. "We talked about that already, right?"

Amelia shook her head.

"Well, let's fix that right now," said Sarah. "Sit down and I'll get your food. Amelia, this is Arnold. Arnold, sorry about the confusion."

"I'm sorry about the dishes," said Arnold. "I should have been more careful."

Amelia sat down, and Sarah put a large plate with a giant sandwich, olives, pickles, and apple slices in front of her. Arnold collected the shattered pieces of the two bowls and the plate that had broken. He arranged them on the table close to their original shape, and then held two pieces at a time together and mumbled something. The two sections grew into each other and reformed like new. Arnold continued with additional pieces until the first bowl was completely restored.

Amelia watched with fascination. Arnold looked middle aged. He had a handlebar mustache and thinning hair. The coat was draped over the back of a chair, but the tacky brown suit with suspenders he had on made him look at least a few decades out of date. He was a curiosity for Amelia.

"I thought we couldn't use our ability in the Dormant

World," said Amelia. "How are you doing that?"

"Same way you get to Carnegie Hall," responded Arnold.

Amelia waited for an explanation until Sarah sat down and said, "She's too young to catch the reference."

"Fine," said Arnold. "When I first learned about my gift, I was told that Learners could only use their abilities in the spheres. I didn't understand why though. Some Creonocens could use it outside of their Spheres, and it didn't make sense that bad guys could do it, but good guys couldn't. I decided to start experimenting to see if I could begin to use my abilities in the Dormant World as well. I didn't have any malicious intent, I just wanted to find out if I could. It took a lot of effort, but I was able to start making progress and eventually things clicked."

"He's a Full Range Learner, or FRL for short," said Sarah. "Very rarely, someone finds that they are able to use their abilities outside of their sphere. Most can only create minor effects. Only a very, very few like Arnold and Jasper are able to fully utilize their abilities in the Dormant World."

"That thinking may need to be changed though," said Arnold. "There have been more cases of it. We are starting to get as many Full Range Learners as we are some of the more severe cases of Creonocens. Jasper says that he thinks that..."

"So you see," said Sarah, cutting in. "I wasn't meaning to confuse you. The vast majority of Learners can only use their abilities in the spheres. I am sorry though. I should have made it more clear."

"Yeah," said Amelia, picking up her sandwich. "I understand."

"Good," said Sarah, a grin back on her face. "Now, how was the festival last night?"

"The rides were fun," said Amelia, evasively. "What are you here for, Arnold?"

"After Sarah finished sharing her research on the pendant last night, and it was corroborated by Angie and David, there wasn't a reason to keep it in Adonei anymore," said Arnold.

"Why not? I thought the Creonocens wanted it," said Amelia.

"They did," said Arnold, piecing the last of the plate together. "But with the conclusion all three researchers had that the pendant doesn't do what it was claimed to do, along with the public release of the full research notes, the actual artifact has become irrelevant other than as a piece of history."

"While the evidence is conclusive, I'm still not satisfied with the answer," said Sarah. "I got permission to

keep it for the time being."

"Jasper thought it would be a good idea to have someone here for the next few days, and I haven't been able to visit for a long time," said Arnold.

Amelia began to eat her sandwich. The distraction had worked, and Sarah and Arnold continued the conversation about "crazy Nancy." It was just background noise to Amelia's meal until a name caught her attention.

"What did you say?" asked Amelia hesitantly. "I think I misheard you?"

"I said that there are some more rumors of the Rha' Shalim," said Arnold.

Amelia had been trying to remember that name for months.

"What are the ra-whatevers?" asked Amelia, trying to sound innocent and ignorant.

"Rha' Shalim," said Arnold. "I think originally, they were something that The Twins were planning to create, but it never happened. Sarah?"

"Exactly," said Sarah. "The concept behind them was to clear out hostile or broken creations and creatures."

"Broken?" asked Amelia.

"Things that Learners of that time would consider deformed or an affront to their sensibilities," said Arnold.

"The Rha' Shalim were supposed to go into people's spheres, using the same gift The Twins possessed, and destroy them."

"The Twins couldn't justify creating something so dangerous or harmful to life," said Sarah. "That doesn't mean that the concept ended. Dark creatures that can break into the safety of someone's paradigm sphere is the stuff of nightmares. They are now in the realm of rumors and scary bedtime stories. Like the bogeyman."

"The problem is that there are many types of dark creatures," said Arnold. "I have investigated hundreds of reports over the last few years, and not a single actual confirmation. A lot of copycat creations and pranksters. Every rumor helps fuel the stories, and the legend lives on."

Arnold stood up and took the three, now repaired, dishes back to the sink and began washing the rest as he had before. Sarah took Amelia's plate and added it to the pile.

"Speaking of pranksters, did you hear the latest about the Jeshua girls?" asked Arnold

"No. What have those three gotten up to this time?" responded Sarah.

"They got stranded in Adonei Bay," said Arnold.

"These girls are all under eight years old and are the daughters of a friend of ours," Sarah informed Amelia, sitting down at the table.

"Well," continued Arnold, "they all worked together to create a giant sea creature and tried to ride on it. Once on top, they found that it didn't have the strength to swim with them as riders. It could only float."

Amelia was amused because Arnold was illustrating the story with some of the soapy bubbles he was creating.

"They drifted further and further away from shore," Arnold continued. "Randal let them scream for help for a while before he rescued them. I think he was hoping to teach them a lesson about being careful with their abilities and testing things first."

"That's what, the ninth incident this week?" asked Sarah.

"Twelfth," responded Arnold. "Top of the list for October were the exploding fireflies, the parasitic wing attachments, and the self-producing sugar pot. This month they are already off to a good start with almost two incidents a day."

Inspired by the story of the little girls, Amelia sat at the table and tried to make a single bubble appear. If Arnold could, then couldn't she? Amelia held out her hands and quietly chanted, "bubble, bubble, bubble," while trying to will it into existence.

At first nothing happened, but after chanting slightly

louder a single bubble formed and grew to the size of Amelia's head. Sarah stood up, walked over to Arnold, and playfully smacked his shoulder.

"Stop teasing her," said Sarah.

The bubble formed into a face before popping. Amelia looked up to see a grinning Arnold put his hand down.

CHAPTER TWENTY-THREE

Hoffy

 "Stupid cow," said Jessica, as she pushed past Amelia to get out of the classroom.

Amelia kept her head down and continued to her locker. She was glad the day was over and wanted nothing more than to get home. She swapped the books she needed and zipped up her backpack. Amelia closed her locker and then jumped in surprise when she found Becky standing next to her. They stood awkwardly, not saying anything. Becky then left. There hadn't been any anger or cruelty in Becky's eyes, only a strange sadness.

As Amelia started to leave the school, Spencer approached her and tried to talk to her for the third time that day. Amelia flatly ignored him and continued walking.

"I'm s-s-sorry," said Spencer, as she left.

Partway through the journey home, Amelia heard a familiar and surprising voice call to her from behind.

"Amelia, wait up!"

Cindy had been just as cold in the morning classes as she had been the previous week. Amelia turned around to see Cindy running to catch up.

"Good. I thought I had missed you. I was trying really hard to get out of band and meet up with you before you got too far ahead," said Cindy, panting a little.

"Why?" asked Amelia, feeling her anger and pain return.

"I'm sorry," said Cindy, looking down at her feet. "I heard about what happened on Friday. I'm sorry."

"Why are you sorry?" asked Amelia. "You didn't do anything."

"I know," said Cindy, looking up at Amelia. "But I wasn't there for you. If I had been a real friend, like I told you I would be, I would have been there and none of it would have happened. I'm very sorry."

"I thought that you were done trying to be friends,"

said Amelia. "You hurt me on Halloween. I was trying to open up, and you didn't listen to me."

When Amelia said this, she saw Cindy flinch.

"I spent all day thinking about this, and I am having a difficult time," said Cindy, tentatively. "I don't understand why you are saying what you are, but I need to be a better friend anyway. I'm sure you have a good reason. I am sorry I wasn't there for you. I am trying to be here now. I still want to make our friendship work."

Amelia thought about it for a moment. She was deeply touched. She was also still frustrated that Cindy wouldn't believe her, at least until a thought struck her.

"Do you have to watch your brother today?" asked Amelia quickly.

"No. My mom is taking him into the doctor this afternoon," replied Cindy hesitantly.

"Great! Come with me," said Amelia, taking Cindy by the hand. "I can prove that I'm not lying."

Amelia dragged a confused Cindy home with her. Arnold was sitting on the living room couch, reading a newspaper.

"Cindy, this is Arnold. Arnold, this is Cindy. Now go call your mom. The phone is in the hall," said Amelia.

"A bit bossy today," said Arnold, as Cindy gave a

quick wave and then followed Amelia's instructions.

"Not bossy," replied Amelia. "We are just in a hurry."

"Well, don't let me hold you back. Have fun." Arnold went back to reading his paper.

Amelia waited for Cindy to finish her call, and then they went upstairs. Once they were in the bedroom, Amelia shut the door and they sat on the bed.

"What do you mean you can 'prove' that you aren't lying," said Cindy, with a doubtful expression on her face.

"Exactly that," said Amelia. "Try me. You're really good at biology, right?"

"I do alright," said Cindy, still looking confused. "But what does that have to do with anything."

"I told you before," said Amelia. "I can create things in my sphere that can't be made anywhere else."

Cindy groaned again and rolled her eyes.

"Look," said Amelia. "I have a proposition for you. If I can create something that shouldn't be able to exist, then you give me a chance. If I can't, then I'll never bring this up again. Deal?"

After a short while, Cindy held out her hand to shake and said "Deal."

"Alright," said Amelia. "What do you want me to make? It has to be fairly simple. I'm still not great at this."

"A frog with wings," said Cindy, with a thoughtful look on her face. "Is that too complicated?"

"No," said Amelia, having a terrifying flashback to an earlier flying frog-ish thing she had created. "I think I can pull that off. I don't know how long it will take though. Close your eyes and count to twenty while I leave. While I'm gone, you can do your homework. I'll be back as soon as I can."

Cindy looked extremely skeptical, but Amelia also didn't want to scare her. Amelia decided it would be best to go through her doorway when Cindy wasn't watching her disappear. That would have really freaked Cindy out, and Amelia wasn't sure if Cindy could handle it right now. After a little more prodding, Cindy closed her eyes and Amelia saw her doorway appear. She ran through it and watched Cindy the whole way to make sure she wasn't peeking.

Amelia found that Bartholomew's ship was again anchored next to Raskiel's island. No one was in sight. She could only imagine how strange Cindy must be feeling, sitting alone in Amelia's room and waiting for her. Amelia wished that she had someone here to help, especially considering the mouse-headed abomination from before. She didn't have much time though, and the thought of going back and trying to talk Arnold into making something appear seemed like it would just lead to more confusion and trouble.

Amelia took a deep breath, closed her eyes, and began to concentrate. In her mind, she pictured a frog with wings. The one she visualized was a big, fat, pond frog with bright white, feathered wings. She focused and tried to feel the creative power work. She opened her eyes as she kept the image in her mind's eye while focusing. Nothing happened.

Amelia tried again. Nothing happened. She tried twice more, and still nothing. On the fifth time, she managed to create something. It was a granite block that was roughly shaped like a frog with wings. It was made of the same granite that she had been working on creating the previous week for protection.

It was maddeningly difficult to create creatures. There was an occasional happy accident, but they were never quite what Amelia was trying for. She needed it to work this time.

Amelia continued trying and was slowly able to create more objects. She was then able to create a few creatures that were getting closer to what she wanted. Most of the attempted creatures hopped or flopped overboard and were eaten up by fish. After the first six, a large school of fish had started to gather along the edge of the ship, hoping for a free meal.

It took almost a full hour to get something that was passable. It wasn't what she imagined, but it would have to

do. Amelia was already worried that she had taken too long in getting back. She was also getting so tired from the exertion that she wasn't sure she could keep it up much longer.

As Amelia stepped through her doorway with the little creature cupped in her hands, she found Cindy sitting on the floor doing homework. Cindy jumped up in shock.

"Where did you come from?" said Cindy, with wide eyed surprise. "I didn't hear you come in. You just appeared. What did you do?"

"I tried to explain it. I came from my sphere. Don't freak out, I'm not trying to trick you right now. Please, sit down."

Cindy sat on the bed obediently. Amelia plopped down beside her.

"Now don't scream," said Amelia. "I know you've been waiting a while. I did the best I could. It isn't exactly what you asked for, but it was the best I could do under the circumstances."

Amelia held up her hands that were cupped together. Cindy began to look excited. Amelia slowly un-cupped her hands and displayed what she had made. She then watched Cindy's excitement fade. It was replaced with a large frown.

"I can't believe I let you trick me," said Cindy. "Why are you so cruel. I was almost ready to believe your story, and

294

all you did was try to hurt me again. Why did I even try?"

"I swear, it's all true," said Amelia, feeling frustrated. "You can see for yourself that it's a frog with wings."

"Yes, but not really," said Cindy, standing up. "It isn't real. You must have run to the pet store and picked up a little green tree frog and glued those poor dragonfly wings on. I imagine the glue drying is what took you so long. How could you?"

"I did not," said Amelia, holding out the tiny frog. "If you look at it closely, you will see that there isn't any glue. The wings grow out of it. It's real."

"No, it isn't," said Cindy, beginning to tear up. "You're horrible. I..."

Before a wet-eyed Cindy could finish her statement, the wings spread out to either side of the little frog and started flapping. Cindy fell back onto the bed in surprise. The frog was only about the size of a nickel. The wings were about three times longer than the frog and had extended clear behind the frog when they were folded. Right now, they were spread out and going like mad to take the frog zipping around the ceiling of the room.

It flew around, bumping into just about every surface it could hit, until it landed on the bed next to Amelia. It then hopped onto her lap. She picked it up quickly to see if it had

hurt itself. This was its first flight, and it didn't have very good control. Amelia thought that it was kind of a cute little thing though. She looked up and saw Cindy's shocked expression.

Amelia was expecting Cindy to scream, and was getting ready to calm her down, until a huge grin suddenly appeared on the wide-eyed Cindy's face.

"That was awesome!" said Cindy, excitedly. "Can I see it? Is it alright? I didn't know, really. I couldn't understand why you would lie. But you didn't lie. This is amazing. How did it fly? How can those wings support it? How does it hop with such large wings trailing behind it? Where did you get it? Oh! That's right! You said you made it. How is that possible?"

Cindy was talking faster than Amelia could respond. The winged frog, which Cindy and Amelia agreed to call Hoffy, continued flying and crashing, practicing its flying while they talked. By the time Sarah knocked on the door to tell them to come down for dinner, they were still talking and now plotting. Hoffy, at this point, was busy trying to catch little bugs by the windows.

"Not a word," whispered Amelia. "At least until I've had a chance to speak to her first."

"Alright," said Cindy, practically buzzing.

Partway through dinner, in the midst of the

conversation, Amelia dropped a verbal bombshell. The table went silent.

"What?" asked Sarah, taken aback.

"I said," began Amelia, once more. "Could you use a biology assistant that would help you with your research?"

"I know that it is unusual," said Cindy, very shyly. "But I learned about everything from Amelia, and I believe it."

"Well, if you learned everything," said Arnold, sounding like he was choosing what he shared very carefully. "Then you would know it is impossible."

"Not entirely," said Amelia, feeling very smug. "There is a way."

"How?" asked Arnold.

"Well, Cindy can't enter the spheres," began Amelia, "but the creatures can come here. Cindy is a wiz at biology and can study them from a Dormant's perspective. She can dissect them and study their anatomy, draw up charts, and do whatever you want her to. That would give you more time to do other research."

"My goal is to do that for a living anyway," said Cindy. "But it would be great if I could work with you on all of the amazing things that Amelia has told me about. I could come over almost every day after school when I don't have to

babysit. I promise that I'll work hard if you'll let me."

Amelia and Cindy looked at each other and then sat in silence while they waited for a response. Sarah thought it over carefully. Then, she turned to Arnold.

"Do you think that Jasper would allow it?" said Sarah, trying to conceal a smile that was starting on the edge of her mouth.

"There aren't any rules about it because I don't think it has been done before," said Arnold, equally trying to conceal some emotions that were starting to creep in. "We better ask Jasper though. I'm not sure what he'll say."

"Alright," said Sarah, looking back at Cindy and Amelia. "Pending approval from the head of Adonei, you will be my new, Dormant assistant."

Amelia and Cindy erupted in cheers and hugs. Arnold even blushed when an overexcited Cindy gave him a hug and a big kiss on his whiskery cheek.

"Now," said Sarah, looking at Amelia. "Are you going to tell me how you explained this to her and got her to believe it?"

At that moment, Hoffy came buzzing down the stairs and landed on Cindy's head.

"Ah," said Sarah, with her usual cheerful smile. "Enough said."

"I hope you realize how fortunate you are," said Arnold to Amelia. "What you did usually doesn't work."

"How come?" asked Amelia.

"Dormants are expert at justifying and explaining away things that are right in front of them," said Arnold. "When their brains aren't ready for something, they will dismiss and forget anything that doesn't agree. Your friend must have made the decision to fully trust you and have faith in you before she ever saw the proof, otherwise she would have left already."

"She nearly did," said Amelia.

"'Nearly' doesn't matter," replied Arnold. "What happens in the end does."

After dinner, Amelia walked with Cindy out to the front porch.

"Just so you know," said Cindy. "With what I heard happened at the Pickle Festival, I don't think that it was Spencer's fault. It sounds like they had been following you during the whole festival and looking for an opportunity when you were away from the crowd. I think that Becky and Jessica set it up without Spencer knowing. Spencer isn't a mean person. He may hang with a bad crowd, but I've never actually seen him do anything hurtful. I think that Spencer may be innocent. I wanted you to know."

"Thanks," said Amelia. "I appreciate it. You have a safe trip home, okay."

"Okay," said Cindy, as she left. "Bye. Take care."

Amelia waved for a bit, and then went back inside. She didn't know what to do with what she was told. Even though she didn't think she could talk to him again, at least it was nice to imagine that maybe Spencer hadn't been out to hurt her.

CHAPTER TWENTY-FOUR

Goody Plates

 Amelia's boots made a satisfying crunching noise as she walked through the snow. She looked at the decorations on the houses and in the yards that were mounded with white. The rooftops looked like they had been generously smothered with sparkling whipped cream, and they were laced with icicles that intermingled with hanging strands of lights. Amelia could smell the fragrance of burning wood as she and Cindy walked along the shoveled sidewalks.

"How's your training going?" asked Cindy. "Wasn't Arnold going to meet up with you to help you practice

again?"

"He said he was busy but might be able to sometime next week," replied Amelia. "I've gotten a lot better because of him."

"Wish I could see it," said Cindy.

"At least you've been able to help Sarah," said Amelia. "That's something. So, what were you going to tell me?"

"Oh, that's right," said Cindy, pushing her glasses back up her nose bridge. "Becky stopped and talked to me after lunch today."

"What for?" asked Amelia.

"She apologized," responded Cindy. "She said that she was sorry for being so mean to me and for making fun of me."

"That doesn't sound like her," said Amelia. "I know she's been quiet since the Pickle Festival, but she didn't seem like the kind of person to apologize. Why would she?"

"I asked her the same thing, actually," said Cindy. "After the festival, she had a falling out with the rest of her group. That's why they haven't been hanging out anymore."

"I've been grateful for that at least," said Amelia, watching her breath form wispy shapes in the cool air.

"I don't think Becky would admit it, but I swear that she's had a crush on Spencer since the fourth grade," said

Cindy. "With him and everyone else not speaking, I think it's the first time she's been alone. Becky told me that she's been trying to apologize to all the people she has hurt. That has to be tough for her."

As they arrived at the house, Sarah was setting out ingredients on the kitchen table.

"I kind of feel bad for her," said Cindy. "Maybe we should try to help her and be friends. I mean, I used to get along wonderfully with her in elementary school. It wasn't until middle school that she started to have problems."

"I don't know if it will work, but it might not hurt," said Amelia.

"Who are you trying to be friends with?" asked Sarah, dusting loose flour off her hands. "Maybe I could help?"

"I don't think so," said Amelia. "It's a girl who's been mean to us since school started."

"But she's going through a difficult time and is trying to be nice now," chimed in Cindy.

"Maybe," said Amelia, feeling doubt rise.

"Well," began Sarah. "There was something I did as a girl that helped."

"What was that?" asked Cindy, while Amelia rolled her eyes at yet another story.

"I had a similar problem," said Sarah. "There was a

girl that picked on me almost every day for a couple of years. It was miserable. She made the thought of going to school just dreadful. Finally, during one of her verbal attacks, I got an idea. I quickly turned to her and cut off her abuse with a question. I simply asked her what she would like for Christmas. She was surprised and didn't know what to say. She asked if I was serious, and I let her know that I was. Despite her suspicions, she told me about something she had been wanting. Thankfully, it wasn't very expensive.

"That evening, I pulled out the money I had saved up from babysitting, and I went to purchase it for her. I went to school the next day and gave her the present. I had wrapped it up in green paper and tied it with a red ribbon. She was shocked and wary at first. She thought that I might have prepared a practical joke in the present. She opened it up cautiously and was surprised to see that I had gotten what she had requested."

"What happened after that?" asked Amelia. "Did she start bugging you to get her more stuff."

"No," said Sarah. "From that point on, we became friends. She also stood up for me if anyone else ever tried to bully me. Her family moved away at the end of the year, and so we were only friends for half of the school year. Even so, I feel like it made a difference in both of our lives. I think

that it might work for you as well."

"That would be perfect," said Cindy. "We could make extra cookies and brownies for all of Becky's gang at school and give it to them as presents. Tomorrow is open activity day and we can hand them out as we wander around."

"That sounds like a great idea," said Sarah, smiling. "We should double what we planned for the peanut brittle and fudge as well."

They both looked at Amelia expectantly.

"What?" said Amelia. "I think that giving them stuff isn't a great idea. Why should I go out of my way to… stop looking at me like that!"

Cindy and Sarah opened their eyes even wider and did pouty faces.

"Fine!" said Amelia, in defeat. "We'll do whatever you want."

"Great!" said Sarah. "Amelia, check the pantry for the colored cellophane sheets. Cindy, check the study for the spools of ribbons. They'll be above the pile of newspapers in the cupboard."

When they returned, Sarah had pulled out a stack of fancy plastic Christmas plates and had the dry ingredients for the first batch of cookies in the mixing bowl.

"Make sure we set aside some extra plates so that I

can take some to Adonei tomorrow," said Sarah.

"Did you get one to Mr. Opal?" asked Amelia.

"Yes," responded Cindy. "That should be the last of the teachers."

"I saw Becky sitting alone and reading in the library when I passed it a bit ago," said Amelia. "Do we really have to do this?"

"Do you think we shouldn't?" asked Cindy.

Amelia thought about it before sighing in resignation and responding, "We should. You're right."

As they approached, Becky looked up startled.

"Becky," began Amelia. "We… I just wanted to…"

Amelia was at a loss for words and looked at Cindy for help.

"I'm sorry," said Becky, shaking. "I know that what I did was terrible. You can probably never forgive me, but I wanted to let you know that I am sorry. I'm sorry I couldn't apologize until now. Spencer had nothing to do with it. When he told us about your childhood, it was to ask us to be kinder. He wasn't trying to hurt you. It was all me, and I'm sorry."

Becky clenched up with her eyes closed, like she was expecting to get hit.

"She forgives you," said Cindy. "We also brought you

a Christmas present. Merry Christmas."

"I was extremely angry for a while," said Amelia, holding out a wrapped plate of goodies. "But I forgive you. I hope that we can be friends from now on."

As soon as the words left her mouth, Amelia felt a weight being lifted. Becky awkwardly took the plate, sitting stunned. Cindy and Amelia quietly left. When the library door had closed and Amelia looked back through the window, she saw Becky bite into a piece of fudge. There was a miraculous reaction. It was the first sincere smile Amelia had ever seen on Becky's face.

After leaving the library, they walked past a classroom where students were cutting out snowflakes, and another room where three of the teachers were at the front singing karaoke Christmas carols to the applause of a mixed group of students and teachers. Near the entrance to the school, Amelia and Cindy saw Bobby, Billy, and Clyde. The boys were sitting and talking.

"Merry Christmas," said Cindy, holding out three of the plates of treats.

"Awesome," said Billy, as he and Clyde each took a plate.

The freckle-faced Bobby just looked and scoffed at their gift. He didn't say anything but made a point to walk a

few feet away to a window and ignored Cindy and Amelia.

"I'll make sure Bobby gets it," whispered Clyde, before taking the third plate from them.

"Any idea where Spencer is?" asked Amelia.

"Probably watching the movie in the theatre room," said Billy. "Someplace he wouldn't have to talk to anyone."

"Thanks," said Amelia.

She and Cindy got partway down the hall before the exchange behind them forced them to turn around.

"But you said you didn't want it," said Clyde, teasing Bobby. "So, I'm going to eat it."

"They said it was for me," said Bobby, having rejoined the other two. "Now give it to me."

"Nope," said Billy, the long-haired member of the group. "You missed your chance, and now it's ours."

Billy and Clyde scrambled to eat as many snacks as they could. Upon seeing this, Bobby started a three-way wrestling match to get a piece for himself. He succeeded in grabbing two of the plates of treats and ran past Amelia and Cindy with a cookie hanging partially out of his mouth.

"Give those back," yelled Billy, as he and Clyde pursued Bobby.

Cindy and Amelia laughed as the boys passed. Amelia was finally feeling like this could work.

308

"Spencer next?" asked Cindy.

"We can head that direction," said Amelia, halfheartedly. She had the start of a plan but wasn't yet sure if she could handle it.

They walked down the hall that the boys had just run through. Some students were chatting, others were moving between classrooms and different activities. Ms. Copnet had set up a makeshift bowling alley down one of the side halls. Becky and Cindy waved to her as they walked by.

When Cindy saw Jessica step out of the art classroom ahead of them, she excitedly ran up with a plate in her hands. Jessica, without a moment's pause, knocked the plate onto the ground.

"What's that supposed to be?" yelled Jessica. "I don't want anything from you. You two morons can get lost. Stay away from me, you ugly, dog-faced jerks!"

Jessica stormed off in a fit of anger, and Cindy was on the verge of tears. Amelia helped Cindy pick up the now ruined present. The red cellophane had come loose, and the treats had been scattered all over.

"At least it seems to be helping everyone else be nicer," said Amelia. "Maybe Jessica is having a bad day?"

"Yeah," said Cindy, with a sniffle. "Maybe. It's just that I was really hoping that this would work."

"I know," said Amelia, stooping to retrieve another broken cookie. She looked up as someone walked toward her.

"I saw that Jessica didn't want her treats," said Clyde, approaching them timidly. "Can I have them? Bobby ate most of mine."

Cindy's sad expression changed. She wiped her eyes as a smile spread across her face.

"Sure," said Cindy. "Don't want them to go to waste."

Clyde helped pick up the last of the treats. He cheerfully walked away with the plate full of broken goodies.

"I got this last one myself," said Amelia, holding up the final plate. "I'll catch up with you in the gym once I'm done."

"Alright," said Cindy, holding up a thumb. "Good luck."

Amelia stopped into one of the classrooms and wrote a quick note on a piece of paper that she folded and stuck in her pocket. She quietly walked into the darkened theatre classroom and located Spencer. It wasn't difficult with how much higher he sat than the people around him. She snuck up, tapped him on the shoulder, and slipped the note into his hands. He stared at her, shocked. The dim light of the movie reflected in his wide eyes. Amelia pointed at the paper, which Spencer opened to read.

Meet me at my locker. We need to talk.

After not speaking to Spencer in so long, she wasn't sure what effect the note would have. His smile upon reading it was a good sign though.

Amelia left the room and quickly walked to her locker. Spencer arrived shortly after. He looked silly. Hands in his pockets, staring at the ground bashfully, and hunching as if he thought he could hide how much he stood out.

"Merry Christmas," said Amelia, giving the plate of treats to Spencer. "I'm sorry I've been so terrible and haven't talked to you. I was hurt at the Pickle Festival and didn't know what to do. I know it wasn't your fault. Can you forgive me?"

"Thanks," said Spencer, taking the gift. "Y-yes, I can forgive you. I don't know what else to say though. This is kind of a surprise. I hope that we can be good friends again. I really was..."

"Just friends though," said Amelia, cutting him off. "I don't think I can handle more than that right now."

"Okay," said Spencer, looking more than a little disappointed.

"And, there is a condition," said Amelia.

"What?" asked Spencer warily.

"If you are going to be friends with me again, you have to forgive Becky and be friends with her again as well," said Amelia. "She is sorry about what she did, and she is the one that let me know that you didn't have anything to do with it. So, you need to be a gentleman and forgive her."

"Alright," said Spencer. "I'll try."

"I don't know," said Amelia, slyly. "If I see your mother at the concert tonight, I might let slip that you weren't exactly being nice to a girl at school…"

"I said okay!" said Spencer, with a lot more conviction. "You d-don't have to threaten. I'll forgive Becky and I'll be nice."

"Good," said Amelia. "She's in the library."

"N-n-now?" asked Spencer, confused.

"Yes," said Amelia. "Please."

Spencer looked conflicted, but finally responded with a weak, "alright." He slowly wandered down the hall, staring at the plate of treats.

Amelia smiled and then sat at her locker. Instead of feeling peace now that the presents were distributed, Amelia was overwhelmed with anxiety.

Did I do the right thing? Is any of this actually going to help? How is this going to come back to hurt me? I'm

trying my best. What am I doing wrong? Amelia's thoughts were spiraling out of control. She took a few minutes to calm down before she could stand up.

Heading to the gym, Amelia passed by the library. Spencer and Becky were both sitting rigidly upright. They were opposite each other at a table and the whole confrontation looked painfully formal. At least they were talking though.

Amelia's mind was racing through her conversation with Spencer again. With it, a new anxiety stabbed her heart. Everyone would watch her sing tonight.

CHAPTER TWENTY-FIVE

The Concert

 Amelia's stomach felt like something had been brought to life. There was a mini zombie walking around in a putrefied state, trying to tear its way through her stomach lining. It became more active with each step that Amelia took.

Amelia found Sarah in the kitchen. Sarah was smiling and singing to herself as she set up an ironing board to press Amelia's choral gown.

"You ready for tonight?" asked Sarah, plugging in the iron.

"No," said Amelia. "Can I stay home?"

"Nope," said Sarah, with a big smile. "You'll be fine."

"I will not," said Amelia, grumpily.

"Anyway," continued Sarah. "How did the presents go?"

"Better than I thought they would," said Amelia. "I need to go practice my piece again though. I don't have time to talk about the presents right now. They're the reason I forgot to practice last night."

"That's fine," said Sarah. "You run along, and I'll make sure that all of us have food before we go."

"Okay," said Amelia, heading up the stairs. She stopped suddenly and turned around as the words sank in. "What do you mean 'all of us'?"

"Hello," came a voice from the study.

Amelia had a fresh moment of panic. She walked into the living room and then through the door to the study. Arnold was in the cushy chair, and Jasper was sitting with a book in a chair at the table. They were all dressed up in suits and smiles. Amelia had been so distracted when she got home, that she hadn't even noticed them.

Arnold was in the same old brown suit that he had been wearing when Amelia first met him. Jasper, on the other hand, was in a dark pin-striped suit that had a matching black fedora with a red feather, a black cane with a golden eagle

315

head on top, highly polished black shoes with white spats, and a red handkerchief hanging out of his pocket. He reminded Amelia of the gangsters she had seen in movies about the roaring twenties.

"Can't wait to hear you sing," said Jasper. "Loved the sweets by the way. They were delicious."

"Mine as well," said Arnold, with a grin. "You better go practice and get ready. We'll be fine here."

Amelia closed her gaping mouth and walked past a smiling Sarah. She turned back and gave Sarah a dirty scowl as she went up the stairs to her room. How could Sarah do this to her? It was going to be hard enough singing in front of mostly strangers and other students, let alone people that she knew.

Amelia walked through her door into her sphere. She was expecting to find Bartholomew so that he could listen to her practice again. No one was on the ship though. If Amelia had bothered swimming to Raskiel's island she knew she wouldn't find them there either.

Whatever, thought Amelia, it's probably easier alone.

Amelia couldn't wait until tomorrow when she could finally confront them, but she had more pressing issues right now. Amelia went to the cabin and brought out the hourglass to keep track of time before she had to return. She then set

down her tape recorder and hit play. The accompaniment music played for her piece and she sang along. With each attempt, she got more and more nervous.

By the time Amelia stepped through her door and went downstairs for dinner, she had no appetite.

"You have to eat something," said Sarah.

"At least try the soup," said Jasper. "It's delicious."

After getting what she could down, Amelia went to her room and dressed in her choral gown. She ran through her piece quietly two more times before heading downstairs. Arnold finished doing the dishes while Jasper helped Sarah clear and clean the table. Amelia put on her winter coat, stocking cap, and woolen gloves and then sat waiting while everyone else finished getting ready. When they were all bundled up, they stepped outside.

"I love this weather," said Arnold. "Nice and brisk."

"We should have another snowball fight," said Jasper.

"No," said Sarah, tersely. "No sense in getting our clothes all wet before the concert."

"Maybe after then," said Jasper.

Sarah glared at Jasper.

"Or not today," said Jasper, dejectedly.

"Maybe tomorrow then," said Arnold. "It was a lot of fun last time."

"Fun for who?" asked Sarah. "You both cheated. 'No abilities,' means 'no abilities.' I can't use them here, and both of you can. It wasn't fair."

"It was just a little fun. It wasn't that bad," said Jasper.

"Not that bad?" asked Sarah, then having to lower her rising voice as she continued. "It escalated into a blizzard, and I was lost in a snow bank for almost twenty minutes before you two even realized that I had disappeared."

"Sorry," said Arnold, hanging his head.

"And you two weren't the one that had to come up with some cockamamy explanation for the neighbors about all the extra snow that showed up in my yard when the sky was clear."

"I won though," said Jasper.

"Keep thinking that, old man," said Arnold doing a little victory dance as he walked.

Amelia felt her heart sink when they arrived at the school. The parking lot was already full. It seemed that the whole town had turned out for the event. They followed the crowd in.

"Good luck," said Sarah, giving Amelia a hug. "We'll see you in a bit."

Amelia watched Sarah, Jasper, and Arnold go into the auditorium. As soon as they were out of sight, Amelia walked

down the dark hall to the choir room that connected to the back side of the stage. She was feeling so nervous, that she thought her eyes must be playing tricks on her as she walked past a side hall. Amelia stopped and went back to double check.

Down the hall were Spencer and Becky. They were standing very close. Amelia couldn't hear what they were saying, but the body language was telling enough of a story as the dim light shone behind them through the large windows at the end of the hall. Spencer leaned in and they gave each other a tender hug.

Starting to feel like a stalker, Amelia quietly and quickly continued to the choir room.

It was packed with other students that were standing around nervously. They were all either chatting about the concert, or quietly practicing their pieces of music. Amelia didn't know what to do. She stood in a corner and started running through her solo piece. She was beginning to worry that she might be over-practicing.

Becky came in, wiping tears away. She was smiling brightly as she went to set her coat in the corner. On her way, she locked eyes with Amelia, and mouthed a silent "thank you."

Mrs. Witherpot came in to give them their five-minute

warning.

The class lined up and started running through their vocal warm-ups as a group. After the five minutes, they went through the door, behind the curtains, and walked out onto the stage.

Amelia wanted to hide but forced herself to follow the person in front of her as she took her position on the raised platforms on the stage. The lights shining in her eyes were unbearably hot and made it difficult to see the darkened crowd. While the rest of the choir was getting into place Amelia scanned the crowd and could just make out Sarah, Jasper, and Arnold sitting next to Cindy and her family. Amelia distinctly smelled mint, pine, and cinnamon permeating through the room.

The lights on stage turned a blue hue, and the crowd began to cheer as Mrs. Witherpot stepped to the front of the stage. She waved at the audience and then turned to the choir. She motioned that they should be smiling wider, mimicking the exaggerated movement on her own face. She then nodded to the pianist on the side of the stage, raised both hands, and the choir started immediately with a bouncy "Dashing through the snow…"

The energy helped calm Amelia's nerves. She wasn't alone, and when she faltered on the words of the second

song, her mistake was covered by the people around her. She got anxious again when the first solo began. One of the senior girls went to the front alone, under a spotlight, to sing O Little Town of Bethlehem. All Amelia could think about was her own number that would be coming up soon, and she ran through the words again in her mind.

Between each number, the audience clapped and cheered. When Mrs. Witherpot raised her hands to start the next number, the audience went robotically silent.

Two more choir numbers, a duet, a solo, and another duet. Two more choir numbers, a trio, and then another solo. They were halfway through the concert, as they began Silent Night.

Amelia began berating herself for signing up for the solo. It had seemed like such a good idea at the time, but not now that it was so close. She looked into the crowd as she sang, Cindy and her little brother were slowly swaying back and forth to the music.

Two more songs and then the world became awkwardly quiet. Amelia's whole body was numb and tingling. Her mind stopped wanting to work, but her legs were moving her to the front of the stage. With all eyes on her, Amelia had never been more conscious about herself as she stood entirely alone at the front of the stage. It was equally

321

terrifying, and exciting now that she was no longer able to hide in the comfort of the group. Maybe more terrifying, thought Amelia now that she could not rely on people around her to carry her through the mistakes. This was all on her.

Time both stopped and rushed past as she indicated she was ready, and the pianist shifted to begin. Amelia could feel her heartbeat as the crowd went perfectly silent and a wave of panic washed over her with the sound of the first note.

Amelia wasn't sure if she would even be able to get her voice to start working when the time came, and the intro was nearly over. She just needed the first note to come out on pitch. She focused all her energy into making sure she could land it.

Right on cue, as she had practiced, Amelia began to sing.

Ave Maria. Amelia had selected it because it was a piece that had always moved her. She started a little more quietly than she had intended, and her voice was shaky, but as she continued singing the knot in her stomach relaxed. Amelia began to feel more confident. She slowly gained volume and momentum as the song went on, building to the highest notes and then fading.

As quickly as it was her turn to sing, it was over. With

the final outro being played by the pianist, Amelia was shocked that she had made it through.

When the piano stopped, the crowd erupted with applause. Amelia hadn't messed it up. She looked down and saw that Jasper was standing up, waving his fedora with one hand, and had the fingers of his other hand in his mouth, blowing wild whistles. Sarah, Arnold, and Cindy were just as loud with their cheering.

From that point on, Amelia was in a haze. She was back and standing with the choir before she even knew where her feet had taken her. They sang another choral piece, had a few more solos, and then had two final group pieces. The choir ended by singing a hauntingly dark and cold a cappella version of Carol of the Bells.

When the song ended, the crowd clapped louder than ever. Mrs. Witherpot turned and bowed, and then she directed the choir to bow. The lights went down on the stage and went up on the audience. The crowd surged to the exit, and the choir members dispersed into the audience.

Amelia went down to meet Cindy, Sarah, and everyone else.

"Amelia, this is my little brother," said Cindy, motioning to the little boy who was now latched onto Cindy's leg. "This is my mom and dad."

323

Cindy's mother was short, thin, and had thick glasses like Cindy. Her father was tall and had curly black hair.

"Nice to finally meet you," said Cindy's mother, giving Amelia a hug.

Cindy's father politely shook Amelia's hand.

"What now?" asked Amelia.

"How about some hot apple cider?" asked Jasper.

"I have some that has been mulling at home," said Sarah, speaking to Cindy's family. "Would you care to join us?"

Cindy's father looked at her mother, who smiled and gave a shrug.

"Alright. Thank you," he responded.

Amelia ran back to the choir room to grab her things, and then met the group at the entrance. They sang Christmas carols as they walked, laughing as they went. Holding her little brother's hand, Cindy dropped to the back of the group with Amelia.

"We have to go out of town and visit family for a few days," said Cindy. "I'll be back in time for your birthday though."

"Alright," said Amelia, letting Cindy's brother grab her hand as he walked between them. "I hope you have a safe trip."

"By the way," said Cindy. "You did great."

"Yes, you did," agreed everyone. Jasper more enthusiastically than the rest.

"Now that school is over, you two can relax and enjoy the break. No more stress for a while," said Sarah.

"That would be nice," mused Arnold.

"Tell me about it," said Cindy's father before starting a conversation with Arnold about the long road to retirement.

Amelia thought it would be nice too, except she couldn't relax quite yet. She was going to be sixteen in less than a week, and she had one more thing that she wanted to resolve before then.

CHAPTER TWENTY-SIX

Underground

Stone began forming. First a light latticework to develop the base structure, and then layer upon layer as the materials in the air coalesced. Amelia concentrated and it seemed as if she was lost in a moment of time where she became connected to the process that was unfolding.

A moment is all that it was though. Almost immediately after it began, the thick granite wall was fully formed in front of Amelia. It twisted and transformed into an igloo like shell around her. Amelia lifted her arms further to help visualize what she was doing.

She had discovered from Arnold that if she treated the creation like a dance, or a physical extension of what she was doing mentally, things happened more quickly than if she was only concentrating on it.

Amelia continued her movements inside of the shell. She lifted her arms higher, and the granite shield lifted and changed into multiple, sharp, jagged rocks. She did a twirl and the whole thing started spinning like a dangerous top. Amelia extended her arms and fingers out in a violent motion that sent shards of rock in all directions. She was very careful to make sure that none of the pieces hit her friends. She then stood up straight and drew her hands back in front of her. The pieces returned and reformed as a protecting shield.

To add flair, Amelia caused the shield to shatter. The pieces changed into multicolored puffs of smoke that quickly dissipated into the air. Amelia wished that she could have turned the pieces into birds that would have flown away, but she was still very, very far from being able to do something that complicated.

Amelia walked over to a stone and sat down to look resolute, while at the same time trying to hide how exhausted she had become with the recent effort. Amelia looked back at Raskiel. Amy, Ohma, and Bartholomew were clapping and cheering at the show. Raskiel was unchanged. He was the final

hold-out.

"We had a deal. You have to let me come with you now," said Amelia. "I can help to protect all of you and keep you from being hurt anymore. Let me be a part of it."

"I can't," said Raskiel. "It's still too dangerous. This is for your own good."

"No, it isn't," said Amelia. "You told me that at Thanksgiving too, but it isn't true. You're being selfish and won't include me."

"And you are being selfish by forcing the issue!" retorted Raskiel, his hair standing up and his size increasing. "We are trying to do something to help you, and instead you wish to be placed in harm's way."

"Exactly," said Amelia. "I can handle things. So, you can just take your vows and toss 'em!"

At this last statement, Amy and Ohma gave little cheers, while Bartholomew started laughing and patting Raskiel's head.

"She's got you on that one, fuzzbucket," said Bartholomew. "It's time. You know it is, Raskiel. She deserves to understand."

"I know," said Raskiel, sitting down on his haunches. "I worry about her. I want her to be safe."

"Have you ever known my pirate queen to play it

328

safe?" chuckled Bartholomew. "Besides, we can't get any further without her, and you know it."

Everyone remained silent, waiting.

"Fine," said Raskiel, watching Amelia closely. "Come on."

Amelia followed Raskiel into his cave, and for the first time ever she was allowed to walk through the open wooden door. Raskiel closed the door behind the group, causing everything to go pitch black. Raskiel's fur began to glow a dim blue-green light. He fastened the series of locks, and then put a large plank across brackets mounted to either side of the door for good measure.

"This is my home," said Raskiel, turning to walk down the lava rock tunnel.

The tunnel opened into a chamber that led to other tunnels and chambers. As Raskiel entered, the wall sconces had a sympathetic reaction to his glowing and began to glow themselves, lighting up the cavern. The walls of the main cavern had hanging tapestries, and a pedestal to one side with a bronze sculpture of two interlocking ballerinas on top. The largest tunnel continued through the chamber and into the darkness, but Raskiel led Amelia and the group down a smaller side tunnel and into a chamber that felt like a Bedouin tent. The walls were covered with woven fabric. There were

tassels and streamers hanging from the ceiling. The floor was covered with layers of rugs, blankets, and woven mats that were piled thick. The edges and center were lined with giant throw pillows. Amy jumped gleefully onto the center pile while Ohma and Bartholomew picked out their own spots to sit.

Down connecting tunnels Amelia could see more chambers. Despite the dim light, or possibly because of it, each room seemed to be more and more curious. One was piled with papers and books that were placed in haphazard stacks. Another had, what looked like, a nest constructed of torn blankets and fur. The third had a rough metal framework, and panels of glass glinting in the darkness. The whole cavern seemed a strange combination of cultured and feral, much like Raskiel himself.

"I guess it is time to begin," said Raskiel, settling down on the floor. "First of all, I will now release you from your vows. As there will be no more secrets, you will have nothing left to reveal."

"About stinking time," grumbled Bartholomew.

"Their vow was to you?" asked Amelia.

"Yes, and no," replied Raskiel.

"Don't give non-answers," scolded Bartholomew. "If I can talk now, then I'm gonna talk."

"I can oblige," said Ohma.

"No, I wanna tell," chirped Amy.

"Quiet," snapped Bartholomew. "Amelia, we talked about how you built this place, and how we all started on the same island. Apparently, some folks got jobs as well. Raskiel got saddled with a whopper of one."

"I accepted it," corrected Raskiel. "It's not like I was forced."

"Is that the secret?" asked Amelia.

"Yes," said Bartholomew. "He monitors the only passage to the underground."

"But we've been underground before," said Amelia.

"Not like this you haven't," chuckled Bartholomew, darkly.

"They had to make a vow to keep the entrance secret in exchange for its use," said Raskiel. "One of the mandates of my position was that you weren't to know about it until you were ready."

"That's dumb," said Amelia. "Who would make an idiotic rule like that just to keep me from being able to explore a part of my own world?"

Raskiel and Bartholomew gave each other a meaningful look and then rolled their eyes as they tried not to directly look at Amelia.

331

"I would be delighted to conjecture," said Ohma.

"Don't you dare," said Bartholomew.

"Right," said Amelia, becoming self-aware. "The shadow creature lives in the underground then?"

"Exactly," said Raskiel. "His name is Fear, by the way. We discovered the name in the process of tracking him down. We have also discovered that he was another one of the beings here at the creation of this world."

"If you guard the underground, how does Fear keep getting out?" asked Amelia.

"That's a big part of the problem," said Raskiel. "I don't know."

"Well, let's go," said Amelia.

"Not yet," said Raskiel. "We still need to talk about the tunnel systems, the flora and fauna, the…"

"Nope! Let's just get headed," thundered Bartholomew, jumping to his feet.

"But we just sat down," objected Raskiel.

"Too bad," said Amelia. "My first day of break and I'm not going to waste it."

They walked back to the main chamber and continued down the largest tunnel. At the end of the tunnel sat a large stone door. The door had been decorated with geometric patterns in relief, and at its center was the shape of a paw

imprint. Raskiel set his front paw on the imprint, and the thick stone door lit up, split in the center and swung open. Once the group had passed, it closed itself and went dark.

"Please, just be careful," said Raskiel, walking past Amelia to lead the way.

At many points, the tunnel split off. There were other caverns and fissures that they ran across, but they continued following Raskiel on a trail that wound steadily downward.

"It's getting hot in here," said Amelia, walking toward the red glow coming from ahead.

She stepped out of the tunnel and immediately understood why. A fresh wave of heat washed over her as she took in the giant cavern. Dropping down a few hundred feet in front of her was a giant pool of magma. The cavern was so large that Amelia couldn't see across to the other side despite the light coming from below.

Amelia jumped in surprise when a giant figure dropped from the ceiling down to a short distance from the lava, opened its wings, and then rode back up to the ceiling to latch on once more. She looked through the smoke and fumes to see more of the car-sized, bat-like creatures floating on the warm currents. Even more were suspended from the ceiling above. One dropped too close to the magma and was devoured by a giant snake creature that rose out of the

333

molten rock.

"Stay close to the center," said Raskiel, leading the way along the wide ledge that ran around the cavern.

"Be careful of the spiders against the wall," said Amy, pointing to the webbing and a few poor animals that were trapped in it. "You don't want to get too close."

"My dearest, they shan't be engaging in your agitation now that we are acquainted with the whereabouts of their personages," said Ohma, while a cat sized spider came out of a hole on the wall to wrap up a gray, furry creature that was trying to free itself. Amy shivered at the sight, and Ohma took her hand in his as they continued walking.

"What's going on with them?" Amelia whispered to Bartholomew.

"Something about the underground," Bartholomew whispered back, as they turned down a tunnel leading away from the large chamber. "He's still as out of touch as ever but seems to have finally found a way to communicate with her. She's been less of an airhead... or more like she's less distractable now."

The longer they walked down this new tunnel, the more the temperature began to drop. There was moist air coming from below, and there was plant life growing on the walls and floor. Some scattered mold and moss at first, but

soon there were clusters of luminescent mushrooms, flowers, and grasses. Amelia even saw a few variations of rabbits and other animals that ran away when the group came too close, prompting Raskiel to say, "The underground is larger and more diverse than the surface."

"They have the cutest animals down here too," piped in Amy. "They have furry snails, wiggling puffballs, and birds with lots of wings."

"Let us not forget the adorable nature of the diminutive, pellucid canines," interjected Ohma.

"Oh, the doggies. I can't forget those. They do tricks and it tickles when they lick my hands," said Amy.

"Seriously, how much have they changed since you guys started coming down here?" whispered Amelia.

The group passed through a cave that had masks forming along the walls, and then through a long fissure into another cavern that contained shallow pools filled with skeletal fish. Amelia panicked when one of the fish splashed nearby, and she created a wall that Bartholomew walked into.

"Watch it with those," he scolded her, rubbing his nose.

"Sorry," said Amelia, following Amy out of the cavern and across a natural bridge that went over a seemingly bottomless chasm.

Raskiel led them into another large, descending tunnel that had crystalline veins cutting through the walls.

"Don't go down these three side tunnels," said Raskiel, motioning to a few of the offshoots. "The air gets bad."

Amelia nodded acknowledgment and kept following. A chill wind was blowing from the direction they were heading, and the walls became coated in frost. When the tunnel finally began to widen, it got brighter as well. The lighter it got, the more Raskiel's fur changed. The luminescence went away, and his coat grew thicker and turned a dark brown.

The tunnel widened enough to expose a large cavern that was only slightly smaller than the magma lake that they had seen above. The snow gave off a blue glow, and the giant icicles hanging from the ceiling and sticking out of the floor were filled with pulsating orbs that reminded Amelia of Christmas lights. These giant icicles made the city in front of Amelia seem small.

"Best stick close," growled Raskiel.

"Why?" asked Amelia. "What's wrong?"

Amy gripped Ohma's hand tightly again.

"Possibly nothing, but there's a good chance you'll see soon enough," said Bartholomew, grabbing a baseball bat

from the nearest porch and holding it in one hand like a club.

"I hope you're ready."

CHAPTER TWENTY-SEVEN

Fear

Snow was falling, moisture crystallizing at the ceiling and dropping as a fine mist throughout the cavern. The orbs glowed and flashed. It was too still. A cold tomb-like chamber where their living flesh didn't belong. Amelia began to shiver.

Everyone moved as quietly as they could. Even Ohma, who usually made noise because of his backpack, was making sure to walk slowly and keep his equipment very still. Despite his attempts, each light clank and rattle made the hair on the back of Amelia's neck stand up.

Raskiel motioned for everyone to move forward as he

snuck across an intersection and led them down a side alley.

"What's going on here?" whispered Amelia. "What is this place."

"You tell us," whispered back Raskiel. "You made it."

It was like visiting her past through a dream. An amalgam of all the places she had lived before. Different homes and apartments, parks, schools, stores, and other buildings all composing a single frozen city. They were moments frozen in time, including the people.

Amelia moved to inspect one of the children on the sidewalk, locked as if flash frozen. Bartholomew, grabbed onto her arm and pulled her back, pleading in his eyes.

"Don't touch them," he whispered harshly. "Don't even go near them. Move quietly and quickly so we can get through this."

"But I know her," whispered Amelia. "She used to play with me in kindergarten."

Amelia paused and looked at the figures. She knew all of them. Many of them were forgotten with each successive move, but the memories were starting to come back in a flood, all of them associated with a negative experience that she had tried to forget.

"We have to keep going," whispered Raskiel, cutting across a lawn.

Each new face that Amelia passed brought back a flash of pain. That one had lied to her. Those two had called her names. That one was kind, but she never got to say goodbye before being whisked off to a new house. All of them, locked in the past. Street after street of frozen memories.

"We're almost there," whispered Bartholomew.

"Where are we going?" asked Amelia, quietly.

"That building at the end of the road," he whispered back.

Upon seeing it, Amelia reflexively pulled back and said, "No!"

The single word, while not a yell, echoed and reverberated through the cavern much louder than Amelia had expected. Everyone stopped and stood still. Amelia could feel the tension and panic rising.

The head of the frozen little girl nearest Amelia, in a sadistically slow motion, turned to face her. Its dark eyes lighting up and a smile spreading unnaturally large across its face. The other figures on the road moved from their frozen actions and turned to face the group.

"Run!" cried Bartholomew.

The frozen people began to change. Down the block, two that Amelia remembered very clearly, Sandy and the

vulture, changed as well. Sandy became a hulking, blobbish ice monstrosity, and the vulture grew long icy wings that took her into the sky. Another figure enlarged, snow transforming into fur, and hands turning into claws as it moved toward the group. Yet another became deformed and reptilian as it charged. The one closest to Amelia had its mouth split open, and fangs appeared as its legs and arms stretched and formed icy scythes.

"Get past them and get inside," hollered Raskiel, sprinting back to Amelia. "I'll hold them off."

Amelia didn't want to go inside. She never expected to see the place again, not after she left it for what she thought was the final time. The home where she'd lost her family.

"Forget it," yelled Amelia, forming a wall to block the closest creature as it lunged toward her. "This is what I practiced for. I'm going to stay with you."

Raskiel tackled the creature that was moving around Amelia's wall. He caught an arm in his mouth and bit down, shattering it. As the other arm moved up to slice him, he quickly planted all four paws in its chest and pushed himself away from it, sending it sliding through the snow until it crashed and shattered against a frozen tree.

Amelia created two more barrier walls to slow down the yeti-like snow creature that was now on them. It stuck its

341

giant toothy head around the wall, only to be met by the bat Bartholomew wielded. The bat cracked, and the creature's head shattered.

Amy grabbed one of the smaller creatures, holding it by its feet, and flew up, quickly dropping it to shatter on the street when it landed. She then began an aerial battle against the icy vulture that was circling the group. Not to be left behind, Ohma had pulled a cast iron pan off his pack and was swinging it wildly to hit anything that came close. His backpack clanked louder and was attracting more attention.

"Keep moving," roared Raskiel, going upright on his two hind legs and increasing further in size. He grabbed two of the reptilian icy creatures and smashed them together, breaking them into pieces.

"No," yelled Amelia again, causing one of her walls to break apart and sending the pieces into a group of the creatures that had started to pour out of an apartment building.

"We have to," said Bartholomew, knocking the legs out from under another creature.

Amelia could see that they were quickly going to be outnumbered as more creatures arrive.

"Fine," screamed Amelia, creating a giant wall to block the end of the street. "I hate this though."

"Noted," called Raskiel, grabbing another creature and throwing it into the crowd.

They started running, and Amelia's legs began to give out. She had overdone it again. Bartholomew saw her falter and propped her up with one of his arms while he swung the bat with his other.

Ohma got a lucky swing with his pan and smashed a creature that got too close. He kept running and let out an uncharacteristic "wooohaaa," his backpack clanking louder than ever.

Amy came crashing into a nearby rooftop, pinning the wings of the vulture together so that it dove into the building first, causing it to shatter. Amy quickly took to the air once more.

"We just need to get a little closer," yelled Bartholomew, breaking off the leg of the blobbish snow creature that had been Sandy. It had been trying to go around a new stone barrier. Amelia was nearly falling over from the exertion, and Amy flew down to help her up the doorsteps to the home.

Amelia clenched her teeth and opened the door, while Raskiel and Bartholomew fought against more of the creatures that had caught up. Amelia was met with a wave of warm air that immediately melted the snow on the steps and

drove back the closest of the creatures. She stumbled inside along with Amy. They were followed closely by Ohma and Raskiel. Bartholomew was last, and he threw the, now broken, bat out as he shut the door.

There were scratching noises from the door, and Amelia was worried that they would be able to get in. Instead, the noises stopped suddenly, and everything became as eerily silent as before.

Amelia sat against the wall. She was out of breath and had to stop. Her body ached, and she was exhausted. She looked around at her group. No one had come through unscathed.

"I thought you could handle yourself?" came Raskiel's low growl, as he licked at a cut on his leg. "Seems to me that was a bluff. You can't sustain your abilities."

"Yeah, well, I seemed to do alright," said Amelia, pulling back her pant leg to reveal a bruise that was appearing around her knee. "Is it always this bad when you guys come through here?"

"No," said Bartholomew, pulling out a handkerchief and putting pressure against a bleeding headwound. "We accidentally woke two the first time we came through, and we've been careful since."

"A reaction to your presence, perhaps," said Raskiel.

"Or just bad luck."

"Maybe," said Amelia, looking around the room.

The exterior had been a reflection of her old home, but the interior was something else. Clay oil lamps, mounted in the recesses in the walls, gave light to the area. The large, rectangular, tan and brown stones that the room was constructed with were covered in ornamental carvings and reliefs. Strange hieroglyphs covered the surfaces along with squared-off imagery. At the back of the room, a large staircase descended into the ground.

"How much further?" asked Amelia, resting her eyes for a moment.

"Just a little," said Bartholomew. "Should be clear the rest of the way."

"Let's get going then," said Amelia, forcing herself up and then regretting her decision almost immediately as she saw Ohma helping an exhausted, and lightly limping, Amy to get up as well.

The battered group slowly descended the stone steps, and then walked through an impossibly long hallway, until they reached the doorway at the end. The hallway was lit with the same oil lamps the room above had been.

Raskiel went to the circular door, carved with ornamentation, and knocked on it with one of his big paws.

A small panel in the door slid open, and Raskiel whispered something through. The panel shut and they waited.

Bright light flooded the chamber as the door rolled to the side, moving along a groove in the stonework above and below it, being pushed along by people in brightly colored, woven clothing. Their hair and hands seemed to be formed of root tangles, some with leaves and flowers growing out of them.

Amelia stepped into the jungle, the humid air and plant life enveloping her. The sun, no, it was a glowing orb that was set into the ceiling of the cavern, gave off warmth and light. A group of the people took Amelia and her friends by their hands and guided them through the trees and toward the stepped pyramids that could be seen above the tree line.

The jungle gave way to farm fields and a village. Hieroglyphic images and patterns covered the Maya-esque buildings. Children were laughing and playing in the waterfalls and streams that ran around and over the buildings and next to the stony pathways. Layers of buildings were built closely together with the large pyramids around the edges, all of it leading down to a tree-lined plaza at the bottom and center of the community.

"For you," said a young lady, placing a flower in Amelia's hair. "Welcome! Is there anything we can do for

you?"

"I'm not sure," responded Amelia, trying to take in everything around her. A little boy ran up, smiled, gave Amelia a hug, and then ran back to a group of kids that had begun to gather.

"We can at least tend to your wounds and give you a place to clean up," the young lady responded.

"That would be appreciated," said Raskiel. "But we came to see the statue again first, if that is okay."

"Whatever you need," said an elderly gentleman, walking to join them. "Will you be staying to have a meal with us? You are more than welcome."

The kids were now taking turns running to give Amelia a hug, and then laughing as they ran back to their group. Hug Amelia had turned into a game. The same children were gathering flower petals by the handful and throwing them in front of Amy.

"Their food is nummy," she said, flapping her wings to blow the flower petals into whirling showers over the children, who laughed and danced.

"We would love to stay for a meal," said Amelia, as another child ran away giggling. "Is there anything that we can do to help?"

"Oh no," said the elderly gentleman. "We are happy

to share. Please, go about your business, and the food will be ready shortly. You can partake any time it becomes convenient for you."

Curious onlookers waved and greeted the group as they walked down to the plaza. With all the warmth and love, the large statue in the center of the plaza felt out of place. It was dark and foreboding. "Fear," as Raskiel had called it. The figure stood tall, and had its sword drawn. The attention to detail on the statue made Amelia feel like it could come to life at any moment.

"This way," said Bartholomew, opening the door at the base of the statue. "Down there is where we're stuck."

Amelia waved goodbye to the entourage of children and followed her friends through the doorway and down a spiral staircase. The stairwell was filled with a faint honey fragrance that came from giant beeswax candles that were lining the walls and provided the only light against the darkness.

"Nothing has changed," said Amy, when she reached the landing at the bottom of the stairs and looked into the next room.

"As expected," commented Raskiel. "Fear still won't show himself, even with Amelia in tow."

"Do I look like a barge?" said Amelia, stepping onto

the landing.

"As much as I would like to watch you continue to torment Mr. Whiskers here, I understand his frustration. It was a bugger to get here," said Bartholomew. "Then, once we finally found the place, we've been stuck for the last month with no clue about how to proceed further."

"But how did you find this in the first place?" asked Amelia. "I mean, it's seriously out of the way."

"I told you, I oversee the entrance to the underground," said Raskiel. "In exchange for access to the surface, and quite a bit of other deal making, I was able to get a lot of information. That led us to the khmets."

"Who?" asked Amelia.

Bartholomew pointed his finger up and said, "They bring Fear food and hold audience with him. They're the ones that told us his name."

"He won't show up when we're here though," said Amy, frowning.

"We have engaged in additional traversals of the subterrestrial to no avail," said Ohma, putting an arm around Amy. "Thus, we oft return to this vicinity."

"That's all right," said Amelia. "I appreciate that you cared about me enough to try. At any rate, I better get this over with."

Amelia couldn't help but smile at the two love birds as she walked past them and into the adjoining room. It was a small circular chamber with a domed ceiling and a clear blue light shining from the opening at the center of the dome. Amelia walked across the room to the large, oval, stone tablet that was mounted into the wall.

It was a blank tablet, but as Amelia approached it, she had a quick flash in her memory of something that made her stomach go into knots. A little girl that she had tried to forget. A little girl she hated and who she blamed for everything bad that had happened to her in her life. The closer Amelia got to the tablet, the clearer the image became.

There was a sharp pain in Amelia's chest. She felt like she was drowning, and she needed to get away from this room.

"Can we head back up please?" asked Amelia, trying to sound as normal as possible.

"That's fine," said Bartholomew. "I'm hungry anyway."

CHAPTER TWENTY-EIGHT

The Two Little Girls

 "Well, you thought it was a giant potato as well," said Bartholomew.

"Yeah, but I didn't try eating it," replied Raskiel.

Amelia laughed as she floated in the water. It was two days before Christmas. Amelia was still having difficulty facing the room below the statue of Fear. Instead, they spent every day of the break exploring and having fun like they used to.

Amelia looked around the lagoon. It was how it had always been. She could see the stars up in the sky, and the glowing coral and fish below. Amelia was so lost in thought,

that she barely looked up in time to see Amy jump off the upper deck.

Amy had a perfect dive. Ohma followed with a flying squirrel belly flop. There was a loud smack as he hit the water.

"Ten points," called out Amelia.

"I'd only give it a six," said Bartholomew. "His last few were much more impressive."

"Speaking of impressive," said Raskiel. "Attempting to eat the ruler of the dahons?"

"I told you, I thought it was a giant potato!" yelled Bartholomew. "How was I supposed to know? How long are you going to keep bringing it up? You wet mop!"

"I would imagine it'll be around for a while," said Raskiel, lazily paddling around in the water. "First, you're the king of the mud pots, then you're a potato assassin. What's next?"

"It all worked out in the end, didn't it?" responded Bartholomew.

"Yes, but next time we go underground, let's pack a lunch instead," said Amelia.

"See, now you're talking sense," said Bartholomew.

"Yes," said Raskiel. "We could pack potato salad."

"And potato chips," said Amelia. "Maybe some mashed potatoes and gravy."

Amy and Ohma swam over to join the conversation.

"We could do sweet potatoes," said Amy, catching on.

"Sweet potato pie, hash browns, and even French fries sound good to me," said Raskiel.

"I desire ham," said Ohma.

This was followed by a long silence. The wise Ohma had disproven himself again.

"We could always do ham on fully loaded, baked potatoes," offered Amelia.

The banter continued, and after a couple hours of swimming and playing, Amelia felt like it was time to leave. She had things that she wanted to prepare before her birthday party the next day. They sailed the ship out of the lagoon, and Amelia returned to her room through her doorway.

After getting a shower, clean clothes, and brushing out her hair, Amelia found Sarah making lunch.

"I was wondering when you would get back," said Sarah. "Nice to see that you made it an early day."

"Yeah," said Amelia. "Sorry about that. I guess I haven't been around much recently."

"Not a problem," said Sarah, with a shrug. "I used to love spending my vacations in my sphere as well. Much more fun than sitting around with nothing to do. Anyway, you ready for tomorrow?"

"I think so. Is there anything I can do to help?"

"I still need you to decide what kind of cake you want," said Sarah. "Then we just need to get some groceries, and we should be done. I took care of everything else yesterday while you were gone."

"Red velvet cake," said Amelia. "With coconut frosting."

"That's do-able," said Sarah. "One more thing, you haven't asked, but your friends from your paradigm sphere are allowed to come to the house sometimes."

"Really?" asked Amelia.

"Of course," said Sarah. "Enion finished his latest research trip and will be back tonight. He's been alone in the common spheres for a long time and could use some company. There are a couple of quick rules though. Make sure that they aren't the kind to destroy anything. Also, unless they look human or like Dormant animals, they aren't allowed outside."

"Would it be all right if they came for my birthday party tomorrow?" asked Amelia.

"That would be fine," said Sarah. "But we better get more food then."

"Great," said Amelia. "I'll let them know and then we can go shopping."

Amelia was standing in front of the blank tablet. It was calling to her. As much as she wanted to run, she felt herself compulsorily pulled toward it. She could visualize the door hiding behind it and could hear the voice crying out.

Amelia woke up in a sweat. The house was silent. She glanced over at the clock and saw that it was still before midnight. She would be sixteen tomorrow, but she wasn't ready for it.

Once again, her door sat open, and she could see the chamber with the tablet. Every night since she first visited the chamber, she awoke to it. She went to close the door again and stopped. She couldn't avoid it any longer. It was time.

Amelia opened the door back up and stepped into the circular chamber. As she walked toward the blank tablet, she could feel someone calling to her from behind it. The vision of the little girl came back into her mind. After fighting off the desire to run away again, Amelia tried to take another step toward the tablet. It was then that she realized she wasn't alone.

Amelia turned around to find Fear watching her.

"What do you want?" asked Amelia.

"To prevent you from doing what you are planning to do," came the whisper of a voice. "I am here to protect you."

"Protect me?" asked Amelia in exasperation. "How are you possibly protecting me?"

"Would you like me to explain myself?" whispered Fear.

Amelia looked intently at Fear and tried to get any kind of a read that she could on the creature.

"I think you had better," said Amelia, after a short pause.

"I was like others and found myself on the lone island at the creation of this world," began Fear. "After a while, I comprehended my existence. As the world shifted and changed, I understood and felt my purpose. Somehow, I knew that I was meant to protect you, even though, at the time, I didn't even know who you were or what you looked like. At one point, I started to feel that something was terribly wrong. It went on for weeks and possibly months. I didn't have a clear concept of time then, but I could tell that something was different.

"Finally, one day, the feeling of danger was stronger than it had ever been. I didn't know what to do. I only knew that I must find you. I saw a shadowy portal open and I stepped inside. I was able to see your face for the first time. Your father had told you and your sister to stay in your room. I watched as you left, and your father and mother invited a

356

man inside to talk."

Amelia was suddenly feeling very uncomfortable. She knew what was going to happen next in the story. She knew the night that Fear was speaking of.

"They confronted him about something, and it erupted in yelling," continued Fear. "I watched as you and your sister came out of the bedroom to see what was happening. I knew that the man was dangerous, and so I tried to warn you both to go back. With all the noise, you couldn't hear me talking. With my pleas having no effect, I jumped out of the shadows in the form you see me in now, and I chased you back to the room and under your bed. I couldn't get your sister's attention enough to get her to go along with you. She had run to your mother's side. You know the rest of what happened. From that point on, I found that I had the ability to use the portal to travel anywhere I wanted to. I could also change my form and appearance."

"I did see you that day," said Amelia. "It wasn't a dream."

"No, it wasn't," said Fear. "I continued to watch over you and tried to protect you from that point on. I generally remain unobtrusive but have worked tirelessly to help."

"If you were so good at staying hidden and protecting me, then why did you make that grand entrance at the

glowing lagoon?" said Amelia. "And why have you been
sending threats ever since?"

"That was also to protect you," responded Fear. "As
soon as you arrived in your current home, I learned what
Sarah was. I knew that you would also be finding out more
about your ability. So, I traveled around through my portal
and discovered all that I could about what you would be
facing. That is when I heard of the Rha' Shalim. Rumors of
dark creatures like me. I wanted to protect you, and so I tried
to dissuade you from returning to your sphere or using your
ability. I was also hoping to find out what threat, if any, there
actually was. Because of that, I sent messages to Amy in the
lagoon, to tap the dormant abilities of the fleora. She had
become too independent for it to do any good though."

"Then what about all the other times?" asked Amelia,
realizing how much Fear had been around. "What about the
singing glade? That could have killed me if I had run the
wrong way."

"That went... differently than I had planned,"
admitted Fear. "I didn't expect you to run like that. I avoided
that tactic later, because I discovered that you could have hurt
yourself in your panic. From then on, I only used my physical
presence to try to scare you away from learning about Sarah.
After you discovered Sarah's secret, I could only stay close to

try to protect you. I did my best to stay mostly hidden, but there were a few times I was careless, and came closer than I intended. It was all meant for your safety."

"Like Halloween, and like..." Amelia paused, coming to an understanding. "That was why you attacked me in Adonei. It was to warn me about the Creonocens."

"Yes, exactly," whispered Fear. "I had to watch you more closely after the discovery of the pendant, to keep you safe. That is also why I wanted you to stop your friends. I have no desire to hurt them. I knew that if they continued, you would eventually come here as well. I don't want to see you in any more danger. I have always sought to protect you."

"Through fear," said Amelia, feeling suddenly angry. "How dare you? You've been manipulating me my whole life."

Fear fell silent and listened quietly as Amelia continued.

"You've been doing it all wrong," said Amelia. "You could have caused more damage than you would have been preventing. I would gladly die if the alternative was to live a sheltered and cowardly life. I don't know if the dangers I would go through by being a Learner are as bad as you think they are, but facing them would have to be better than cowering and trying to forget about my friends and

everything I've seen. I appreciate that you saved my life, but you had no right to try and make me think I was crazy, or to try and control me."

"I know," whispered Fear.

Amelia stopped. She wanted to keep yelling at it, to convince it about all it had messed up. The fact that it agreed with her, took the fight out of her argument.

"Fine. As long as you understand that," said Amelia. "Now open the door so I can get this over with. I have to get in there. She's calling to me."

Fear was silent. There was a long pause before it spoke.

"That is not in my power," said Fear, somberly. "The tablet and the sealed room beyond were not me. This was of your own making. You created this and placed me here to guard, though I doubt you knew that is what you were doing. I accepted the task."

"I made this?" asked Amelia.

"Well, yes," said Fear. "The tablet was a creation of yours and a reflection of what you must face before you can move forward."

"So, I wanted to be scared away from ever opening this door?" asked Amelia.

"A natural instinct for creatures to protect themselves,

is it not?" responded Fear.

"Not for this 'creature,'" said Amelia.

She was done being controlled. She walked up to the tablet and tried opening it. She couldn't find a switch, or a latch. Pulling on it didn't do anything. It was firmly set in the wall. The image of the girl burned into her mind so firmly that she had to fight the instinct to run. She couldn't let that instinct control her, and she was done piddling around.

Amelia backed up two steps. She created her stone wall, formed it into spikes, and sent a barrage into the tablet, breaking it apart and revealing the door behind. Amelia walked through the door and into a crypt. There were four stone coffins on the floor of the tiny square room.

There was a man sitting on one of the coffins, weeping. He was a sad, pathetic man. As Amelia got closer, she began to panic. She knew this man. It was the gardener. She felt anger, fear, anxiety, and horror all at the same time. Amelia jumped when she felt something touch her shoulder, and then backed away as she saw Fear had come up behind her.

"Calm," whispered Fear. "What will you do now? Isn't it time to deal to him, what he dealt to you? Won't you use your newfound powers to teach him a lesson? I am sure that you could truly hurt him if you were so inclined."

Amelia looked at the gardener. He wasn't moving. He wasn't attacking. He was sitting and weeping, unable to do anything beyond that. She remembered him with such loathsome memories that she was waiting for him to do something evil and terrible, but he didn't.

He seemed to be in torment over what he had done. Amelia wanted to hate him, but she couldn't anymore. He wasn't an evil demon. He was a very messed up, disturbed, and sad individual.

Amelia reminded herself that, in the end, he had taken his own life. Whatever had happened wasn't the result of a healthy mind. She couldn't begin to justify his actions, but she didn't feel like she had to continue to hold the hatred and anger that had been eating at her for years. It didn't do anything to get back at the gardener. All it did was damage her.

"No," responded Amelia. "My fear would make me attack him, but I won't hurt other people anymore just because I'm scared. I need to find another way to make things better."

"How will you do that?" whispered Fear.

Amelia wasn't sure. She didn't know how to change hatred and fear into something else.

"Wait," said Amelia with an image of a tray of sweets

popping into her head. "I think I might know."

Remembering Becky, Amelia knew what she had to do. To let go of the damaging emotions inside of her, she had to forgive the gardener. She didn't want to. She wanted to hate him for all that he had done to her and her family, but it was the only way to finally heal. It took her a moment to build up the strength necessary to say the words. Once she did, the pain in her chest began to ease a little.

"I forgive you," said Amelia, through tears. "I want to let go of this anger and pain. I forgive you, whether you want me to or not."

The crying figure stopped. It turned and looked up at Amelia. The gardener, and the coffin he sat upon, dissipated into a dark mist. With the gardener gone, Amelia finally noticed the sound of someone else whimpering and crying. It was the voice that had relentlessly been calling to her.

Amelia knew who it was. This one was going to be much harder to deal with than the gardener. She loathed this person. There was a reason that she locked them up in here. They were meant to be forgotten. Weren't they?

Amelia looked at the far corner where the sound was coming from, and saw a little girl curled up and rocking back and forth, tears soaking her face and dress. Amelia's own tears started to flow at the sight of this child. The rage and

loathing replaced with compassion.

Amelia stood silently for a moment to regain her composure and waited until her tears had started to slow down. She then walked slowly toward the small figure that was wearing a little black dress. It was Amelia when she was four years old.

After watching the younger version of herself for a moment, Amelia crouched down to hold the little girl and give her a hug. Amelia knew that it was exactly what she had needed most at the time.

"Are you okay?" asked Amelia.

"No," came the little girl's reply. "I'm not."

"What's wrong?" said Amelia with as much love as she could.

"Don't want to talk about it," said the younger version of Amelia.

"I understand," said Amelia. "Some things can be difficult to talk about. I had something terrible happen to me once that I still have difficulty dealing with."

"You too?" asked little Amelia, looking up and wiping her tears. "What happened?"

"Well," began Amelia, "there was a man that did something terrible to me and my family."

"That's the same thing that happened to me," came

the little girl's reply, as she started weeping once more. "And it's all my fault."

Amelia wasn't sure what to say. At the time she was four, it felt like her fault. She felt like everything the gardener had done was because she wasn't strong enough to stop it. But, now that Amelia saw this poor little child crying, she could see clearly that there was no way a child that age could have had any control over the situation.

"No, it's not," said Amelia, holding the child even closer. "You are a good girl."

"I am not," said the little girl, sobbing. "Mommy, Daddy, and Sister are gone because of me. I messed up. I should have told Daddy about the gardener sooner. I was scared. It was my fault."

Amelia didn't know what to say. She knew how stubborn the child would be, because she knew how stubborn she herself would be. Amelia held her, rocked back and forth, and sang a lullaby to calm the little girl down.

"I love you," said Amelia, once the child had settled down enough to listen. "I love you very much. I am here for you, and I understand what you are going through. You will never be alone again because I am here for you and I love you."

"Really?" asked the little Amelia, through sniffles.

365

"Yes really," said Amelia, through tears as she continued to hold the little girl and rock back and forth. "And even though you feel like it is all your fault, I want you to know that I forgive you. I love you and you are wonderful. Even though it isn't your fault, I forgive you for anything that is. I forgive you. I forgive you."

Amelia continued to hold the child for a while longer until the younger version of her dissipated into the same dark mist that the gardener had. She wiped away her tears and looked at Fear, who was now in the middle of the room between the three remaining stone coffins. The lids of the coffins were dissipating into a dark mist.

"Looks like you locked away more than you may have suspected," whispered Fear. "Your childhood-self left you some presents. Likely, these were locked in here at the same time as she was."

Not knowing if Fear had a morbid sense of sarcasm, Amelia walked forward in trepidation. Her heart leaped when she saw that they were, in fact, actual presents. In each of the coffins were mementos of her family. In one was a doll that she and her sister had shared as children. In the next, she found her mother's diary. In the final one, she found a picture album full of images that her father had taken.

"I thought this stuff was lost," said Amelia, through

tears of joy.

"Apparently not," whispered Fear, in its cold voice.

Amelia picked up the items and held them close, making sure they were real and hoping that they wouldn't disappear in a dark mist along with the now dissipating coffins.

"On to business," said Fear.

"What?" asked Amelia. "What business?"

"Come now," said Fear. "I have outlived my usefulness. This form no longer suits me. I told you, I have the ability to change my appearance. It is high time that I return to the one I began with. The 'business' is that I ask that you give me a new name once you see it. My old name no longer fits my purpose or function."

Amelia watched as the darker than black mist poured off the creature, and its shape fell away. In its place sat a precocious, strawberry blonde, little girl who was wearing a full-length summer dress.

"Raskiel said you were a boy," blurted out Amelia.

"Shows how much he knows," came a chipper and strong little feminine voice. "Oh, that's weird to talk normally again."

Amelia couldn't help but stare at the little girl who, seconds before, had been an evil and menacing creature.

"So, what's my new name?" asked the little girl excitedly. "Now that 'Fear' isn't appropriate."

Amelia thought about it for a while, and finally said, "Hope."

CHAPTER TWENTY-NINE

Hot Chocolate

 The sun came streaming through the window, warming the quilt. Amelia yawned and stretched, looking around her room. She didn't want to get up. The sunshine was too nice. Between her birthday party and Christmas, she was still exhausted. Amelia chuckled as she remembered them.

"What's so funny?" asked a drowsy Hope.

Amelia looked at the floor where Hope was still curled up on a makeshift bed of blankets.

"Just thinking about my birthday," responded Amelia.

"What about? Your friend with glasses that couldn't

stop staring?"

"Yes," said Amelia. "About everything else too. I'm still amazed at how fast Ohma and Amy accepted you."

"Yeah, well, the other two still haven't warmed up yet," said Hope.

"They will," said Amelia. "What do you expect after being 'Fear' for so long?"

Amelia picked up her mother's diary and the picture album that she had left on the floor the night before. She started flicking through the picture album and absorbing the photos of her family.

"Christmas was fun too," said Hope. "I had always wanted to try it sometime. I still don't understand why Sarah wouldn't let us open presents before we got showered and ate breakfast."

"I think it had something to do with the fact that she didn't know you would be staying here for Christmas when everyone else went back to the paradigm sphere. She had to come up with some presents for you," said Amelia.

"But Enion stayed too," said Hope.

"She had planned on him," responded Amelia. "Your new pajamas are cute by the way."

"Thanks," said Hope, grinning.

Amelia got out of bed and put the journal and album

on the bookshelf, next to her sister's doll and the little plush rabbit that Spencer had won at the Pickle Festival.

"Did we really have to go deliver all of those things though," whined Hope, rolling onto her belly.

"It was Christmas everywhere," said Amelia. "Sarah's friends in Adonei were happy to receive her presents. I think they enjoyed us caroling to them as well."

"Humph!" uttered Hope. "Caroling stinks."

"I told you I would help you learn the words to the songs for next year," said Amelia. "I didn't make you sing when we went to deliver presents to Bartholomew, Ohma, Amy, and Raskiel, did I?"

"No," grumbled Hope. "But they could have gotten me something in return."

"Maybe next year. For now, I'm hungry."

"Okay, I'm getting more sleep first," said Hope, rolling back onto her side and cuddling into the blankets.

Amelia walked over to the large terrarium Arnold made for Hoffy, and she checked the food and water. Hoffy happily flew around and hopped in appreciation.

Amelia went downstairs to find Sarah singing, preparing breakfast, and wearing her usual smile. Enion was sitting on the floor, staring at the cartoon playing on the television.

"Morning," said Sarah. "Breakfast is almost ready."

"Morning," replied Amelia. "Good morning to you too, Enion."

"Quiet," said Enion, unmoving. "Wait till the commercial."

"He's missed his cartoons," said Sarah, setting down a plate of pancakes on the table. "Haven't you, Enion?"

"Shush," said Enion, eyes fixed. "Be quiet."

Sarah and Amelia exchanged a look, and finished setting the table. Once Enion's cartoon had ended, they said a prayer and began to eat. It was mostly silence at first, but Amelia was thinking about how much had happened since she moved in.

"Did you mean what you said when you first met me?" asked Amelia. "Do you still want me around?"

"Of course I do," said Sarah. "Why?"

"It's just that I've already been here a while," said Amelia, poking at the egg on her plate. "I was wondering when I would be asked to move on to somewhere new. I know that it isn't a rational thought, but I haven't ever had a permanent place."

Sarah laughed a comforting laugh.

"Well, it will likely take some time to get used to it. I want you around, and that isn't going to change," said Sarah.

"I told you before that I am here for you. We are family now, and I intend to keep it that way. I love you."

"I love you too," said Amelia. "Thanks."

"No problem," said Sarah.

"If you two are done, can one of you turn on my cartoons again," interrupted Enion.

Amelia finished eating and started up the stairs, passing a bed-head Hope who was walking down.

"Mmmmm, breakfast," mumbled Hope.

Amelia's doorway was already open when she got to her room. She stepped onto the deck of Bartholomew's ship and sat down next to him.

"Hello," said Bartholomew, turning momentarily to see who it was.

"Hello, Binky," said Amelia.

There was a deep sigh in response.

"I was wondering when that was going to start up again," said Bartholomew, setting down his fishing pole. "I knew it couldn't have really ended."

"No," said Amelia. "But things sure have changed."

"Yes," said Bartholomew. "They certainly have. With all your newfound friends, I guess you won't be needing me as much anymore."

"What makes you say that?" asked Amelia, surprised.

"I thought we resolved this after we found out that I wasn't crazy."

"You are crazy," said Bartholomew, with a grin. "But that's another story. I'm glad you still want to spend time with me occasionally."

"Always," said Amelia. "That's why I came to visit you right now. I have something that I wanted to tell you."

"Really?" said Bartholomew. "What's that?"

Amelia gave him a big hug.

"Thanks for always being here for me and for being so good to me," said Amelia. "I love you and truly appreciate you. I'm sorry for not showing it more often."

Bartholomew hugged her in return.

"I love you too," said Bartholomew.

Bartholomew turned and discreetly wiped his now wet eyes. Amelia pretended not to notice, and they sat quietly watching the ocean as Bartholomew returned to fishing.

"Sarah is looking for you," came Hope's voice.

Amelia turned to see Hope coming through a black portal onto the ship.

"She said she wants you to help her make layered cookie bars."

"Fun," said Amelia. "Then you can stay here for a bit and have Binky teach you how to fish."

Bartholomew glared questioningly at Amelia.

"You need to get to know each other," whispered Amelia.

"Why?" quietly grumbled Bartholomew.

"I'll bring back some cookie bars this evening if you do," responded Amelia.

"Not a great reason," said Bartholomew, his voice back at a normal level. "But it'll do. Come over here, squirt."

"Do I have to?" asked Hope.

"Yes," said Amelia. "I'll braid your hair for you later if you do."

"Fine," responded Hope, stomping over to sit next to Bartholomew.

Bribery firmly in place, Amelia went to help Sarah bake. When the cookie bars were done, Sarah went upstairs for a nap. Enion was still entranced with cartoons, and Amelia didn't want to interrupt Bartholomew and Hope's bonding time. She decided to go for a walk.

Although there was still a lot of snow, the sun was taking the edge off the cold. Amelia wandered around town and waved to people that she saw.

Eventually, she found herself over by the school. She had gone into autopilot mode. She walked this path so many times, it just felt natural to travel it. She was reminiscing about

her time in Pickleton and wasn't paying attention as she walked around the side of the building.

"Oh great! The freak is back," came a voice.

Amelia looked up to see a group of kids sitting at the swing set. She realized that it was the same group that she had met when she first visited the school. Bobby, the freckle-faced boy, must have been the one talking because Becky punched him in the arm.

"Shut up!" said Becky. "Hello, Amelia."

"Hi," said Spencer, Billy, and Clyde.

Jessica glared daggers at Amelia while Bobby quietly rubbed his arm.

"Hello," said Amelia, hesitantly.

"You wanna hang out for a bit?" asked Spencer.

"I don't know," said Amelia. "I was going to stop by Cindy's house."

"Alright," said Spencer.

"Are you sure?" asked Becky. "We were going to get hot chocolate and go sledding up the canyon later. We'd be happy if you could join us."

"Maybe," said Amelia. "Could Cindy come too?"

Jessica gave a disgusted sound and rolled her eyes, but otherwise kept her comments in check.

"That would be fine," said Becky. "We'll head over to

Pearl's Café in just a bit. You can meet us there."

After picking up a very surprised Cindy and heading to the café, Amelia found herself in a situation that she would not have thought possible only a short while ago. She was sitting and drinking hot chocolate with a group of school friends.

It wasn't perfect by any stretch of the imagination. Jessica and Bobby were still very rude on occasion, and there were moments of awkwardness. Becky was kind, Cindy was engaging, Spencer was quiet, and Billy and Clyde were surprisingly funny. As Amelia sat, sipping her drink and laughing with her new friends, she realized that all of life was that way. It was a messy mixture of good, bad, and everything in between.

Despite the pain and problems that she had experienced, there was a great amount of change and good that had come from it. Amelia was finally able to come to terms with herself and face her inner demons. She had learned that she could have faith in herself and be kind and loving, regardless of other people's actions. She was finally able to confront her past and let go of her guilt and anger. Most importantly, she could now start to allow herself to feel loved instead of immediately discounting it.

Amelia smiled as Billy stole one of Clyde's

marshmallows when he wasn't looking. She took another sip of her hot chocolate and just let herself be in the moment.

Amelia wasn't naïve enough to believe that she wouldn't keep having to deal with her past, or its effects. She also didn't believe that she wouldn't have some bad times to go through, but something had changed inside of her that seemed to be giving her strength to continue.

Amelia watched and listened to her group of schoolmates chat, argue, laugh, and have fun. As she was enjoying herself immensely, and finishing her drink, Amelia had one thought sticking in her mind.

Life isn't perfect, but it's definitely worth it.

Acknowledgements

I would like to give a special thanks to my wife for all of her love, support, and encouragement over the years. Thank you for giving ideas and suggestions and regular feedback during my writing process.

I would like to give thanks to my children for their love, for being constant sources of inspiration and material, and for their willingness to sit through multiple readings of the book at different stages.

Thank you to all of my family and friends who took the time to read this book and offer feedback so that I could improve and polish it.

Thanks to Julie Jeffery for being an early proofreader and for helping me realize that I shouldn't use the word "however" in every other paragraph.

Thanks to Cindy Beatty at Proof Positive Papers for being my final proofreader. I am grateful for the extra set of eyes and even more grateful for your encouragement and support.

Thanks to Marcelo Vignali for being such a powerful inspiration, ally, mentor, and friend all these years. You helped pull my scattered explorations together to create cohesive visual direction, allowing me to finally push this project across the finish line. Thank you for helping make this possible.

I would like to give thanks to all the other authors at various stages of their literary journey who took the time to offer advice and support as I continued on mine.

Reading Guide

Here are some things to think about yourself, or ask
in classrooms, reading groups, or clinical environments.
These are not the only questions you should ask. Instead,
these are meant to be a springboard for discussion, and you
are encouraged to develop and ask additional questions of
your own.

-What are the themes that you noticed in this book? Not just
the theming – a contemporary fantasy – but the themes. The
relations, connections, and lessons that you find in the story.
What can you learn from the themes and how do they apply
in your life?

-A paradigm is a specific worldview, perspective, or way of
seeing things. Not everyone's views or way of seeing things
are the same. How might your worldview either compete or
correlate with those around you? How can you find a place
of support and understanding when you have competing
paradigms?

-Amelia's paradigm sphere was a reflection of her interests,
thoughts, and personality. If you had a paradigm sphere, what

would it look like? Where would you go, what would you see, and what would you be able to do?

-If you had friends in your paradigm sphere who reflected aspects of your personality, what would they look and sound like? How would they act? How would those different aspects complement or compete with each other?

-Amelia had to deal with bullying. What did she do well? What could she have done more effectively?

-The subject of honesty and sharing things about yourself appeared a lot in the book. When is it appropriate to share things about yourself, and when is it not? Are there people in your life who you can talk to and discuss things with who can help you discern the difference?

-How did Amelia develop and grow over the course of the story? How have you changed and grown even over the last few years?

-While we can often see our own growth, it can be hard to see growth in the people around us. How did the people around Amelia grow and change over the course of the story? How are the people around you changing and growing?

-Sarah loved and cared for Amelia even when they first met. How is that possible? Do you believe love is a choice or that it is something that just happens? Why or why not?

-Life is tough. Things can get really dark and really difficult. Amelia was able to push through and find support even when it seemed all hope was lost and she felt absolutely alone. Who or what do you have in your life to help with similar dark times? If you don't currently feel like you have proper supports in place, what can you do to find them? This would be a good time to talk to a close family member, mentor, teacher, or friend to help set up supports so they are in place before the tough times hit.

Thank you again for reading. I encourage you to continue asking questions and looking for lessons you can learn.

Therapy Guide

This book was written around the theme of managing trauma. The goal was to have a book for use as a reference and example in a clinical setting for younger, and possibly even older, patients who may have difficulty understanding tough concepts. My hope was to create many "You remember when Amelia..." type scenarios to draw from.

Here are some of the book's concepts, ideas, and therapies. This is not an exhaustive or complete list, but it is a good place to start as you look for yourself, or for someone around you, so that you have relevant examples as you go through the process of healing and/or helping others heal.

Here is the list in no particular order:

-Meditation/Becoming Centered

-Creating a Safe Space

-Developing a Support Network

-Honesty and Dialogue

-Humor as Therapy

-Reframing

-Exposure Therapy

-Healthy Escapism

-Emotional Balancing

-Breathing Techniques

-Inner Child Work

-Journaling

-Empathy

-Social Awkwardness

-Dissociative Amnesia

-Re-traumatization/Re-living (PTSD)

-Depression and Suicidal Thoughts

-Addressing Cognitive Dissonance

-Stages of Healing Trauma (Identifying, Addressing, Confronting, Accepting, Forgiving, Healing)

-Self-Acceptance (Embracing all aspects of yourself both good and bad)

-Facing Fear

-Finding Hope

There are also some examples from the book of what not to do and used as warnings:

-Unhealthy Escapism

-Controlling Through Fear

-Shaming/Guilt (The ghost story is a clear warning against the dangers of guilt and shame.)

-Bullying

-Violence

-Abuse

-Self-Harm

-Unhealthy Silence (Closing lines of communication)

-Unhealthy Solitude (Shutting out support networks)

Please feel free to reach out to the author through his website if you are a therapist looking for additional ideas on how to use this book.

Author's Note:

If you or someone you know is struggling with trauma, or any other kind of physical, mental, social, or emotional issues, please reach out to those around you for support. It is a good and honorable thing to do. You are not weak for needing help. It takes bravery to speak up and own that you need support.

People can't help you if you don't let them know that you need it. Please reach out.

About the Author

Henry Elmo Bawden is an explorer, experimenter, and active creator in many mediums. He currently lives in Ohio with his wife and seven children. He is a professor at a local community college where he directs the Video Game Art and Animation program.

This book is Henry's debut novel. To see updates about upcoming books and projects, visit his website at bawdenstudio.com.

About the Illustrator

Marcelo Vignali is a husband, father, and enjoys being surrounded by a multitude of pets and plants. He is a commercial entertainment and illustration artist and has worked for Disney, Sony, and many others. He has worked on a wide range of products, and in various positions, for television animation, feature animation, video games, cards, theme park rides, and more.

Made in the USA
Middletown, DE
16 October 2023

40886900R00239